AN HOUR OF REDEMPTION

DOUGLAS W. ACKERMAN

For information regarding permission, please write to:
info@barringerpublishing.com
Barringer Publishing, Naples, Florida
www.barringerpublishing.com

Cover, graphics, and layout by Linda S. Duider
Cape Coral, Florida

ISBN: 978-1-954396-83-8
Library of Congress Cataloging-in-Publication Data
An Hour of Redemption / Douglas W. Ackerman

Printed in U.S.A.

For Gordon and Jodi

DOUGLAS W. ACKERMAN

PROLOGUE

Jack lay there panting and heaving when a late spasm churned. He thought he was finished, but like an old billy goat, he'd somehow knotted his loins too hard and struggled to unclench his achy, old prostate—his blissful brume tainted with white-coats and waiting rooms. Then, finally spent, the planks buckled in his back, and he rested on top of her. He flushed fleeting thoughts of biopsies and MRIs from his mind and lay in peace.

She'd orgasmed three times already and loved his old torso's full weight on her—from quivering to inert, surging to sated, writhing to wrecked, and now static, thick, and masculine.

"Wrap your legs around me. *Please*," Jack said, the bone-lessness in his calves, feet, and toes reassuring and comforting him that conditions were normal.

She'd forgotten again but from the first his request had been simple—wider so his hips would fall deeper into her hollow, then out and around but more around his thighs than waist. There was too much space there, and now, reminded of how she'd been asked this before, she wanted to rub her calves against his hamstrings down near his knees and back up while her hands worked his vertebrae one by one. This loving procedure was one of the few things he'd ever asked of her.

It was the most wonderful five minutes of her life, and she'd been having lots of them lately. He pulled out, lay on his side, and now she was the helpless one as he pushed one arm under her, hooked it around her and enveloped her like a bicep curl then the other arm, lower, around all the way to the same bed sheet. Doubly encircled, he gently squeezed her tightly. His blue eyes, inches from her browns, speaking patiently. She produced a smile, then looked up at the ceiling.

Then, he whispered. "You're the most delicate cherub in the firmament," his normally strong voice sounding like it came from the basement. But there was no basement in Jack's house where they were, northeast of Orlando in Geneva, Florida.

She smiled again but said nothing and stared up.

She was twenty-nine. But who would ever say that to her again?

The chess game they hadn't finished was in the corner, below the oversized poster of the 1980 US Hockey Team. Jack's tennis trophies littered one side of the bedroom—small, unimportant, local—chickenshit for desperadoes like me, Jack would joke. Her cello was out of its case near the other corner by her big bags, purses, and shoes.

It was July 1, 2019, his birthday, 7:47 a.m. He was forty-nine. She had no presents for him but figured he'd just received one. She was unsure what to say, if anything.

The fireball from the East was off the Atlantic, across the St. Johns River, across Lake Winter Breeze, and beating on the blinds of Jack's bedroom. There were no clouds, and early rays pushed under the blinds and lit the cello's scroll and upper neck; they seemed disembodied so bright was the sun compared to the darkness in which the bouts rested. He pulled her tighter, nibbling. The air conditioner clicked on. She frowned at the old Florida buck on the wall above her. She'd been there the prior winter when the windows were open but somehow it seemed colder now with the A\C; she burrowed against him and pulled the single sheet up. He pulled her in still closer, nosing.

Jack wanted to marry her. He imagined that he had survived the risky visit with her parents. He had put all his cards on the table and told not a single lie. He knew he'd never love more deeply. It wasn't the age; he often forgot about it. It wasn't her body; it wasn't as good as she thought it was. It wasn't her face; it wasn't as good as she thought it was. It wasn't the sex; his best sex was long gone. Silence—it was the silence. He rarely felt on stage, rarely felt a need to insert conversation, rarely felt a moment that was uncomfortable, rarely felt a need to pose. He couldn't say "never" to any of these; and "infrequently" was perhaps more accurate than "rarely."

Long, long ago, he'd looked for a woman like this but never got close. Decades after that, he'd given up looking and stared instead at the options actually available. Again, he never got close. Perfection in love, he was sure, was unattainable. Love was euphoria versus toleration, and the latter always won. So be it. He was redeemed. He would never let her go.

Chapter One

A MILLENNIAL READING DOSTOEVSKY

They had met at the tennis courts; the same courts Jack had been playing on since he was twelve. It was January 2018, and all the leagues were starting up fresh. Jack loved this time of year. It was cool out, and he had just gotten the biggest check of his life after working extremely hard for all of 2017. But his singles match, Lonnie, had uncharacteristically bailed out, and it was either go home or do doubles. Jack wasn't in the doubles league. But they always needed guys for no shows, or they couldn't get the matches in. He hated men's doubles, but it was better than the couch. The local badass, Mike, was in charge and not too sympathetic. Jack pitied the poor bastards like Mike who had to constantly recruit fresh players to keep the never-ending doubles leagues going. Though he thought they were friendly enough, he'd spurned Mike's overtures to become a regular quite a few times. Anyway, it was 65 out with only moderate humidity, and Jack always enjoyed some fresh air. What was the worst thing that could happen?

Mike paired up the groups and sent them off, and Jack gradually realized he was going to get screwed again as no one picked him. He registered that several guys intentionally took players worse than him. Shit. So, they think I'm an arrogant asshole, do they? thought Jack. Well, then fuck 'em: doubles junkies, cheaters, score keepers, pushers, hackers, slashers, never took lessons, never worked on their games, numbnuts. Jack did standing two legged jumps and absorbed the rejection.

Finally, Mike said something Jack never thought he'd hear: "Well, Jack . . . mixed doubles?" Shit. Shit. Shit. He'd hit millions of tennis balls but had never played mixed doubles in his life. But he'd seen it played, and it made him sick—the total lack of athleticism; the preposterous chivalry juxtaposed against the near mandatory picking on the girl; the limp banter; the newly giggled rules. Shit. Shit. Shit. Plus, he didn't see anyone around.

"With whom?"asked Jack.

"My wife and a friend from her office," said Mike. "They're over on 6."

"Better than sitting on the couch."

Jack started walking over to the court. He pulled up his file but couldn't quite remember Mike's wife's name. He knew she was a lawyer, like Jack, but they didn't run in the same circles. It was either Erin, or Evelyne, or Eve. He had his ears on so he could pick it up from someone else. He saw a big head of dark hair in front of him when he got there.

"Honey, this is Jack," Mike called to his wife forgetting they knew each other distantly.

Darn it, Jack thought, he didn't use her name.

"Sure, everyone knows Jack Forester" Mike's wife said. "Great. This is Jen. We work together, and Jen just moved down from Connecticut."

"Virginia," Jen said, while everyone seemed a little confused, "school in New York at Cornell."

"*Purnell?*" Jack said.

"*Cornell*, Jack, sorry Jen," Mike's wife said.

"Hmm. Is that school, what do you call it . . . ah . . . accredited?"

"Jack," Mike's wife said.

"What brings you to Orlando?" Jack looked at Jen.

Jen replied, "I hate cold weather."

"Any family or friends here?"

"No."

"So you took a job in Orlando for the sole reason that you don't like cold weather?"

"Jack, this isn't a deposition," Mike's wife said.

"You're right. I'm sorry."

They'd been standing on opposite sides of the net, and the couples retreated to the baseline. Jack was irritated that he couldn't remember Mike's wife's name but smiled his way through it. Everyone knows Jack Forester? He thought. What kind of dig was that? Anyway, he got a good look at Jen as they paired off: 5'8" maybe a little more, white shoes, long white legs, white skirt, white arms, white blouse, and big head of dark hair. She looked at him and did not smile, like she wasn't exactly looking forward to it herself, deep dark eyes, longish face, pretty girl. "Nice to meet you, Forester." Jen said. "Same here, Jack Forester." Had she picked up that he couldn't remember Mike's wife's name? Holy shit, Jack thought. Why is everyone calling me "Forester"? This is going to suck.

"So you work with Evelyne?" He said to Jen trying to be soft because he still hadn't heard her name and wasn't sure "Evelyne" was right.

She looked over and he motioned with his eyes for help.

"Erin," she intentionally said loudly and grinned at Mike and Erin, then, "Same firm; different practice."

"You're a lawyer?" Jack looked over at Erin who gave him a mild glare. Fuck, she busted him. Jack thought he might have met Erin twice in his whole life, and now she was glaring at him because he couldn't remember her name and saying everyone knows Jack Forester? God you're a dick, he thought to himself.

"I'm sorry, Erin, I called you Evelyne 'cause it's prettier. Forgive me?" Jack attempted.

"Cheeseball line" Erin said, "but it happens to all of us."

"Call me an inconsiderate lout. I know you want to."

"Inconsiderate lout."

"Hit me. I deserve it." Jack turned his cheek as if to receive a punch.

"Enough," said Erin

"Yes, just started." Jen said, changing the subject.

"Interesting. Yeah, come down from Vermont?" He gave her his best straight face and talked too loudly.

"New York," Erin said loudly. Jack was going to make a Puerto Rican joke given that Jen most certainly was not Puerto Rican but didn't think the timing was perfect enough.

"I know. I know. I'm sorry I forgot your name, Erin. Why don't you train your husband to use it more often to help me out with my social problems?"

Mike smiled at the needle. Erin glared at Mike now.

"Virginia," Jen said, refusing to get sucked into the tiff.

She smiled and he could tell she wanted to say something but wouldn't. Jack loved games, gave her another smile, and kept quiet. She didn't speak. Jack waved at Erin across the net, and she smiled back. She will forgive me, Jack thought. "I'm sorry I forgot your wife's name, Mike," Jack said.

"Well," Mike said, "I'm somehow sure it will never happen again."

Mike and his wife were about the same age as Jack, but Jen was at least fifteen years younger, maybe more. It seemed like this generation of girls wanted to look super young, while in his day girls of that age tried to look a touch older—the feminists to be who turned into the feminists in your face. Jack's older sister's name was Jennifer, called "Jenny" frequently, but never "Jen." "Jen" was a new name for the same shit. Moved down from New York to Florida—same shit he'd heard since he was five years old. Virginia? Same shit: these pretentious assholes didn't even remember they were in the Confederacy at this point. And correcting what's her name and where she was from and where she went to school as though someone gave a jolly rancher. Geez, Jack thought, you're either a Gator, a 'Nole, a 'Cane or an "other" in Orlando. Will they never learn?

And Jen was a definite Millennial as she checked her phone after the warm-up. What the fuck for? Jack thought. The recipe for Coke, or "took a nice shit just now, check in with u later." Jack saw the little pocket it went into and calculated how stealthily he could spill his water into it from waist height. Otherwise, he'd have to watch her check it on every changeover. It looked like quite a tough shot. Oh well, he thought, let's get to work on this sweat.

He could tell from the warm-up that fitness was the goal tonight. But he wasn't going to be a dick anymore. This was social tennis, he signed up for it, so let's make the best of it. He'd done this one thousand times in his life. He was waiting for the first words from anyone suggesting they quit after one set or even less. Mike's wife had made no awkward attempts to signal Jack and Jen that anything should happen between them, which Jack appreciated. The ease with which women signed up men to do their work for them had always irritated Jack. Geez, he thought, you really are an old asshole. You're lucky this tall, gorgeous Millennial will even stand next to you.

Oh well, let's work on that sweat. After only four games, Mike's wife started commenting on the normal but unbearable Orlando humidity. The wind had died, and even in January it was sticky.

"No need to continue if it's not fun," he offered, but it came out condescending.

Jen said nothing.

Mike said nothing.

They kept playing, and it became apparent that Jen was pretty good, and no one knew it. They went ahead 5-1 in only thirty minutes. When he was serving, he got some good looks at her as she played the net in front of him. She'd certainly had lessons somewhere. They attempted no strategy between points, and that saved him from having to communicate with her. She made no giggles or small talk. She didn't ask any stupid questions. She didn't over-compliment anyone. Jack noticed her stance, grip and posture were perfect.

They broke to close out the set at 6-1 and took a sideways look at each other as they walked to the benches. She gave him her first smile—a smile he never forgot; it came with steady, hard eyes. Where was that phone for her to check when he needed it? He smiled back and guzzled water—sweaty indeed. He made note of that smile.

"Switch partners?" Mike said.

No one said anything for too long.

"Geez, do we need a subcommittee?" Jack said.

Everyone chuckled, and they switched partners.

They played the second set, and he could see again that Jen previously had lessons to go with her natural talent. She was a graceful mover, unhurried. On one point, she sprinted behind Mike to retrieve a lob over his head, cupped the back of her wrist concave and hit a perfect counter-lob diagonally to the opposite corner where Jack was. Jack had been measuring his strokes the entire match to avoid any awkwardness. Men's doubles were awkward enough; he didn't want to risk hitting a woman with a tennis ball. But now, he was very deep in the court from her lob, and decided he'd let the big forehand go. Sure, he was older than shit, but he'd always had a big forehand. So, he pulled his left shoulder around all the way, relaxed his neck completely, sunk into his thighs, uncoiled, and let it ride back at her. She shanked the return, and it squeaked over in front of him, winning the point.

"Oopsy," she said with racquet twirling like a parasol, but the laugh was noticeably sarcastic not girly, almost like "fuck you, big prick."

Everyone laughed, and then it was over. Back at the benches, she did not check her phone. She went in her bag for her keys and pulled out *Crime and Punishment* while digging for the usual girly stuff.

"You're kidding?" Jack said, glistening and steamy in the chilly but humid conditions.

"Huh?"

"Dostoevsky?"

"Sure."

"How old are you?"

"Twenty-eight."

"Well, then there is no 'sure' after the question—Dostoevsky?"

Jen laughed. "I guess you're right. How old are you?"

"Ever heard of Rip Van Winkle?"

She laughed again. "Pretty big forehand, Rip."

"Thank you, Jennifer. It was a pleasure playing with you."

Mike and Erin smiled. Everyone smiled.

They all left, and when he got home, he realized he could officially quit mixed doubles and say he'd played one match, and it hadn't been bad. That Jen, boy, she'd be sure to torture souls before it was over, Jack thought. He saw a big furnace in his mind, with Jen, naked but with perfect hair, even a baby barrette in her big pubic bush, shoveling pleading men into the fire. "Here go your little hearts," she sing sang to them as she tossed them in, "Momma said you're only little farts." Not a giggle to be found. Dead souls of dead men.

Jack laughed. He was glad a Millennial was reading *Crime and Punishment*, thought how his back was hurting, and didn't think much more before he blacked out. About ten years earlier, Jack had been diagnosed with chronic obstructive sleep apnea. The drain it had put upon him was relentless; there was no way to win, only draw or lose. He woke up at 3:17 a.m. and realized he hadn't worn his CPAP at all. He got up, urinated outside the back door, got a breath of chilly air, and put his CPAP on. Jack was asleep in ten minutes and never thought of Jen again.

Chapter Two

PRECEDENTS CANNOT BE IGNORED

That same January of 2018, after the longest break in the lawyer's year, Jack resumed his normal work and play schedule. He worked from 8:30 to 6 or later. When he was a younger attorney, he had worked many many weekends and many many nights. This had earned him the respect of his bosses who were also workaholics. Even back then, they were already talking about the decline of the practice of law. "We used to think about law; now all we think about is billable hours." But back then they were only a little afraid. They knew they'd make it to the finish line.

From the start of his career to the present, Jack had billed his life in six-minute increments. One hour was sixty minutes, and a lawyer divided that sixty minutes into ten segments, every hour, every week, every month, every year, forever. Jack realized very early that time had to be put in every day, or he would waste time trying to recover time. Postponing the recording of time only made the recording of time worse. Consequently, Jack had been a religious timekeeper from the beginning and even tried to get three lawyers fired over the years for not putting in their time.

His early bosses had certainly been correct, and the practice of law had indeed gotten significantly worse since Jack had started. There was more greed, more lying, more cheating, more stealing, less honor, less honesty, and less interest. The worst thing from Jack's perspective was the decline in the law itself. The trial judges were less and less prepared and more and more political. And the appellate judges couldn't write anything without so many qualifiers hanging off that it amounted to no law at all. As the years went by, the murky soup bowl of equity turned into a lake and threatened to turn into an ocean. Jack had dedicated himself completely to the law, and he found his efforts increasingly frustrated. He had not studied extremely hard to master areas of law that were slowly being turned into "totality of the circumstances" garbage. As the years went by, he found himself unable to tell his clients anything meaningful about their case. It did not matter that he knew their case inside and out because the law to which it was applied turned increasingly into mush.

When *A Few Good Men* got mentioned amongst lawyers, Jack had joked that the only realistic line in the whole movie was when the judge walked in and said: "Gentlemen, what do you have for me today?" The joke had worked for two decades or so. But Jack was concerned that the Millennial lawyers hadn't seen the movie, so the joke was destined to fade away. Plus, Millennial lawyers didn't seem to have much of a sense of humor anyway. They all seemed a bit tame and weak and programmed. He wondered what they'd do if he put an old Richard Pryor stand-up routine on.

Plus, was it even funny anymore now that lack of preparation was ubiquitous? Anyway, Jack considered it his job in life to keep the jokes going, so it depressed him that one of his old standards was in decline. He'd need new jokes. Regardless, unprepared baboons in black robes did not impress Jack. Their numbers were steadily increasing. They were smugger and smugger. In twenty-three years of practicing law, Jack had never been asked by any judge, ever, how judges were doing. Every Bar Journal article had a pile of bullshit in it about diversity, inclusion, slavery, lactation rooms and other nonsense, but not one article, survey, or pool on judicial incompetence. Every appellate seminar featured the same pretentious asshole appellate judges, and they all had the same lines: "The workload is too much (if you don't like the job quit), respect for the judiciary as an independent branch of government (you're the ones who made fools of yourself), and please more money (fuck off)." But not one appellate judge ever asked or talked about how terrible the opinions were, how mushy and murky the law had become, how the breakers of the procedural rules were rewarded and the followers punished, and how anyone could always get an extension for anything, lest the judiciary should ever have to get off its ass and work. The bottom of the barrel were the lectures on "civility" from the same judges who ripped each other apart in their appellate opinions, preening for all the legal world to see just how stupid they thought their colleagues were. And, if Jack had ever been asked, which he hadn't, he would have said adding "with respect" is extremely unimpressive. "With respect, I must say you are a very dumb and/or corrupt piece of shit." How "civil" they were—happy horseshit.

This was rough stuff, and it had beaten Jack down slowly but steadily. So, for the last ten years or so, he'd resolved to never work nights or weekends unless he had to. But Jack had other interests. Jack was about 6'3" and 240 lbs. As a young man, he'd been an inch taller and forty pounds lighter. He'd been something of an athlete his entire life. He'd seen video of himself lately, and he knew he walked with a little stoop already—just like his father had. Jack's father had been English, tall and lean, but Jack's mother, nee Polachek, was from Eastern Europe somewhere and Jack had a strong dose of the stocky torso and square head. Jack had medium brown hair, and he could grow a good beard. But an old girlfriend, Betsy, on New Year's Eve 1987, told him he looked better clean shaven. He'd clung to that for all these years. He had little else to which to cling.

Though he wasted his prime on basketball, he played tennis a little as a kid and competitively for over twenty years as an adult. At this point, he was over the tournaments and the leagues, but he'd done minor damage while he'd been in them. He also hunted and fished his whole life. His father, one grandfather, and two uncles had taken him hunting and fishing his entire life, and he couldn't imagine life otherwise. He loved anything involving nature. His father had taught him to sail as a child, and even though Jack did not have his own boat, he had friends with boats and kept sailing regularly.

Jack had been a constant reader his whole life, and he still read every night before bed at a minimum. Jack loved music and was a decent violinist. He had played off and on, mostly off since he was 15. Jack had always loved the fine arts but had not been a regular attender. He almost never had anyone to go with, and usually got stuck with "Bud Light, Saturday

Night" and all that hung off it. Those nights had never really yielded anything to Jack. Yelling at women over the din of loud music for two hours did not excite him. Certainly, they were not excited by him.

Because Jack had never been married, and had no children, these pursuits filled his calendar. He had always been an excellent scheduler. When he was 15, he had gotten his first job as a dishwasher and still remembered vividly that the manager had been impressed with his organization of "the pit" which is what the dishwashing area was derisively called. His organizational skills were honed and rehoned over the years. Everything could be made better even if only by a millimeter was Jack's motto. He had proven himself correct many times.

Jack was from a family with many women. He'd known both his grandmothers very well before they passed, had his mother who was still alive, had one aunt with whom he was fairly close and another not so close, had five female cousins, one sister with whom he had been extremely close, and a younger brother who was married to what seemed to be a nice girl. They had individually, collectively, and occasionally in duos and trios and more beat him up about women from high school to the present, though there was now a general resignation that he was a "goner," "hopeless," etc.

From the earliest periods of his life, Jack had struggled with women, felt they did not work, held up obstacles, and wasted enormous amounts of time. And for what? He'd wondered since he was young. In his twenties and thirties, Jack's energy was nearly limitless, and he felt no pressure, but realized he was no good at whatever "dating" was. It seemed to him to be essentially a series of lies and euphemisms organized at an extraordinarily slow place—all for the benefit of the female.

"Lie a little," his family had told him but what they really meant was "Lie a lot and lie continuously and never stop." This hurt Jack increasingly as the years went by. Jack prized honesty and endeavored to be honest. "Lies only delay the truth," he would say. Actions always spoke louder than words to Jack Forester.

But he had been proven wrong, repeatedly, and he had to admit it. Lies worked. Lies were effective. Women wanted to hear certain things, and whether those things were based on truth did not matter. Worse, women took all the horribles and liberally euphemized them into something gentler sounding: death=moved on to a better life; fuck=slept with; shit=poop; piss=pee; slutty=inappropriate; big tits=nice figure. There was no end to it. They'd turn "cancer" into "chance to find oneself" if they could get away with it. The mangling of the English language did not appeal to Jack.

This was rough stuff and had beat Jack up early and then in tandem with his career. In his late thirties, the on-line dating thing got going, and Jack gave it a try. However, after four or five attempts, he decided on-line dating was a fraud. It was good at getting Jack dates, something he'd never had any problem with, but the date itself remained unchanged from the old days. It was like Vince Vaughan tearing up the phone numbers in *Swingers*. All the on-line dates were both shorter than advertised and fatter than advertised. The pictures posted dramatically oversold the goods delivered. One lady had said she was interested in classical music; on the date that meant she'd heard of Canon in D and not much else. She admitted she only posed because she figured rich guys were more likely to list classical music on their profiles.

Another girl listed sailing but then told Jack she'd never even been sailing once, just was generally "interested" in it.

And so on. The dates themselves were just the same as they'd always been: Jack had to do everything. Jack drafted the ideal profile for his woman and told everyone to let them know when they found her: "Very hot girl with very tight butt looking for mediocre dufus to rescue; willing to initiate virtually everything, not make any cutesy faces (except ironically) and giveth not a shiteth about man's net worth. Call Destiny at 1800BIGTITS."

By the time Jack was in his forties, there were fewer than ten days a year for which he had nothing planned. The hunting and fishing seasons planned themselves, and Jack planned around them. He tightened the screws more each year determined not to waste any time of his precious life.

And so, if he worked Monday through Friday, 8:30 to 6 or so, Jack also had a violin lesson one night a week off and on for thirty years. True, years without playing had occurred. Instructors had come and gone, but Jack loved the instrument and always found a new one. Jack played tennis 2-3 nights a week and for years played tournaments on weekends. And Jack would practice other pursuits as the season dictated: archery, skeet shooting, fly tying, fly casting, etc. There was always something coming up on the calendar or something being put on the calendar. Jack loved it, and every year he packed it fuller and fuller.

On top of the fun, Jack never had a housekeeper or landscaper. When he was thirty, he bought six acres in Geneva, Florida. No one had approved of it, and the mortgage was big. It was in the country, on Lake Winter Breeze, near the St. John's River, and not that far from the Atlantic. Jack recalled his father shaking his head, "you're going to go under" on the mortgage, but Jack was resilient. He scratched and scrapped for ten years, even borrowed a small amount of money from his father at a low point. Then he got lucky, the crash of 2008-09 happened, and Jack refinanced at half the previous rate. He was in the clear. Five years later, the rates dropped even more, and Jack refinanced to a 15 year at 2.9 percent. I'm a genius he told everyone at the office. Of course, they'd all refinanced, so no one was impressed.

From the beginning, Jack loved the property. He had a little piece of rural Florida. It was quiet. It was dark. There were deer, turkeys, and ducks. All the neighbors minded their own business. He cooked all his meals. He cleaned the little house. He did his laundry. He fixed the endless things which needed fixing. He bought a fancy lawn mower and mowed the lawn; he especially loved to do this during the long summer when it wouldn't get dark until eight or later. He'd get home from work at 6:30, crank off fifty sit-ups for his tennis game, put the earmuffs on, and mow the lawn in the twilight. Frequently, there was an East wind off the Atlantic making the heat bearable. Jack's big decision at thirty had proven correct.

Jack did all of this because he liked to keep busy, but also because it kept him distracted from the central agony of his life: his failures with women. He loved women, but they did not love him. He had a "Leave it to Beaver" childhood, and his parents were very happy, though Jack had lost his father in 2015. It was the worst experience of his life. He had been close to his father and considered himself a colossal loser in comparison.

He did not know exactly why he repelled women. As a young man, he had very much wanted to get married and have children, but he never got close. Objectively speaking, he came from a good family, he was highly educated, he had a track record of keeping and excelling at jobs, he could always make people laugh, his mother had told him he was good looking but no one else had so he thought he was better thought of as not so ugly as to be a deal killer. In his whole life, he had never hit a woman. He had never called a woman a "bitch" or a "cunt" or anything abusive. He had raised his voice at women, but never without reason or chronically. He had never thrown objects at women. He had never played financial games with women. No, his relationships had always failed quietly and with little drama. "Not a good fit," "let's be friends" or some horseshit, they would always say.

He did know that he had serious personality traits which were repellent to women: he treated them equally, he expected them to participate in the relationship, he expected them to love him, he expected them to care about him. As Jack had learned, these were all dead on arrival. None of them wanted "equality," except when it benefited them. Otherwise, they wanted to continue to enjoy the privileges of being a woman. Participate? All of them wanted him to make all the decisions and come up with all the ideas. Their idea of "participating" was to bitch and complain about his ideas, having produced no ideas of their own. This seemed most acute during the early dating phase when they derived enormous amounts of enjoyment at doing absolutely nothing except expecting to be catered to while they came up with gems like "whatever you'd like to do." Another lie of course. Why not start the relationship on a lie? He guessed they thought.

Love and care for him? Shit, days and weeks would go by without them saying anything nice to Jack. He had had girlfriends for which he had never figured out why they were with him to begin with. Sex? When they want it; how they want it. He could recall on two hands how many times women had performed sexual acts with him that they had clearly been uninterested in and had done only for his benefit.

Most infamous was Carolyn from his undergraduate days. Jack had had a ferocious sex drive and was in possession of a raging hard-on with a creamed tip one morning. They had been drinking the night before, and they were both hungover. But Jack was twenty-one years old, and his gonads weren't hungover at all. They had already been having sex for months, and there was KY lube right on the dresser as they lay there. Just please let me spoon you, he had begged her, after she aggressively and negatively announced she wasn't interested. But he kept after her, and she'd finally relented (as though the ten minutes this would take was tantamount to her receiving a prison term in Siberia). She was dry as a bone, but Jack dutifully lubed everything up and slide right into her. "Ouch" she said, but that was bullshit. She only said it to hurt him. His cock had slid into her like warm butter. He only took five minutes so engorged were his loins, and he could still hear her say in her husky, Marlboro light voice, "Hurry up and come, *Hero*" to try and ruin it for him. She only said it to hurt him. He wanted to hit her, but he hit her ass instead. She was on the pill, so Jack had no reason to pull out nor had he been doing so for months. But Jack was pissed. Well, Jack never had much luck. He pulled his twenty-one-year-old cock out, writhing and angry, put it on her hip bone, and a little spurt lept out and landed on her flank. No problem. But then the big kicks came and the second spurt—18 inches long—landed on her neck, ear, and hair. The third, just short of her chin, and the fourth back on the hip but more voluminous.

"What the fuck? You bastard, animal!" she said, laced in jism. "I told you I needed it," he said. "You fucker—what is all this?" and she looked at him with cold hateful eyes, as though he had murdered her mother with malice aforethought. He was so hurt, he wanted to scream "Take it you fucking cunt," but what good would that do? Yeah, these are my balls, they have to *work*. Learn some basic biology. He thought all these things as he glared back at her. The glaring went on for a minute or more without speech. She reached over the side of the bed and pulled his T-shirt from the floor and wiped off. Jack didn't tell her what a shitty job she did as she had a big strand of semen on her hair, suspended, that apparently, she didn't even realize. She went back to sleep with that big toothpaste shot on her head. Fuck you, Jack thought. She always whined that she was tired anyway.

Then he passed out and dreamed of a woman who would say *"It's okay. Go ahead. I know you need it, and I love you."* The relationship was over a week afterward, and he'd never met such a woman as was in his dream. Jack often wondered what became of that ice-cold, selfish bitch Carolyn, probably married the douche of her dreams, had three kids, and is getting the cottage cheese liposuctioned out of her ass right now.

Jack could recall every girl he had ever kissed; there were 24 of them. He could recall every girl he had had sex with; there were 17 of them. He could recall every girl he had considered a girlfriend; there were 11 of them. He could recall every girl he had had a relationship which lasted more than eighteen months; there were zero of them. He could recall every girl he had ever wanted to marry; there were zero of them. Well, maybe Vivian from his senior year in high school, but could he really count that? He had loved her, but they were so young. Anyway, at best, he could put one in the love column.

Jack's excellent memory reminded him of both the quantity and the details of his failures. What was he going to do, make himself forget? He had been naturally analytical prior to law school, but as a result of his training he was now hardened and objective. Jack read all the majority opinions, all the concurring opinions, all the dissenting opinions, and all the footnotes. His patience for unrealistic nonsense narrowed with each passing year.

As his failures began to accumulate, Jack started to refine another fundamental problem he had with women; they never did anything; they had no pursuits, no interests, no avocations. From kindergarten to twenty-five, that didn't matter much. Jack's boner was so big, they could have worn Ronald McDonald's outfits, and he would have stuck it in their red nose just for relief. Never did they ever realize this. They either had no idea how strong the male sex drive was, or, worse, realized it but considered their role in relieving it to be *optional*, as though masturbating was a *cure* rather than a compounder and aggravator of failure. Worse, they didn't seem the slightest bit curious about this massive force of nature. They'd rather talk about a new restaurant that just opened! YAY!

From twenty-five on, his failure with women became a bigger and bigger problem, and one to which Jack had become extremely sensitive. He realized that women wasted their evenings on bullshit, wasted their weekends on bullshit, and wasted their vacations on bullshit. It wouldn't have mattered except that they had to drag Jack into their lameness to be with them, wallowing in sloth and laxity. "Relaxing," they called it a lot, as though they had something to relax *from*. What to do? His friends, even the happily married ones, were extremely tough and cynical. "Better than being single," was about as positive as it ever got. Others were "shitty," "sucks," "I've got kids," "she's not too bad," "I guess I've gained some weight too," "in too deep to get out", and "yeah, you just have to do all that bullshit; otherwise, you'll never get any." How true these turned out to be.

Again, law school had exacerbated the problem. Jack loved judicial thinking and now all his past failures were "precedent." Although he did not have to adhere to them the way judges did, they were nevertheless neatly categorized and organized in Jack's mind. Each new girl he met, whether he dated them or not, was adjudged against these existing categories, and as the years passed, Jack was horrified to find that very rarely did any new precedents get made. Jack was horrified at how perfectly many women fit into the existing categories. My God, he thought, they are all the fucking same. Jack loved games and resolved to try and intentionally pull women out of the existing categories. Rarely was he successful and even then, only temporarily. Once the stimuli which only he supplied was removed, they would quickly revert.

He recalled Lynn, a big bra-burning, feminist Nazi, who talked a big game about equality in law school. Jack had met lots of these at law school. They seemed to think that by merely announcing a wish it became so. They never could answer how many wars women had won over the millennia. If we can kill you, Jack would ask them, what difference do the theoreticals matter? And why all these separate categories of competition, one for men one for women? His favorite to hammer on was a separate "chess rating" for women? Come again? Don't you feminists find that extremely embarrassing? No answers came but some gasps did. It had taught Jack to love gasps.

Well, Lynn reminded everyone how she liked to work out a lot. The woman was about 5'4" 105 lbs., and Jack could have picked her up and thrown her across the room like a doll. She fit the "Angry Bitch Who Won't Discuss It" precedent, but Jack liked her. She was funny in her Janis Joplin roughness and tried hard. But Jack had observed that such women could not admit and reconcile themselves to their physical inferiority. Somehow in their mind, it was the man's fault that men were physically superior. Rather than appreciating a superior being who loved, cared, and was prepared to die for them, somehow in their minds men should be punished for the superiority which mother nature handed out. And oh, by the way ladies, please identify the other species in the animal kingdom where the sexes were "equal"? Please correct us, but isn't it true that every species has a "dominant" sex? Ah, but merely because you want it pronounced somehow, we, the most pretentious of all species, have attained what no other species has? QED. Maximushorseshitmus!

He invited lovable Lynn to start playing tennis. She was already a pretty good athlete and had a fair amount of coordination. Jack drilled with her, and she improved rapidly. Jack predicted and feared she would challenge him one day, lose, and somehow make Jack out to be the asshole. To avoid his fear, Jack determined to steer Lynn toward female competition, and, if male competition was inevitable, at least to steer her away from a direct confrontation with Jack. If she persisted, he would beat her ass and neither apologize nor gloat. And so, it came to pass after about six months that Lynn popped a new can of balls and threw them at Jack. "Best of three?" she said.

"Lynn, you're progressing so well, there's no point in playing me."

"Afraid?" she glared.

"Lynn, please, let's drill. Your volley is really coming along."

"Pussy?"

"I do like pussy, yes."

She laughed too loud.

"Bring it," and she strutted back to the baseline.

So, he crushed her 6-0 6-0 and could have donated a point here and there but resolved to make the ass-kicking complete. He even pounded two big overheads at her on purpose—you want equality, here comes my uterus!

"Wow, I guess your dick is bigger than mine," Lynn said, sitting down after the match.

"An elegant sentiment," Jack said.

Then, she sulked and pouted on the bench. He offered no words of consolation. She refused his offers to drill over the next few weeks and then stopped communicating at all. Nearly two years later, he'd run into her at the grocery store, and she said she had not played tennis since and "was not interested" in the game anymore. What a waste, he thought, and for what?

The years passed. The precedents got stronger and stronger.

He'd pretty much given up the idea of kids by 35. Almost everyone was already married and already had them. He knew the odds of finding a woman who wanted them were declining, unless he tried for girls in their 20s. But shit, he thought, girls in their 20s weren't interested in me when I was in my 20s, so why would they be interested in me now?

In the meantime, his legal career took off and became relentlessly more demanding. At the same time, his interests filled more of the schedule. Gradually, whether to pursue another woman (for they would never ever pursue him at all) came down to: Tuesday night, play tennis with _____ and have guaranteed good time and stress-relieving physical activity or go on date with _____ and be faced with more work (she will do nothing), pay money (she will pay for nothing), more stress (she will do nothing), and get home late (big day at work tomorrow)? As more and more Tuesday nights ended up in the "did-all-the-work, paid-all-the-money, and ended-up-jacking off-alone file," that tennis match started to look better and better. When hunting and fishing got going, and there was a 3 or 4 a.m. wake up call on the calendar, that too started to make decisions very easy.

By the time he was in his late thirties, his married friends started consistently with the sexual horror stories: no blow jobs; no morning sex; no sex if the kids were around, which was always; no blow jobs; fewer girl on tops; no blow jobs and no blow jobs. Some of them were having sex once a week or less. Some less than that. And some almost never. Their wives had married them only to get someone to pay the bills for what they really wanted—kids. They were now on sexual rations just enough to keep them paying the bills, and maybe a blow job on their birthday. Geez, Jack thought, am I unlucky or lucky?

And so, Jack was the ordinary morning of February 25 at 8:41 a.m., when he received a text.

"Hello, Rip. It's Jen. I heard you play violin. I play cello. Want to play?"

Jack read the text four times. He'd waited for such an invitation his whole life. She played cello? The girl with the Dostoevsky novel in her purse? The girl with the concave wrist and the diagonal lob? The prissy coquette who thought she was hot shit? The girl who never giggled? Who told her he played violin? Must be Erin, but how did Erin know? Well, what did it matter? It was no secret.

How old was she? Jack tried to remember if there were any overt clues, e.g., how many years out of law school had been mentioned at the doubles match. He couldn't think of any. Wait, hadn't he asked her? Yes, he vaguely recalled he had but couldn't remember the answer. She'd been a bit of a smart ass, hadn't she? He googled her firm. Her name was on there—"Jennifer Fairfield," but the bio said "pending." He went to the Florida Bar website. Same thing: listed, but very little information.

Maybe the text was an internet joke, some "bot" or some horseshit? Jack wondered. He was contemptuous of computers and could not believe how the Millennials swallowed the big internet dick no questions asked. It was so obviously designed to program the species, Jack could not believe the allegedly "educated" arts and science folks could let this get passed. Where was the critical thinking that had dominated his education? Surely, at least, the lawyers would rip it to shreds. The internet/computer thing was a million times worse than "Fuck the Draft," but none of these Millennials seemed to care. They were utterly obedient. Dissent was not welcomed. Ideas were not exchanged, and they seemed not to care at all. Worse, their music sucked, their painting sucked, their sculpture was both nonexistent and omnipresent, their theatre sucked, their TV sucked. They had killed the arts and didn't even care. They were sullen, self-righteous, ignorant prigs—the worst kind.

For Jack, it was both a horrible realization and easy plinking. There were so many targets. They were so easy to hit. He loved it especially when a weak, ignorant, self-righteous vagina was the only sentry on duty.

"Don't you think women should be drafted just like men?"

"Of course."

"So you think women should die on the front lines in combat?"

"I don't believe in war."

"Please answer my question."

No audible response. Eyeroll. Hand flutter. Huff. Puff. Time to change my maxi to a mini. Dinosaur Dismissed!

No Camille Paglia was to be found anywhere. Indeed, they hated Paglia—the self-described ambivalent carpet muncher whom Jack loved reading. Any girl who'd publicly admit that she hated pink pussy hats was okay with Jack. She wouldn't sing in chorus and had to be destroyed, or in Millennial tactics, ignored. Jack had never heard a single Millennial engage in self-deprecation. In school, they all got A's in "Advanced Self-Esteem Building w/o Attendant Accomplishments." Jack was part of the hiring process at the law firm, and he'd requested undergraduate and law school transcripts. The top of the class was taking "The Meat You Eat," "Growing Fruit for Fun and Profit," "The Insects," "Post-Modern Genderism," etc. No one was taking history (except racist history), literature (except racist literature), philosophy (except racist philosophy), or logic (course discontinued for lack of interest). Sure, there had been a little farting allowed in Jack's day, but mostly meat and potatoes was served. Jack's partners had asked him to please stop asking "Jefferson Davis" questions in the law firm interviews as none of the best and brightest knew who he was.

Jack took a deep breath and went and got a cup of coffee from the firm's kitchen. He couldn't think straight until his anti-millennial rage dissipated. Jack loved coffee. It was so strong and assertive. It literally coated everything it touched with skank and cack and scum and yak and never apologized. It was the heroin of not-too-potent drugs, but still it tagged everything it came in contact with. Your carafe needed cleaning, so did your reservoir; your cups were black, imagine what your gut looked like? And it made your urine brown like your organs were decaying.

There were three ladies in Jack's law firm's kitchen: Vanna, Lysa, and Cathy. He loved them all; they were such good girls. They all giggled at Jack, and Jack cracked a few jokes for them. Cathy was a little older, but Vanna and Lysa were good looking girls in their 20s. None of them were married, but two of them were on the "I'm waiting for my boyfriend of NINE years to propose" program. He had noticed they never asked questions other than possibly "how was your weekend?"

Jack joked with them, and they giggled their little chicken heads off. Jack girl-giggled back at them, and they really roared off. He could make his eyes wild, make voices, etc. He told them how tired he was, and how he wanted to "get to the weekend" so he could, wait for it, do nothing, you know sleep in. They pissed their panties YAY. I'm always tired Jack said, and Vanna said "bullshit" but her eyes were laughing. Jack loved to make women laugh. Jack loved to make men laugh. Jack loved to laugh himself. "I need a wellness day," Jack said as he shook his old ass at them leaving, "because I'm *not* well" and they chicken-headed off at the old loser with no kids and no wife, the fifty-year-old harmless loner who showed up at every firm event without a date. He would die alone, and they did not care at all.

Similarly, they would waste their lives for sure, Jack thought. What nice girls. He must be like a church elder (wait they didn't go to church) or an old Hollywood actor like Kirk Douglas (wait they thought history started with Bill Clinton) or I know, Jack thought, like a Harry Potter fictional freak show. Yeah, old man Jack, twenty-year-old clothes, old man's flat ass, creaky back, receding hairline. What a good porno it would make, Jack thought. He'd title it *Semen Seriatim* and bend them all over in the law firm library, making them chant "jism justice" while he administered his big purple cock from behind, different colored lipstick for each of them with a matching Lady Justice blindfold, Jack with a powdered wig on and those funky, white, calf stockings circa 1776.

His fantasy leaving him, Jack barked like a dog and made fun of himself one more time for their amusement and took his coffee back to his office. They were nice girls—just like all the ones who'd never given him the time of day.

Geez, he thought, Jen just wants to play music. You stupid son of a bitch. Get a grip. She'll never ever touch you, old Geezer. All of his normal apprehensions with women receded, and he laughed at how ridiculous he had been in thinking the harmless text was anything sexual. Sure, he'd been waiting for it all his life, but he was too old now to take advantage of it. Sure, he was a proponent of the "men and women can't be friends" law of physics, but shit, she was just too young. Had he asked her how old she was? He had but he couldn't remember. Thirty? What did it matter; she was well out of range. He laughed again, and his secretary, Karen, called him and asked him if anything was wrong because he was laughing so much. He made her laugh and got back to work. The Robbins file had a particularly interesting needle, and he knew he would thread it with gold.

After lunch he'd gathered himself and decided this was an excellent opportunity. Never in his life had he had a cello player on a consistent basis. This was rare, and all his decades of yearning might actually yield fruit. However, he hadn't played in a couple of years, so he'd have to get back to work. But that was no problem. If there was anything Jack could do, it was work endlessly toward an unattainable goal. An odd hope battled his hoary precedents and won. He was, after all, a real lawyer, not a Millennial, someone willing to reconsider arguments which previously had not prevailed. Only an idiot, Jack thought, refuses to debate, reconsider, and decide anew.

Chapter Three

A SECOND BEDROOM TO PLAY IN

"Thunderstruck!" he texted her later that day, "Schedule? Wednesday or Friday night would work here, but I don't want to kill your date with the Governor."

"Wednesday. 7 p.m.?" She texted back in under a minute.

"Confirmed. Location?"

"Is there a brothel in town?"

"Millennials are not allowed to use the word "brothel" as the word fell out of fashion prior to 1992 when recorded history started."

"Ha. Long text. They told me you were out there." She shot back.

"Confirmed. Et tu?" Who was "they" Jack thought?

"Confirmed."

"Is your voice as mellifluous as your cello?"

"Confirmed."

"Then prepare for the dreaded telephone call." Jack sent a flamboyant tongue emoji.

Who was this woman, he thought as he called her. What on earth did he have to lose? So, he called her.

"Isaac Stern, sans yarmulke, here," he said.

"Yo, Yo, Yo, Yo," she street-spoke, but Jack detected something.

"Did you just make an allusion to Yo-Yo Ma?" Jack said.

"Confirmed."

"Now, you can't use my own lines against me, Yo-Yo Ma."

"You had me at mellifluous," she mocked.

"Jerry Maguire?"

"Ratified."

Jack laughed hard. Who was this woman? "Well, where shall we attempt to play?"

"Attempt?"

"I mean. You realize I'm terrible." Jack said.

"I doubt it. Maybe mediocre, but not terrible."

"Hmmm," she continued. "Well a cello is kinda tough to tote around?"

"Good point." But Jack thought, it was not that hard really.

"Being from up North, you probably have an anteroom or something you can invite me to without being wildly inappropriate?"

"Inappropriate?"

"Well, pretty young single girls from up North cannot have a red neck geezer from the South actually present in their abode, can they? I mean they can't even be *seen* with such a creature, can they?"

She laughed. "Hmmm. That's a lot of adjectives, Jack."

"Ok. You pick."

She ran out of game, and there was a small silence. "You're right. Let's play at my place."

"Address?" Jack said.

"I'll text it to you."

"Shit."

"No, thank you."

Hmmm, Jack thought, as he hung up, it makes only a little sense. There was only one Millennial attorney at the firm that he could stand—Elan Carter Fields. Jack had voted against hiring Elan but had been overruled by his partners. Although a textbook Millennial, Jack did notice that Elan was a bit of a sneaky shit, and Jack liked that. He asked him to come to his office.

"Elan, help a Geezer out."

"Sure."

"We might have a case against Robbins Mortons, and they got this new attorney, Jennifer Fairfield, from up north, thinks she's hot shit, you know the usual unbearably arrogant Northeasterner."

"GATORS!" Elan duly growled.

"Yeah, so do me a favor and stick a knife in her for me. I want a full social media profile, you know Facebook, Instascram, TikDik, drunk photos, pot smoking, keep the nudes for yourself, all that shit, alright."

"Cake walk."

"For you, badass. Then, she grew up in Virginia and went to Cornell law, so check the Virginia and New York Bars and see if she is admitted and if so when."

"How old?"

"Late 20s; your age," said Jack.

"Got it."

"Then, you know she had to pass the full background check to get into the Florida Bar, right?"

"Of course."

"But they won't give us all that info. However, see if you can find out when she applied for the Florida Bar and when she was accepted." Jack loved poking around.

"You mean was there a suspicious gap suggesting she had some double murders to account for before they'd let her in."

"Stud. That's why I like you, buddy."

"Ok. All this just because we might have a case with her?" Elan revealed that he was a Millennial.

"All what? How long will this take a badass computer guy like you?"

"Probably an hour."

"Ok. Well, keep this just between the two of us, write up your time to "professional development," and I'll give you a pair of Magic tickets and a couple hundred bucks so you can take your babe out and have some fun."

"Deal. They say you have a big heart, Jack."

"True. That and nine dollars will get you a cup of coffee at Starbucks. When can you work your magic?"

"Less than a week?"

"Deal. Keep your mouth shut."

Jack was going to play music with her regardless, but the story didn't make sense. Who moves to Orlando solely for shitty weather? He liked having Elan sniff around, maybe it was nothing, maybe it was something. Jack hated being ignorant.

He showed up, March 3, 2018, Wednesday night at seven. She was a wonderful cellist. He hadn't seen her at the tennis club in the interim and hadn't thought of her at all. She was a lawyer so Jack had opened a tiny file "May see again professionally," but that was it. He was waiting for Elan and what did it matter now? Their first piece was Ave Maria. After 2-3 abortions, they found their tempo and played the piece pretty well all the way through. Jack thought he had died and gone to heaven. Then they played "Meditation" by Massenet, and it was pretty good. Then they played "Red River Valley," "Theme from Love Story," and "The Swan," for which Jen had a good arrangement that Jack had never heard before. Because the cello had the melody, most of the arrangements had a very pared down violin part. Or worse, they'd take the melody from the cellist and give it to the violin, a horrible felony in Jack's view that should lead to open revolt amongst all cellists. But Jen had found an arrangement with an exchange of melody and accompaniment with long notes rather than the usual eights. Jack was in heaven, so he struggled to sight read it. But he heard the glory and promised to practice it. Regardless of arrangement, they both agreed the cellist had to have at least half the melody. Jack played it cool, but deep down couldn't believe he was even having this conversation. Jen did not know Jack from Adam, yet she seemed not the slightest bit nervous at having a strange man in her apartment. She must have done some internet search on me, he thought, and it came up "no known convictions" or "harmless dufus."

Even though she was a Millennial, the sheet music was all paper and much of it weathered. There were notes from fifteen and twenty years ago. Jen had been playing these pieces since she was a young girl. Who would have suggested them to her at such a young age? Did she pick them herself when she was seven to ten years old or so? Jack was in heaven.

The apartment was in upscale Winter Garden just off downtown "shit city." Jack had driven past it most of his life but had never given it a moment's thought, three preposterously pink salmon buildings, only nine units, and surface parking. How did she get in here? She had two bedrooms, but no roommate. So, the second bedroom had been turned into a study or den or something like that, and tonight a music room. Jack had walked right up and rang the bell with no security. Jen had answered, wearing sweatpants, a Cornell Law sweatshirt, and no shoes. Her hair was double bunched like long pigtails with frayed ends. The carpeting was royal burgundy with a medium nape, and she was sockless. She wore no makeup and was filing her left hand when she answered the door. Despite his ingrained habit of observational detail, Jack did not tarry. He was also a perfect gentleman. Rather than ogle, he immediately asked, "Where shall I go?" and was sternly motioned into the second bedroom which was the first door off the foyer. The kitchen was opposite, but Jen didn't offer him anything.

All women were cockteases. He knew that unequivocally. He had zero chance at sex with this nice young woman who had invited essentially a strange old man into her apartment, and he simply would not give her any reason to doubt his bona fides. Of course, she would try to tease him. But he would not go for it. On the contrary, he would cultivate an asexual attitude toward the entire situation. Jen was Aunt Matilda with a triple neck supporting a ragged grey head of hair, numerous C-section scars on two spare tire bellies, gigantic fleshy buttocks and a vagina so dry and squeezed from the pressure of the wrinkled flesh around it that its only purpose was urination. If she could urinate out of her anus, then the vagina could be stitched up tight, once and for all. He forced himself to think this. She drank pinot noir and offered him a glass. He declined. One of the few advantages of being a loser

Jack had learned over the decades was that you could act like a hot girl didn't arouse you at all since you weren't going to get any anyway. This drove them crazy. Like everything else, Jack had refined this little game and, depending upon the situation, he might even innocently drop in "I'm sorry; are you ok?; it looks like you've gained weight" or compliment much uglier women in front of the hot woman or, if the timing was absolutely perfect, Jack's favorite: "Geez, you look like shit! Can I help?" He didn't need any of these tonight, so he went stiff and formal.

Well, that was the plan, until she started with "Ave Maria," one of Jack's favorites which she couldn't possibly know. Jack closed his eyes and was transported to another world. How old was he? How many years had he waited for a woman to play music for him? Why was *this* woman playing music for him? Had he rented a whore and forgot? What on earth was he to do? Why was he on earth? Why did he eat? Why did he defecate? Maybe Icarus would not fall? She said nothing. Her fingers on her left hand worked hard, and her bowing arm was vigorous. Her giant head of hair seemed damp, thick, musky, like a mushroom on her head. Stay cool, Jack thought.

But then, Jen did something that very few women, including women with whom Jack had been lovers, had ever done. "Here, Jack. Here's your part," she said. This simple gesture reduced Jack's anxiety, salved his insecurities, and returned him to the rational man he was. Finally, a woman who would help him in a tandem effort.

"Thank you," Jack said.

And so, they played. Jack started to play horribly below his normal level and kept looking at his left arm to see whose it was? "I'm not really *this* bad," Jack apologized. She shook her head without stopping playing, "Big breath! Exhale that tension." Again, this small act of patience made Jack feel better, and his playing got a little better.

There were many mistakes, but it was only their first time. There were moments of glory, moments that Jack had dreamed of since he was 12 or 13, moments that had never happened to Jack before, moments that Jack had given up on ever having, moments of peace, of relaxation, of contentment. In a blur, it was 8:30.

"Thank you, Jennifer Fairfield," he said as he was leaving, "I can play better."

"Oh, no one calls me that."

"Jennifer? What is your middle name?" Jack had to know.

"Scarlett."

"Oh, Rhett?"

"Ok. Wishful thinking. It's James," she said. Jack surmised that no one had ever asked her.

"Jennifer James, thank you for a lovely evening."

"Oh God, no one has ever called me that."

"What kind of Millennial makes an allusion to *Gone With the Wind*?" Jack raised an eyebrow at her.

Big smile. Or was "big" the right adjective? No audible response.

He left without even a handshake. He did not touch her. He did not ogle her. He treated her with the utmost respect. Outside the weather was a perfect sixty degrees with low humidity and a gentle breeze. Jack went home and sat on his patio with his beloved bourbon and coke. He looked east while a half moon glided in front of him. He could not remember when he'd had a grander evening. After a while, his apneas started poking at him, and he brushed his teeth, and strapped his CPAP on. For once, the mask did not breech, and Jack slept very well for the first time in months. When he awoke, he thought he was thirty years old for just an hour or so in the morning.

At the office, he locked eyes with Elan across the way who smiled and nodded him toward Jack's office.

"Wow. Granny!" Elan exclaimed.

"What does that mean?"

"This her," Elan showed Jack a small print out.

"Yes."

"She's not on social media. This is it. Facebook page "inactive" with just her name.

"Impossible." Jack was stunned.

"No, just rare."

"Wow."

"What's your instinct say?"

"Nothing. There are still some grannies around, very unusual. Plus, there is nothing suspicious about the Bars, neither a member in Virginia nor New York. In Florida, she applied, took the first Bar Exam, and was admitted without any delay, so I smell nothing. She's twenty-eight so possibly got a little late start or took a year off or something."

"Yeah, the Bar would have drilled her if there was anything serious."

"I would assume."

"What else can you dig up?"

"Need a Social security number or driver's license number, but I mean what's this all about?" said Elan. Jack thought: again, the uninquisitive Millennial strikes.

"What did I tell you the hallmark of a good lawyer is?"

"He's always inquisitive."

"That's right. So, either she's a 'granny' or something's amiss," Jack smiled at Elan and looked at him hard. The young man was telling him the truth. That, he could see. No evidence for anything nefarious existed. Elan looked back at him.

"Great work, Elan," Jack said, "which game do you want—Atlanta or Charlotte?"

"Charlotte," Elan answered.

"No problem. Here's a couple hundred for you."

"Jack, please, you don't have to; it only took me fifty minutes on my lunch break."

"Nice detail. What did I teach you?" Jack was irked.

"Always take the money."

"Good. Now take it. Of course, you'll have the circumspection to never mention this to anyone."

"Certainly."

"Thanks, Bud. And keep your notes. I may need an update some day." Jack smiled at the young man but doubted whether he ever got through.

Jack worked the rest of the day and pondered the situation every now and then. So, she did appear to be some kind of anachronistic woman captured and contained within the ever-increasing electronic age. Interesting.

Chapter Four

THE INADVERTENT ESCORT

Then, a strange coincidence befell Jack. It was late March of 2018, the Ides of March, the Winds of March if you sailed— one of Jack's favorite months. Jack had always thought he was unlucky, and more than one person had told him over the course of his life that he was unlucky. "Give it to Forester," they'd say at the office if a horrible case came in or "Turd du Forester" or "Bucket of bullshit" or "Blender of bullocks" or just "Fuck. Geez. Jack, how did this shit find you again?"

Once he'd had as a client a large hotel chain being sued by a professional plaintiff in a wheelchair for not complying with the *Americans with Disabilities Act*. The professional plaintiff had intentionally showed up at three in the morning, been shown wheelchair accessible rooms, but declined them because allegedly the shower would not allow a wheelchair in it. He'd then left. To go where was one of Jack's first questions. It was a test case, a stroke off, a pile of bullshit, a reason to hate lawyers. The plaintiff's attorney was also in a wheelchair, and at the first hearing in the case, the judge, clearly a black, female, affirmative action appointment who

43

did not understand the basic concept that no evidence is taken on a motion to dismiss, had blurted out, "Well, my mother is in a wheelchair, and I had an assistant in a wheelchair. Does anyone feel uncomfortable with any of this?" After the plaintiff's counsel warmly announced he had no problem, Jack asked for permission to think about it. The stupid judge allowed it, and Jack was back at the office asking anyone if they had ever disqualified a judge? Howls of laughter and derision were aimed at Jack.

They were renewed a week later when the transcript of the hearing was passed around the office. Larry, one of the senior partners whom Jack had known for twenty years, came into Jack's office palpitating and red-faced with laughter. "Jesus, Jack. I was constipated when I came in today, but after reading this, I shit my brains out just now. And a black judge who doesn't know the standard of review on a motion to dismiss to ice the shit cake! My God, this is so unlucky, there are no words." And Larry left snickering. "Helen," he screamed down the hall to his assistant, "get me a wheelchair. I've just been with Forester! The bastard won't let me take a shower!" Steve, the other Senior Partner, barked from his office: "Is anyone uncomfortable with any of this? God forbid lawyers be put in an uncomfortable position, right Forester?" Laughter. A younger partner, Melanie called from her office: "Most litigation is comfortable, isn't it Steve?" Howls of laughter.

Such was Jack's life at the law firm and in general.

Jack had analyzed it and concluded that although he was generally very lucky in the big things in life—family, intellect, education, and temperament—he really was unlucky on the little things. Jack would play the odds in poker and lose. He'd play the odds in backgammon and lose. If there was an obscure injury to get in tennis, he'd get it along with the conventional injuries. Russian Roulette? Fuck, Jack would be sure to get the bullet on the first trigger pull. No woman he'd ever met in his entire life had ever made things easy. Ever. No woman had ever had too much to drink and asked him if he needed a lap dance. Jack never found a 100-dollar bill on the sidewalk. He never had a waiter miscalculate his bill and leave the shrimp cocktail off. He never played the lottery, but if he had, he would never have won.

But, three days after playing with Jen, some little thing finally went Jack's way. While checking his emails, a tickler from Bob Carr auditorium came up: Yo-Yo Ma was playing with the Orlando Symphony Orchestra! He didn't know how he had missed it. He was not a season ticket holder, but he checked periodically. It fell out of the sky. He rang Jen.

"Rip here. Sorry for telephoning. I hope you're not embarrassed in front of your friends."

"Well, I did answer, so co-conspirators I guess?" said Jen

"True. Excellent point, counselor."

"Well, Prufrock?"

"Huh?" Jack thought his ears had deceived him.

"You were just about to roll the universe into a ball or something?"

"You know that poem?"

"Rhett dear, where I came from they *made* us read." Jen laughed.

"So you want me to call you Lolita?"

She laughed. "Don't get carried away, Sting."

"Hey, I'm not that old." Jack protested.

"Who said anything about age?"

Jack laughed. Who was this woman? She *got* the Lolita allusion? Impossible.

"Well?" She said.

"Yo-Yo Fucking Ma!"

"And?"

"Thursday, April the 11th—one night only. He's flying in from some godforsaken place up North which I'm sure you think is great."

"Here?"

"Bob Carr."

"Who?"

"It's the name of the theater."

"Wow. I just googled it. Not exactly the Met huh?" she said. "You're right. The Thursday after next. Hmmm. Now why would you think of me?"

"Oh coy coquette. Here we go."

"Well?"

"Dear Jennifer James Fairfield, would you have any interest in going to the Yo-Yo Ma concert with me?"

"Just friends, of course."

"Of course."

"Yes." She said but without any enthusiasm.

"Dinner?"

"Hmmm. Thursday 7:30 I must work and so do you. Sounds like pressure."

"Agreed." Jack said. "Meet you there at 6:45?"

"Good. How much?"

"How much what?"

"For the tickets?"

Jack laughed. "Oh, I'll bring you the receipt for a full accounting."

"Good."

"I guess I should hang up?" Jack said.

"Huh?"

"Well, your friends must be concerned that you're talking on the phone?"

"I've only been here three months. I don't have any friends." But she spoke with a strange tone—as though it didn't bother her that she had no friends.

"Noted. Ok. Music this week?"

"I'm sorry, Jack. I can't."

Jack thought: No friends but "can't?"

"No worries. The following Wednesday?" He said.

"You do like to schedule."

"Yes. It gets things done."

"I just can't say right now." But her tone gave her away because she was lying. But why?

"Ok. May I say very directly I loved playing with you?"

"Oh, thanks. Better some culture, than none."

Jack thought: Say what?

"Goodbye, Jennifer James."

"Bye, Jack."

She neither committed nor de-committed on playing music together on the Wednesday before the Yo-Yo Ma concert, and that pissed Jack off. She was a lawyer. The issue was simple, clear, and discreet, yet no answer came. While the days went by, Jack remained distantly irritated by Jen's failure to communicate, but figured she wasn't his girlfriend and would never be his girlfriend and so what? Even if she were, how would it change anything? Jack could remember all his girlfriends, either because he had a good memory or because there weren't very many of them, and decisive decision making was not a strong suit anywhere, unless the answer of course was "no." Thus, would you like to attend the conference with me next Thursday would be met with "I don't know" or "I'm not sure" or "let me check" or endless other horse shit. But would you like to take your clothes off and ride my hobby horse? got a succinct, pellucid "no," perhaps "no, asshole" or the *tour de force*, "fuck no, asshole." So, they *could* be clear and decisive, that much Jack knew in theory.

Plus, Jen was a Millennial. These Millennials were all slackers anyway. He'd seen young attorneys like Jen. If you mentioned working nights or weekends, they looked at you like you were from another planet. That was like a horse and carriage to them; they vaguely knew it had existed millions of years ago. They came in at 9:00 a.m. or later right out of law school. Jack had started work at 6:00 a.m. out of school, moved to 7:00 a.m. a year later, and moved to 8:00 a.m. a year after that. He remembered sweating that he was going to get fired for the first three or four years. Even now, he came in almost every day at 8:30. Now they breezed in at 9 or so, and Jack wasn't even sure they realized they could be fired. A lower energy group of twenty-year-olds was tough to imagine. Jack wondered whether they would storm the beach at Normandy, panties around their necks so they didn't get wet, white panties, in a dark tide swell. Easy soft targets plodding. Dead before any stress even got to them. They'd check their texts just before the Higgins ramp dropped.

Yeah, these Millennials had no work ethic, so why would Jen be any different? He had the concert calendared. She didn't communicate, so that was it. He would not play concierge for her. Fuck it. He'd go alone if he had to. He had done that a hundred times before.

On the morning of the concert, he texted her: "Tickets in possession. Rendezvous 6:45 at Bob Carr. Please confirm?"

"Confirmed. But I might be a little late."

That too pissed Jack off. He knew it was complete bullshit. But she wasn't his girlfriend and never would be. If he made her angry, they'd never play music together again. He also had a full day of work ahead of him, so he worked. He would work until 6:30 and go straight to the show. He put a twenty-year-old sport coat in his truck for the show, and that was it.

He got there early, and she texted that she was running late. How would he get her the ticket to get in? He decided to let it ride. Fuck this non-communicative bitch. This was exactly the kind of small, easily fixed issues which really pissed Jack off when they weren't fixed and left to linger. In any event, he had the tickets, he was already inside, and he'd let her deal with it.

He was upstairs on the second floor when a little flash went through the ground floor: it was Jen and an old lady usher looking for him. So, Jen had *conned* the usher into letting her in without a ticket—impressive. Jack waved, and there seemed to be a small light in Jen when she saw him and waved back. He had wondered what she would wear. She had looked good on the tennis court, and she had looked normal for the music session. The women in Jack's family were all low-key dressers with a limited dynamic range. There would be a little lipstick, a little high heels, a decent dress, and an extra curl in the hair. But here came Jennifer in a form fitting, black satin, cocktail dress and shiny, black, spike heels, a silver-sequined clutch, a big diamond necklace, and her famous hair piled way up. She was noticed all right. Jack suddenly felt queasy and inadequate looking down at his ten-year-old shoes with five-year-old polish. This was *his* date?

"She's an FBI agent," he whispered to the usher who clicked the ticket with the scanner.

"Sorry, I made it so hard," Jen said to the usher.

The lady usher who was in her late sixties gave a long contemptuous sneer and left without any pleasantries. Jack's lightbulb went on. My God, Jack thought, she thinks Jen's an escort and I'm the John. Jack thought Jen must have noticed it, and he looked at her. It must be hard to be all alone in the South, but then to go to a concert with a much older man and have the usher think she was a whore? Oh, that was so bad. Had she noticed? He kept looking at Jen and could see her normally impenetrable veneer had been breached. She was a little shaken and hurt.

"I'm sorry," Jack said.

"About what?" Jen said, but she wouldn't look at him. He paused his gait, made her stop, and looked at her. "Don't play dumb because I know you're not."

"Not your fault," Jen said. She looked right at him not believing he'd noticed. They exhaled.

"I had no idea you were so beautiful."

She laughed hard and wiped away a little tear. He could see she didn't like crying; to her it was weak, a loss of control. Then she laughed again and clenched and unclenched her shoulders, arms, and hands.

"That is so funny, Rip."

"I'm sorry. Really. That was so terrible. I thought I was in New York for a second."

"It's okay. I should have told you I liked to get dressed up." She said.

"Well, what an immodest coquette you are indeed, and what a lucky motherfucker am *moi*," he mock bowed. "Champagne?"

"That'd be going in the right direction," but she couldn't keep a straight face and laughed hard.

He got her the champagne. She rebounded quickly, and very shortly it was time to enter the theater.

"I've been coming here since I was a kid," Jack said.

"Really?"

"Yes, my dad's practice had season tickets, and the family would come all the time. Our seats are over here somewhere."

"Wonderful."

Jack was not good with computers, but he'd always been good at getting tickets. He'd gotten on Stub Hub and put them in the second row, just left of center. But he'd never told Jen. He wanted to surprise her. As they walked down the aisle, he once again felt an odd sense of hope and goodness. He felt terrible for Jen and wanted to make her happy. But why? She didn't care about him. The old usher hadn't meant anything. It was just a reflex, but sometimes that's the most hurtful of all—like a kid saying you're fat.

She was in front of him and tall in her heels, and it was fun to see her checking the rows to see which they'd go down. But he just smiled at her, slow-played it, and acted dumb. But she was too smart and figured out he was up to something a few seconds before he showed the tickets to a different usher. The seats were fantastic.

"Wow, Jack. These are awesome," she said.

The orchestra was quietly warming up in front of them, and Jack smiled and nodded.

"Are you okay?"

"Yes. Thanks."

He gave her the softest touch on the shoulder and said: "Thanks for joining me."

She smiled at him. He'd summed up the minor incident and made it all go away and seem utterly insignificant without detailing or dwelling on any of it. She'd recognized and appreciated the whole thing. "Fuck that usher" was unsaid between them. They were reset, and she smiled again. He filed away a potential joke for later use: "I like *only* high-class whores." He knew the timing would have to be perfect to pull it off, but it was still better to have it ready.

Chapter Five

I DOUBLE YOU

As far as he could tell, she loved the Yo-Yo Ma concert, and as they had left, he knew there would be at least one moment of confused sexuality. But he'd already decided the evening had gone well, and he would not lose her over some parting nonsense. Over the decades, he had fumbled this sort of occasion frequently, it being always, forever, and without explanation understood that he was obligated to manage the situation with grace while the bitch in question did, of course, nothing.

He remembered Mary Lou, the first year of high school at Sadie Hawkins. Of course, she didn't actually invite him but got her friend to ask Jack for her. At the age of fourteen, Jack already hated social occasions, but Mary Lou was the cutest girl in the freshman class. Jack had said he could not and would not dance, but when a slow number came on Mary Lou had convinced him there was nothing to it. True, but there was one problem: Jack's massive leaky bowed archer and its refusal to deflate. The only thing redder was Jack's face as he felt waves of embarrassment crash over him. Of course, he had

53

never touched Mary Lou before, was monstrously aroused, and kept poking Mary Lou with his yard stick, which only made it bigger. She knew how much he was suffering but what was there to do. The song seemed longer than "Free Bird" and Jack feared he would either ooze out the top of his waistband or actually fire out the top and hit and hold on Mary's billowy, lacey, cum-latching, lavender dress. Couldn't she have just sat him down?

He froze up the rest of the night, didn't make her laugh once (it was why she had 'invited' him to begin with), and then tried for a big hug and kiss at the end when, of course, she did nothing. He got a big push off and a glare.

There was Susie in senior year of high school. Her folks had moved from Chicago, and they'd gone to the Grateful Dead together, Jack lying to his parents or they would never have let him go. Again, at the end, Jack had tried for a kiss. She ducked, called him an 'asshole' and "couldn't believe" that he thought she wanted to. Bullshit, Jack thought. The same girls who would say "of course" I like you when I go to a concert with you are the ones who also say "of course" we were just going as friends. With females, there's always lots of "of coursing" in lieu of actual communication, Jack thought.

In undergrad, Courtney had gone to a poetry reading with him, yet still he got the stiff arm at the end. What was sexier than a poetry reading? So, Jack had been beat up, and he would neither fuck the Yo-Yo Ma concert up with any ham-handed parking lot maneuvers nor would he sit and stammer while she did nothing.

Jen had Ubered, so there was no car to walk her to. Certainly, he wouldn't dream of offering to drive her anywhere in a million years. Best for a quick, even stiff, good night.

"Thank you, Jennifer," he said formally and stuck his hand well out.

"I loved it. Thanks, Jack." Her cards were snare drum tight.

"Have a good night."

"You too. Thanks."

And it was over. Perfect, Jack thought as he drove home. She can't burn him at the stake over that. Although it was extremely late when he got home, Jack's chronic obstructive sleep apnea wouldn't let him sleep. He thought of the smile she gave him when he had figured out the "whore/John" thing and made it quickly go away. There was a tiny light in that smile, he decided. But no, it was nothing, he tossed in bed, just a surprising disaster and she had probably never had any similar experience in her life. What did a woman think when another woman thought she was a whore? Jack laughed at the absurdity of the questions—as though he could ever know— and went to sleep.

But now he still had no girlfriend, but he was a little distracted. He felt some connection to Jen.

The Kowalski trial was on the docket in about thirty days and Jack didn't think it would settle. He liked the case about the air-conditioner equipment seller (his client) against the general contractor, Robbins, Inc. It was a shitty apartment complex that everyone was going to stuff their pockets on. But Robbins hadn't been able to find a decent air-conditioning sub, so being the greedy sons of bitches that they were, they decided to cheap it out with a young company. Worse, ordinarily the A/C sub would supply its own equipment, but this one didn't have a thousand dollars in the bank. So, Robbins thought it would get cute and order the equipment directly, convert the markup into their profit, and smile rapaciously at the end. However, the equipment was chronically late arriving, some was incorrect, and the errors blew the whole schedule, as there was air-conditioning equipment in every single unit in the entire complex. The project was way, way late, and everyone refused to step up and honorably take responsibility. Jack loved the case for his client Kowalski. The ordering by the GC had been all wrong, there was little paper in the way of guaranteeing delivery dates, and the Robbins corporate representative deposition had been spectacular as they had been forced to admit that they had never done this before in company history. Also, the case was nonjury, and Jack knew the judge pretty well—a cranky, old bitch who had been around the block, and smart. Opposing counsel was Larry Friedman, a giant, arrogant asshole from one of the biggest firms in town. Jack hated big law firms and their big dickheads. Jack had told everyone at the office: "I'm going to rape his wife first, in front of him, then rape him, and even then, he'll find a way to look back at me and tell me I didn't go to UVA law. Ha!" Jack had everyone laughing and red-faced at the office.

But he thought of Jen a lot, and he couldn't find one reason why.

At 4:11, she texted him. "Great show. Want to play Thursday at 7?"

Jack panicked. He had a giant day Thursday, and a hearing at 9:00 a.m. on Friday. The Kowalski case was on his mind a lot. He hadn't practiced his violin. He needed to play tennis. Jack panicked a little more. He got a glass of water from the firm's kitchen. Little Gretchen was in there; she was one of Steve's daughters, probably sixteen years old, doing some "work." She gave him a sly smile. "You look stressed, Jack."

He had to tell her to call him "Jack" three times, but she kept calling him "Mr. Forester" until he said "Gretchen, dear, if you call me Mr. Forester again, I'm going to have to tell your father you are stupid."

She had laughed, "ok, ok, ok."

"Say it."

"What?"

"Jack."

"Do I?" said Jack, pleased with the memory.

"Oh, yeah. I felt tension as soon as you walked in here."

"Geez. I'm sorry."

"What's wrong." She asked but did not look up from her phone. This was the longest conversation they'd had in the six weeks she'd been working there.

"It just burns me up that Contessa Perdono is only two and half minutes long. You know when you strip away the fast parts. I want to milk that soprano and unison for at least another 90 seconds, so gorgeous." Jack said.

Gretchen giggled and giggled.

"I'm a fool aren't I?" Jack gave her a big smile. "Imbecile? Dummy? How do you say 'asshole' in Taylor Swift?"

Gretchen laughed loudly and shrilly as only a sixteen-year-old can as Carolina walked in. "Hey, what's so fun in here?" Carolina asked, twitching her hips a little and fluffing her hair with both hands.

No one said anything. "Aw, c'mon."

"Well, tell her Gretch."

Gretchen turned pink and red but couldn't stop smiling. "Jack just said the craziest stuff. I don't even know . . . was that *shampoo* or something?"

Now Jack laughed devilishly. "You don't like my shampoo?" No response. "Call me when you get a pencil," and he left in an exaggerated fashion.

"Shampoo?" Carolina said, shaking her head. "Pencil? What's funny about that?"

Back in his office, Gretchen had relaxed Jack.

"Yes," he texted Jen, "confirming for seven on Thursday." He'd man up and practice extra and stop whining.

It was April 2018, and their second session, and it went very well. Jack intentionally wore the same thing he'd worn the first time. He knew it was not a deal killer, and he wanted to see if Jen would notice. If she did, she never said anything.

Jack noticed that Jen had put a little more effort into her appearance. Having shown off at the concert, Jack mused that she couldn't just work the Cornell sweatshirt anymore. Still, Jack thought, it doesn't mean anything. Girls will dress up for the fucking mailman. Don't get confused, you dumb shit, he thought. Just because you haven't had sex in three years doesn't mean Jen has any interest in helping you with your agony. Focus on the music, Horndog.

She'd pulled her hair up into a big bunch in back, but there was still plenty hanging down her sides. But it was way off her face and even her ears, which he'd never seen before. She offered him tea first, and in the bright kitchen lights, Jack finally got his first good look at her. She had no discernible make-up on. She had very white "from up North" skin, etched eyebrows very dark, a longish face but not aquiline, and a wide mouth. Her ears were tall and oval, not small and round. She had on a diaphanous lavender blouse, and rich girl blue jeans, and flats. She liked being watched, he figured, but so did all of them. She must have known he was checking her out, but there was no tension, no nervous giggling, no wrong words. She knew the lights in the kitchen were on high, but it almost seemed like she wanted to let him see her to get it over with? You can look, but you'll never touch, Jack imagined her thinking. God, you are stupid, Jack thought; it doesn't mean a thing. Never for a second has she thought about your cock and balls.

"Earl Grey," she joked as though it was a TV commercial.

"I prefer Lady Grey," Jack didn't miss a beat.

"You're kidding," she broke character.

Jack held his hands out in confusion.

"*I* always liked Lady Grey better," and she shook the box of Lady Grey at him as she brought it down from the cabinet. Who is this woman? But it was only tea, thought Jack.

"Lovely. Is this your family?" he motioned to a small photo in the kitchen. What kind of Millennial even knows what Lady Grey is, he thought to himself, but he let it roll off.

"Yes, Mom and Dad and my brother David."

"Older?" Jack asked.

"Mmm."

"So you're the baby, oh Lord, we all know what that means."

She smiled and stuck her tongue out at him. "I've heard that before," she admitted.

"How many times?" But it came out a little harsh and blunt. She paused.

"Two or three." She allowed.

Jack filed the answer away, but he knew he'd hit a little nerve. The answer was probably fifty or something. A spoiled little brat, Millennial, he thought. Well, what the fuck did that have to do with him? Pluto was closer to him than her clitoris.

They played, and it was a little better than the first time. Again, Jack was transported during "Ave Maria," and overall, everything got just a little bit better. A few moments of beauty were created, however fleeting. Jack saw some cups in the second bedroom where they were playing. "You've been practicing?" he said.

"You don't miss much."

"Sorry." Jack shrugged.

"Let's work on the second melodic repetition, see here, bar 19."

"The repeat, yeah." Jack nodded.

"Should it be louder or softer than the first time through?"

"Hmm. That's the most exciting thing anyone has ever asked me," said Jack.

They smiled at each other.

"What do you think?" Jack said.

"Well, I asked you."

"I think the highs and lows only should be accentuated, more vibrato at the top and bottom but even in the middle," said Jack.

"Hmm. Let's try it." Jen said.

They did and they both agreed it was better.

"Now, let's try softer on the first time through against what we just played" she suggested. Jack could tell that she liked taking the lead on this.

Also better they both agreed.

They played another hour. Jack never once thought about the Kowalski case. Between pieces, he could see her neck and shoulders tensing and flowing with the music. They'd positioned themselves directly opposite one another. But Jen had a way of turning her head to her right when she played, so her long white neck was continually exposed. Jack wanted to get a tape measure and check out in detail that white flesh from the bottom of her chin, down, down, down, to where it disappeared below her second unbuttoned button. Brother was that some flesh, he thought. Her expensive flats looked huge, but Jack knew some of that was the preposterous jeans which tapered ridiculously tight to the ankles. Of course, the cello blocked her crotch and chest, but that didn't stop Jack from wishing he were the cello. A woman's hands on the cello had to be one of life's most beautiful things. Jen's were long and thin, her tips seemed to have "squared" up. She had been practicing, Jack thought. Jack had had girlfriends with short fingers, and he didn't like them. It was purely physical; he just didn't like them. Why couldn't his cock be as long as that cello neck with Jen's hands and fingers moving up and down and around it for all eternity or at least until Jack's scroll trembled and straightened and shot a quart past the moon. Get your shit together, Jack thought, God you're a mess. She's leaving you in the dust.

During a break, Jack noticed a bookshelf which hadn't been there the first time. Jack was forever checking out bookshelves his entire life.

"Oh, no," Jack said, "that's not the family backgammon set passed down from Thomas Jefferson?" He pointed to a set on the top shelf.

"You play?" she said.

"I mean I suck, but yes. It's been a long time. No one plays backgammon anymore. Gosh, Florida will tear that up, you better not take it out into the humidity. How old is it?"

"It's a twin set from around 1900 from my great-grand-mother," said Jen. "This one is brown, and the other one is black. My parents have it."

"No kidding? Whoever heard of matching backgammon sets? You're shitting me?" said Jack

"Ha. 'Shitting you'? You're a funny guy, Rip. How could I poop *that*."

"I double you," he said.

She laughed. "Some other time. Thanks for playing tonight."

"I loved it."

"You watered my old well," she said it softly but he had a feeling something was coming and her words went in deep, deep, and deeper.

"Your cello?" he tried to diminish her sudden exposure, but again she just looked at him with the "here it is" look.

She nodded yes and led him to the door. Again, his hand went way out, far away from their bodies, and she shook it with the same hand which had bowed the cello. A little jolt went through Jack as they let their shake last longer than last time. It didn't matter how old he was, her old affair with her cello, apparently long dormant, had been rekindled by Jack. That was rare; that meant something. Jack was elated.

Jack worked hard the next day and took his tennis gear to the office with him. He'd done this about 400 times. He ate a protein bar and guzzled water. He played Lonnie, one of his regulars, and it was their usual brawl in the Florida humidity. Jack got home at 9:40 and thought, Who is this woman? Most women would tell you if they had a boyfriend or husband within 45 seconds of meeting them. Jennifer had not said a thing. She was twenty-eight and beautiful. Whether she'd been in Orlando for three months or three minutes, all she had to do was go to any watering hole and the jackals would be all over her. Plus, she was a Millennial, and they had all the computer dating/sex stuff, endless. Plus, she worked with lawyers, notorious meeters and greeters, bloviating blowhards, endless agitators, stirrer uppers. He'd lived in Orlando all his life, and knew without question she could have had any number of dates within a week of arriving. Yet, she hadn't said a word. Be rational, Jack thought as the last of his strength ebbed.

He looked at his mantel where his tennis trophies sat, his sunroom with the brass sailboat he and his father had won at a regatta when Jack was a kid. He was brutally dehydrated but drinking a Foster's Lager oilcan anyway. Jack tried to think of something besides sleep, of which he thought continually.

Option A, she was not interested. Certainly, this was the most rational option due to their extreme age difference. Even though he hadn't told her exactly how old he was, the difference was clearly huge. His date of birth was on the Florida Bar website if not numerous other online sources. She clearly knew enough to decide whether anything sexual would happen. But this confused Jack. If she clearly under no circumstances was not going to have sex with him because he was too old, then there were a million ways to let him know. First, she could just flat out tell him. "Just friends," she'd said in re Yo-Yo Ma, but Jack thought hard. She hadn't said "just friends" or anything analogous since. Second, she could just make up a boyfriend even if he didn't exist. Jack would either get the hint or question her in which case he'd *really* get the hint. Either way, it was a subject that was easy to clarify. Jack drifted off in his confusion to the big kick serve he'd hit early in the second against Lonnie. God, you are an old loser, he thought, sitting alone in your shitty house, at 48, and jerking off to some stupid kick serve that no one on planet Earth gave a shit about. He brushed his teeth thoroughly and fell in bed. But his brain wouldn't let him sleep.

Option B, she is interested, including sexually. It seemed impossible, but c'mon, Jack, you're a lawyer, make an argument. "You watered my old well." That's the nicest non-sexual thing any woman had ever said to Jack. But was it non-sexual? "Well," could easily be a metaphor for "vagina," and "water" even easier could be "moist" or "wet." Had she told him "You make my pussy wet?" Jack chuckled in bed with the very last moments of the day vexing him.

Open file: May/December relationships do exist in Western culture; maybe Eastern, too, Sure, there were a lot of men older than their wives up to about ten years, but how many regular men can you think of that are twenty years older than their wives or girlfriends? Jack chuckled again as he staggered to bed. He was dead tired, and his chronic obstructive sleep apnea would not win tonight. He fell asleep quickly and woke up with a big erection, feeling great, but he had no specific dreams of Jennifer. It wasn't like his sixteen-year-old erections; those had to be dealt with as they were not going away. Now, he could have a horrible conversation with his erection and talk it into waiting another day. Why go on living, Jack thought? But he had to get to work.

She didn't text or call for six days. Jack was a little hurt, but the Kowalski case sucked him in a little more. Larry big boy had called and let Jack know just how stupid he thought Jack was. Jack played along and said they should have lunch at Buchenwald's, which the dumb fuck didn't get, confirming

AN HOUR OF REDEMPTION

to Jack that Larry scorned every word from Jack's mouth. He loved that more than anything all day. He wanted to preserve the musical relationship with Jen. That's what any rational man would conclude. He'd never had one with so much potential. They were very rare. What to do without coming on too strong? He didn't know.

"Backgammon and bourbon?" she finally texted on Thursday at 4:38 p.m. How'd she know bourbon was his favorite? Coincidence? Jack was at work and again needed to gather himself. She'd "missed" Wednesday when they would have played if they had a set routine, which they didn't. In fact, they'd played Thursday the last time. Get your shit together, Jack thought, there has never been a set Wednesday schedule except in your mind. She hadn't said anything about missing music, which kinda hurt. How about "wish we'd been able to play but _____." No mention of time or place, but since it was Thursday obviously the weekend was suggested. Again, no clarity on the sex issue, but she suggested they drink alcohol together? Hmmmm? Jack was very confused. Jack had trouble being rational. These questions were so easy, and yet she must know she was making them difficult. Why? What was the point? Jack checked his schedule. He was going offshore fishing Saturday at 1:30 a.m. and that would cook him all that day. Sunday was fairly open, but if the fishing were really good, he'd gladly clean fish Sunday a.m. So that meant Sunday p.m. was open. Friday night? He didn't have anything, but she must. But then, he caught himself, why must she? She's inviting me on a Thursday. Jack was very confused.

Jack went into the firm's kitchen to get water. Carolina and Susan were there. "Shampoo man!" Carolina said. They gave him big smiles, and he hunchbacked around pretending to shake dandruff out or some shit. Somehow, it had become a little firm joke. *"Gretchanna, Perdono!"* he said fluffing his imaginary head of big hair and standing erect. The girls laughed. He mock sang "Susanna Perdono." He figured they were laughing at him, the old loser, the unmarried guy, nearly fifty, no kids, lots of crazy ideas, but hey, kinda harmless. It's not like his finger was on the nuclear bomb. He knew the women in the office thought he was a loser, but he still liked hearing them laugh. He knew where the buttons were, and he pushed them all the time. It certainly seemed like they needed pushing.

Jack went back to his office. Be objective, he said to himself, use your brain. You're supposed to be a lawyer, dumb shit. He went back to Professor Van Sternberg and his "screens" he had taught in school. One screen at a time, he'd yelled at them, only one. They are all irrelevant to one another. Because the argument made it through one screen is irrelevant to all other screens. Then, Jack recalled deposition advice he'd given over the years: "If they ask a stupid question, just give them a stupid answer." Jack had taught his clients that not every lawyer could put a fine point on the salient issues. Why help them?

"Love to!" he texted back "Details?" Let the onus be on her. He'd answered the question.

"Tonight. University Club. 6:30?" she texted within twenty minutes.

Oh, so she'd joined the University Club? Wow. That was pretty aggressive. Jack was not a member but had been there a dozen times or more over the years. Lovely place. Pretty low key, but gadflies about. Ah, Jack thought, it's only blocks from her apartment. Location, Location, Location.

"Confirmed. How much money do I need to bring?"

"1000. Small bills of course."

So, he met her after work, without showering or changing his clothes, just literally rolled in off the street. It's not the clothes, it's the man, Jack's father had said or maybe he'd just gotten away with it. Jack thought the odds of meeting someone he knew there were low but quite possible, maybe 20 percent. Again, she threw him a curveball. He'd suspected her breasts were bigger than she'd shown, but now finally she showed them. They were fantastic. She had on a tight-fitting white top, heavier material than the lavender blouse routine, but bra lines and curves everywhere. Plus, it didn't tuck in. It was low enough to get away with not being called a "midriff" but still there would be tugging and some showing for sure, some of that lovely goose flesh was going to pooch through. He wondered if she'd pop some headlights for him, but these new bras they had nowadays, Jack lamented, it seems like you don't get nearly as many nipples as in the old days. The same rich girl jeans, but this time jet black. Heels but only moderate. Again, respectable girl with a dash of slut.

"You look very aggressive this evening," Jack said.

"This game is all luck."

"Mmmm, hmm." Jack did his best Bobby Bowden, but doubted she got it. He loved messing with Northerners. All his life, he'd been introduced to these pompous asses from New York, New Jersey, Massachusetts, etc. The Midwesterners weren't so bad, but the northeasterners really were unbearable. Jack made fun of them every chance he had. "Feel free to head on back," he'd often say to the nearly always unsolicited advice they'd way too frequently offer.

She already had the board set up in the members' area back behind the general seating. There were quite a few members playing cards, and there were two pool tables but no one currently using them. No music, so it was nice and quiet.

"Well," she said, "five dollars plus doubling cube?"

"Hmm. The girl from up North? Big girl? Fancy pants? Are you sure five dollars can get any blood flowing? What's a doubling cube?"

"Yes. And I know you know what a doubling cube is, Rip, so quit it."

"Okie. Dokie. Now, go easy on the old guy."

"Oh Rip, you're not old."

"God bless you, urchin."

The old set was oversized with really heavy, old chips, marvelous. It was rough leather, almost canvas on the outside, but velvet and brilliant on the inside. What was that old Emily Dickinson poem? Gossamer? Tulip? Oh shit, he would fuck it up. Let me use the men's room and then I'll drop it on her, Jack thought. Tulip? No, that's wrong, he was sure. Anyway, what was he thinking?

She went up very quickly. "Double" she said.

He declined and put a fresh five on the bar. "Ah, Abraham," he said.

She got up again in the second game, tried to double and again he declined.

"Where's this bourbon I heard about?" Jack asked.

"Ah, damn southerners."

It was the first time she ever swore in front of him. She marched off. Her gait, usually long and smooth, had a peevishness to it. Her black jeans disappeared in the dark room, so that it looked like a white-shirted ghost went into the main room. She came back.

"No service in here. What would you like?" She frowned.

"Goddamn southerners!" Jack laughed. "I'll help you."

"No. I'm the member, so what'll you'll have." Jack could see she was a little pissed.

"Southern Comfort, ma'am." She frowned again. Jack loved fucking with Northerners, but he could see he was pushing it too far.

She stalked off to get the drinks, her pumps pounding into the old wood floors.

She came back, put the drinks down, fluffed up her massive hair, put on a vampire face and said "Now, I'm ready to kill. What kind of club makes the members get their own drinks?"

Jack giggled. "Ah, these southerners are killing you missus Scarlett?"

"Your move."

But this time he got ahead of her and doubled. She accepted, a low percentage play so Jack knew the bet wasn't high enough. He rolled a couple of turds, and she rolled double fives and went way ahead.

"Double," she said.

"Jennifer, dear, it's not your turn."

She smiled, and he rolled acey ducey.

"Justice," she said grabbing her shaker.

"Double?" she said after looking at the board for a minute.

He surveyed the board. Yes, she was up, but not as much as she thought.

"Accepted."

She rolled double 4's and screamed.

"Carpetbaggers," he mock moaned.

But then, he rolled double 3s, and then double 3s again. It was very close. He looked at her. For the first time ever, she was animated. Her guard was down a little. She wanted to win. Well, his mother's voice said to Jack, you should let her. He smiled.

"Double?"

"I accept," she said. There were 5s, 10s and 20s all over the bar of the set, and she rolled a 5 and a 2, but it was decent.

"Now for the real fried chicken. Oh Gawwwd, yes," Jack said as he mock shook, but he only rolled a 6 and a 3.

"Doubles" she said, but only shook out a 5 and a 4.

It went down to the wire, but eventually it played out that Jack was slightly ahead of her.

"Double?" she said. Now, he knew the bet had not been big enough. Doubles meant nothing to her.

"You're joking," said Jack.

"Huh?"

"Well, any lawyer can see you're behind and the odds are against you, so why would you double? Plus, the bet is already huge so what's up?"

"Ha."

"Ha 'Fairfield, concurring in my judgment,'?" Jack mocked.

Jen laughed harder than he'd ever seen.

"Ok. I mean I must accept. How can I not?" said Jack.

She rolled a 5 and a 4 again. They continued until the very last roll. Only double 4s or higher would win for Jen. So, she rolled double 6s and won.

"Whoooo, red necks everywhere, I am your champion," she said.

Jack couldn't believe his ears. "Did you just make an allusion to Amadeus?"

"Of course."

"How do you even know what that is?"

"There once was a story of a redneck named Jack . . ." and her eyes were filled with verve, lightning, and laughter. She'd only had one drink.

"Geez."

So, she had won every game, but things were just beginning. It was only 6:45. Slowly, Jack ground her down with percentages, but he could see she was looking bad. Jack had been trained as a child by his Uncle Bob, who had played tournaments in Vegas. Jack spotted some bad moves she made; of course, he continued to play the dolt. Her giant mountain of cash had dwindled, and she had had two drinks for the first time Jack had ever seen. It was 7:45. Jack excused himself and went to the bathroom. Emily Dickinson went through him again, but he couldn't come up with it. Tulip? Horses' heads? Eternity? Better not fuck it up, he thought. If he were a millennial, he'd pull it up on his phone while he was taking a piss; then come back all suave and drop it on her. But fuck that. If your chops weren't sharp, the old Reagan kid thought, you don't deserve that goose flesh.

He cleaned up and resolved to let her win if the dice didn't allow her to win naturally. A handshake was in the future, and he washed his hands thoroughly. He'd never seen her so happy, and he wouldn't send her home on a downer. But, how to throw a game if it came to that, without her knowing? Never in his life had Jack shaved points.

But when he came back, a waiter was there. If things were slow up front, servers would sometimes make their way to the back room, Jack knew. The waiter was in his sixties, possibly seventies, and looked like he had worked there since President Nixon had been in office, and had indeed served President Nixon at one point in time. He gave Jack a long look. It was obvious he was unprepared.

"For the . . . uh . . . ," the waiter glanced at Jen for help, but none was forthcoming, "Gentleman?" he finished. Jack could see the waiter had seen old male members with young female guests, but had not had too many young female members with old male guests. He was "mister smooth" in perpetuity but had made his annual fumble. As he looked in vain at Jen for help, her big smile came out, but no words. Again, Jack noted the smile, which seemed faker and faker.

"Nothing for me, thanks," Jack said.

He left and Jack sat down to continue playing.

"You could have helped him out." Jack said

"What?"

"You could have helped me out," Jack said.

"What?"

"Both of us know perfectly well that the 'gentleman' was struggling to address me appropriately, looked to you for help, and you let him twist in the wind."

"God, you're out there."

"And? You disagree?"

She looked at him. "No," and she proffered her big smile. Jack did not smile back but changed the subject back to the game. That smile worried him more and more.

Luckily, she won the next one and that was enough. The cash was also clearly in her favor.

"What a blast, Jen, thanks."

"You let me win."

"That's absurd. How could a rube like me ever compete with a brilliant northeastener half his age?"

"Bastard!" She punched him in the shoulder.

They walked out together. Although they'd made quite a bit of noise, everyone seemed self-absorbed so they didn't have to deal with any officious inter-meddlers. Plus, they were in the backroom where Jack knew it was an unwritten rule that everyone mind his own business; they'd probably gambled millions of dollars in that backroom over the years. The poor waiter was forgotten by Jen, but not by Jack. Anyway, he wasn't around when they left.

"Well played," and he punched her back as they parted. But his punch was different. He broke his wrist and rolled the back of his hand up her shoulder, feathery, round, warm. Jack had always had skillful hands; he knew that since he played four squares in kindergarten. He tried to transmit it to her. Still, they had never gotten closer than four feet, and the parting was clean, sterilized, and asexual.

Chapter Six

THE GENTLE VACUUM SUCCEEDS

It was May 2018. Jack lay on his couch and deliberated. What to do with this wonderful woman? Of course, this was always the problem and had always been the problem. As much as Jack had read, he'd never read an answer. Most of the great philosophers didn't even address it. In fact, Jack couldn't think of any that had. In those days, survival was paramount, and men and women married very early and stayed married to try and survive. What's with all this "dating" bullshit they would have asked? Socrates? Aristotle? They wouldn't even understand the question. Chaucer? Jack thought. That was 1300s, and still there was some ribaldry and little more. No, Jack searched his mind for something, the earliest? It must be English sonnets right around Shakespeare and including Shakespeare. At least the specter of having to deal with the female mind had started. He recalled his professor in grad school saying that most sonnets had been written to try and get laid. Still, in terms of history, that was yesterday.

Things were quite different starting around 1900, Jack speculated, and the problem of course was the women. Men had changed very little, did not need, or even want a woman to spend a lot of time with, and jeez what was all this bullshit? But the women didn't need the men to survive anymore. Thrive? Maybe, but not survive. Somehow, they'd convinced themselves that men *wanted* to be with them, *wanted* to cater to their bullshit, *wanted* to listen their nonsense, etc. The reality that the sexes actually had to put up with one another for a greater good was lost to the fantasy that there must be some man, or at least a subset of men, who actually wanted to "get coffee and go shopping. YAY!! Let me get my skinny jeans on and we'll go!" Jack laughed aloud as he lay on his couch thinking of Jen. He thought he might love this woman, but he knew he hardly knew her so that was just stupid. He had never been so relaxed around a woman in his life. There were even times he didn't feel like he was even *working* with Jen. Amazing. Yet, as always, the problem was what can we do? He'd noticed that though Jen played the independent Millennial, she was, alas, much like the women of Jack's generation and indeed all generations Jack had been exposed to: she had nothing to do. Other than playing music together, which Jack scored an 11 on a scale of 1 to 10, she'd come up with little. Nights and weekends came and went, and she had nothing planned, ever. Though he had faced the same problem every time with every woman, Jack did not want to give up on Jen. She was something special. Now they had backgammon, and that was pretty big in Jack's mind, easily played at any time anywhere in the world for a lifetime. Hmmm, Jack calculated, two hours per week for thirty years until he was dead or worthless was a lot of time spent together. The harder you work, the luckier you get, Jack's father had told him. Jack had begun to question the accuracy of that in the last ten years or so, but for now he worked for Jennifer James Fairfield.

"Sailing?" he texted her one Thursday morning at 6:07 a.m.

"And? So?" She was up and responded. Jack noted another small thing: they were both morning people.

"Would you like to go sailing?" Jack texted.

"You know how? Is this a joke? I'd love to!"

"Sunday morning?"

"Sure. Where?"

"I need to make some calls because I have no boat."

"Well, any man I'd be with would have a yacht or something," Jen texted with a unicorn emoji.

But it wasn't funny. In fact, it hurt Jack. Why would she say something like that, he thought? Plus, "man I'd be with" sounded pretty sexual. If they were just friends, then why would she say that? If she wanted more, then why not clear up the elephant dick in the room? Jack imagined them talking while his detached cock, impossibly engorged and lengthened to six feet with balls like cantaloupes, hung on the wall like taxidermy listening in, waiting for exhumation and revival, empurpled. Poor cock, never an answer for you and never a reason why there was no answer. Just bullshit and emojis.

But after some serious sweating, he resolved to be rational. They didn't know each other that well and had been fond of throwing bullshit at each other from the beginning. She was just texting and let one fly. Don't get hung up, he thought. Keep going.

"I'll make some calls," he texted, after forty-one minutes. Whenever she said something weird or hurtful or similar, he always remained quiet a long time in hopes she'd fix it or at least try to fix it. So far, she never had. He tried to recall any apology she'd ever made; there were none. Any splash of self-deprecation? None that he could recall. Humility? None. No, like all Millennials, she was extremely pleased with herself.

"Oh good," Jen texted. Like her smile, this was a common tool of hers and Jack started to think it meant something like "that means that *you* will take care of it while I, Jen, sit on my *derrière*." She never said "Oh, bad," so the lack of antonym resonated with Jack that "oh good" was code language. But, again, she was a lawyer. Why use code language? What was the endless point of the endless bullshit? Why even go to law school if one was going to revert to speaking like a non-legal person? In fact, how was it even possible to make it all the way through law school and *be able* to speak like a non-legal person. They were supposed to beat that out of you. Jack ruminated at length.

Jack had done a great deal of sailing, and he knew there were a lot of options. They were in Orlando, within range of two oceans and dozens of lakes. Starting with his father when he was no more than five or six, Jack had sailed big boats, medium boats, and small boats. His uncles, too, took little Jack sailing. Even his mother, who started to play old maid in her 50s, had taken Jack sailing quite a bit when she was young. She had joked that she'd call her boat *The Little Jack*, because Jack would get scared and put his head up the back of her shirt when the wind kicked up. Jack had a big head.

His favorite was small boats. He liked to get close to the water, haul ass, get sprayed and feel in close contact with the elements. He was forty-eight. She was twenty-eight. Although he was well past "ordinary," with Jen, ordinarily he would go for it with such a young crew; let's get wet; let's tip over; let's kick ass; let's leave it all out there. But he kept thinking. Once, when he was about twenty-five up on Lake Michigan, he'd taken his aunt's maid's son who was probably about twelve-thirteen sailing. It was a shitty, old sunfish, but Jack loved the big lake and had just come in. The housekeeper was from Chicago and brought her two children, an older daughter and the son. They were Latinos and Jack tried to remember their names, but he couldn't quite pull them up, just that the son had an anglicized nick name "Bobby." When they got there, the son had infamously asked, "why is there no noise?" They'd never been out of the inner city. They were brown and stood out on the white beach with its very white people, many eager to burn themselves for the only time that year. Anyway, Jack beached the sunfish, and Aunt Margaret asked him to take Bobby out. The 5'1" mother smiled. The 5'3" older daughter looked askance at the big chop and heavy air coming off the lake, but she didn't say anything.

Jack's big balls were frozen tight, and he didn't even think about it. He took 4'11" Bobby, and they went. The chop right off the beach was big and Jack told the kid to hang on while big buckets of icy water hit him in the chest and face. "WHOOOO!" Jack yelled in delight. Jack was busy trying to get them through the chop off the beach, so he didn't have a chance to check on Bobby—just looked at the back of his head from a foot away. Once they got out to where the conditions were heavy, frothy, cold rollers from heaven, he smiled hugely over at the kid, and Bobby looked back at him. The kid was whiter than a sheet of notebook paper. "Ohh, it's okay Bobby," Jack said, but the kid shook his head no and said, "back, back." He'd been baptized and was scared shitless.

"The beauty of sailboats," Jack's father used to snicker, "is that they don't have motors!" So true. What was Jack going to do, snap his fingers and transport Bobby on the beach in a toasted blanket? Besides, apparently the kid didn't have a father, Jack was twenty-five, the lake was rocking, and fuck it let's party. Time to grow some sack, young man! The old sunfish was smoking along—or at least as much as a sunfish can—and Jack miss angled one of the snow- capped rollers. Over they went and quickly. "AHHHHHHHH!" Bobby started screaming when he popped up *under* the sail. Jack quickly lifted the boom, and yanked Bobby by the life preserver out from under sail. "AHHHHHH! BAAAACCCKKKK!" Bobby continued to scream, going from thirteen to three. "Calm down," Jack yelled but he kept screaming. He checked him out, and the kid was fine, no blood, limbs intact. It was all fear. "Stay here" Jack ordered, and slipped under the boat and righted it. Jack climbed in from the windward sign and yanked Bobby aboard from the leeward. "Please, please, please, please, please back," he softly implored to Jack. "Please, please, please, please, please." Wow, Jack thought, this kid actually thinks he's going to die today. Jack's big heart melted, and he wrapped his big arm around Bobby and hugged him tight, "Ok, little guy. Back. I've got you." The kid did not smile but he focused all the way home, which was downwind. Jack knew he'd have to make only one gybe to get back to the beach, but what a hairy gybe it would be. Jack loved hairy gybes, but he thought of Bobby. Jack decided to come up on the wind, tack rather than gybe, and then bear away home. It was an absurd way to sail, but much more under control. If they tried a hairy gybe, Bobby might shit himself. So they did. Bobby's whole body was shivering as he had been soaking wet the entire sail.

The water was probably 60 degrees. But now, Bobby could see colors on the beach, and his thirteen-year-old mind figured out the angle was good. "Please, please, yes." He pointed at the beach. Jack gave him another big hug. "YES." Downwind, they were there in less than ten minutes, and Jack pulled the centerboard up halfway, rounded up, jumped out and grabbed the bow. "Get out!" Jack called but Bobby was frozen and shook his head violently no. Jack started walking the boat in and pointed down. "Shallow" he called. Bobby figured out Jack was standing in about three feet of water, jumped out, and moved faster than a cat thrown in a swimming pool to his mother and sister on the beach.

As Jack recalled the story, it occurred to him how much the country had declined. The mother let loose a stream of Spanish at the kid to the effect that he'd been disrespectful to Jack and then apologized to Jack profusely in broken English when Jack got the boat back on the beach. Today, he would have been thrown in jail. Jack gave the mother a big smile and said, "no problem." The sister had a towel around Bobby, and he was shivering with hard eyes as Jack approached him. Poor Bobby, first some crazy man nearly kills him, and then his mother yells at him. Jack got down on one knee and pulled Bobby in tight. "Safe," Jack said, and the kid softened a little and popped a couple tears as he shiver-shook in Jack's embrace. Jack wiped them off with the towel, "Big guy, you're safe," and tussled his hair and gave him one last squeeze. Jack never saw any of them again, but Aunt Margaret had seen the whole thing, and the story went immediately into family folklore.

Jack knew he couldn't get Jen in any remotely comparable situation.

Jen was a blue blood from up North who had never sailed, which was odd because there was a huge tradition of sailing up North. Certainly, for hundreds of years the sailing tradition in the North had dwarfed anything in the South that had existed. Like a lot of things, maybe it had died or gotten very tight and narrow. Anyway, what to do? Having a discussion with Jen on sailing history certainly would not solve the problem.

As always, Jack played the percentages. He didn't really know this woman, and she didn't seem to want him to know her. Everything was a short bowling alley with her, a quick sentence, a dead end right away. Why? It was the opposite of law school, and she was a lawyer. She should have been trained to make and counter every argument, every permutation, go down every rabbit trail, turn over every stone, look in every cabinet, examine each eyelash on the gnats, etc. Ah, ha! There it is at the bottom of the pit under the blanket! He could not figure it out. But she had let her hair down during backgammon—a little and with the "Well" comment more than a little. Maybe law school hadn't been a one-way portal for her; maybe it was just treading water with nothing else to do? Also, Jack frequently liked the silence between them so maybe he was greedy wanting it both ways?

Still, it was very early; play the percentages he thought. So, he rented a J24 at Lake Fairview in Orlando. He'd been to Lake Fairview fifty times at least. It was safe. A J24 was a slow tugboat, but dry. It would never tip over and would have plenty of room. Even though it was a day sail, he imagined Jen arriving with bags of bullshit everywhere. So be it. Better, they would be on a lake in the interior of Florida. Jen would be familiar with such lakes. While things could get dicey on a lake, the risks were nothing compared to going in the Atlantic or the Gulf. No, he'd play it safe. She wouldn't care, and why risk bad weather and potential extreme conditions? C'mon Jack, he thought, be a big giant pussy just like they've been telling you do since you were ten.

While musing, Jack pulled up a nightmare in addition to "Bobby and the Sunfish." He remembered Karen from undergrad, a brown beauty with a big, beautiful rack, and a quick smile. More than anything, he'd wanted to suck her tits and die doing so. Why couldn't he just put his head in her lap and suck those tits until the end of time? She'd heard he liked to sail and inquired. Jack knew her a little and got very excited. But he hadn't played it safe. He took her out in Biscayne Bay on a Hobie 18, flipped it over twice, pitchpoled once, and in Jack's mind had had a rip-snorting, good time. Jack was twenty-one. She was similar.

"Whooo! Buy you a beer, Karen?" he'd said after checking the boat back in at the rental place.

"You mean an ambulance?"

"Oohh, it wasn't that bad, c'mon."

"I thought I was going to sit and drink beer, not train for the Olympics."

Jack saw she was serious. They never talked again. Later he learned she had liked him but couldn't believe he treated her like a "dude." But she'd never said a word about safety, fear, assumptions, or anything, and she approached him, so Jack dismissed her. How was he supposed to know she wanted to sit on her ass and drink beer. Speak up, bitch! He was twenty-one; his dick would be hard forever; this was no pattern destined to repeat itself, he thought.

"Lake Fairview, Sunday, 10:00 a.m." Jack texted Jen later that day.

"Why ten a.m.?"

"Well, that's when our reservation for the rented boat starts."

"Oh, that's sweet, Rip."

"Sweet?"

"You're the boss," she texted back.

Of course, he wasn't the "boss;" in fact, he felt more like the donkey who carried all the packs. But she was so beautiful. He tried to control himself, but he wanted to hold her uncontrollably. He wanted to comb her hair. He wanted to nuzzle her neck. He wondered if her nipples were big and round, like silver dollars, or tight and long like eraser tips? He thought about that a lot. Why couldn't sailing be over so he could rape her and get it over with? Typically, she never answered the original question. She had all the time in the world to waste. All these irrational thoughts went through Jack's head for hours. He went and made some coffee. Geez, loser, get it together, he thought.

"Deal," he mustered eventually.

"You mean ten a.m.?

"Yes."

"Ok."

"Do you want to play Cleopatra or do you want me to teach you?"

"Cleopatra," she texted with goofy emjoi. So, there *were* moments of clarity, but what did they mean? So, she could use the English language with precision, but why elect not to most of the time? But maybe it was he who had been precise, and she only had to say yes or no; that was much easier than *broaching* a topic with precision or *developing* a topic. Again, Jack was totally at a loss. But again, he had nothing to lose.

At 10 a.m., she was all smiles and big eyes. That smile seemed awful ready, Jack thought. He didn't trust it anymore.

The weather was fair. The boat was slow (though she didn't realize it). And he did all the work. It was an old J24 with a handheld rudder, no wheel. The winches were good, but not self-tailing, so he told her to stay away from the winches and the cleats and that was that. Down below, she had indeed brought two bags of bullshit. She was the answer to the question "Why did the folks on Gilligan's Island bring so many clothes for a 'Three Hour Cruise?'" But there was plenty of room.

It was a lovely day.

The little canal out to the lake was thick with weeds, narrow, and the slight breeze was behind them. Jack knew they would flounder on the way out, but it was really bad. There was no spinnaker, and the sails didn't want to fill in the light air. He even spun them around once at 1 mph. Jen knew something was wrong but stayed calm while Jack made a monkey of himself fore and aft. Eventually, they slid out of the weeds and into open water. It was a keel boat, so Jack knew the weeds would slide off in deeper water, if he could just get the damn thing moving. She smiled and stayed calm and quiet. He liked that about her and recalled she was the only woman he'd ever met with whom he could enjoy silence without apprehension and the desire to fill the air. For thirty minutes, she said nothing while he floundered and flailed.

Finally, Jack got them on a broad reach in exceptionally light air; the boat going slow but at least under control; both the genoa and the main partially filled with air. Jack was able to get back into the cockpit with Jen, take the handle on the rudder and sit for a moment for the first time in a long time. He was sweating like crazy and must have looked like a madman when he glanced at her and said: "See how much fun, your highness?" She burst into laughter and grabbed one of the seventeen towels she had brought and wiped his face and neck down and gave him a super quick kiss on the shoulder and a huge smile. "You're *intensely* interesting, Rip," she said. "You're an *animal*." She'd touched him. She'd kissed him, sort of. But her timing was perfect, and she had made it decisively nonsexual somehow. Jack guzzled water and thought of his next move. He liked being in complete control. She'd given it to him; he accepted. As usual, he'd never seen towels as nice as the ones she'd brought.

After a while, Jack's brain locked in and he had the breakthrough moment he'd been waiting for his whole life; in fact he'd given up on ever having it. She sat quietly paying close attention. Again, the lack of palaver was appreciated. The boat was crabbing a little faster. She didn't say anything stupid. She didn't giggle. She didn't "wheee." She smiled at Jack again, and Jack relaxed. For some reason, this woman always made him feel he could make a comeback. Their broad reach had them too close to the shore to feel much of the wind, but the boat had momentum now and was sailing. Jack could see the wind out on the lake; he knew it was there. She watched, and she smiled. He punched her shoulder.

He knew when they gybed the boat would head out to the middle of the lake, and he could come up on the wind and get to a beam reach. That would hook her, he thought. When they'd first started, he was too anxious and unnecessarily so while they floundered. She had always been patient. Now he could see her face, and that she was starting to enjoy herself. He checked all the lines and milked the broad reach while he planned. I have a feeling this woman is going to love sailing, he thought, and I'm going to be the one who introduces her. He had no particular reason, really no reason at all except the lightness of her touch he'd witnessed in other areas.

"Jennifer," he said, "come sit on this side; we're going to gybe." He knew this would prematurely put her on the wrong side of the boat, but it was better than having her on the high side when the sail flipped over, and things started happening. She complied without comment. He could tell she liked the word "gybe."

"Okay. I'm going turn the boat; the sail will go over your head to the other side; and when I hand it to you, please pull on this line," he motioned to what would be the new genoa sheet.

"I couldn't pull that in a million years and I don't have any gloves," she protested.

"Do you think I'm stupid, Cleopatra?" He looked at her, full of sweat and smiling.

"No." She hesitated. "Oh, you want me to trust you."

"Very much."

"Ok. Ready."

"Gybing," Jack called. He turned the old J24 away from the shore and out into the lake, the boom started to swing, and he caught it briefly by the main sheet to deaden the jolt when it got over. They were going quite slowly, but still there was a jolt. The genoa started flogging. Jack quickly picked out a new course; tightened and cleated the main near where it should be required. There was no autopilot, so he had to pull the genoa around in big armfuls, hold with one hand, control the rudder with the other, let go, and take another armful. But once the genoa got around the forestay and blew itself out the other side, Jack knew they'd be fine. He cleated it and gave her a smile.

"Perfect," she said. Again, she made no hysterical noises while all of this happened. She was the picture of repose.

"Not yet." He raised his eyebrows at her.

"You didn't tell me to pull."

"Soon," teased Jack.

The main was pulling fine, but it was still too far out. He trimmed it and cleated, picking out a giant white house on the other side of the lake as their course. He knew the main was near perfect, and the boat heeled a bit and picked up a little drive. He popped the winch handle in and handed her the line.

"Don't pull until I tell you," said Jack

"Roger." Who was this woman?

He uncleated the genoa sheet, took a single wrap around the winch and pulled hard.

"Now," said Jack.

She did. "Nothing happened."

"Stop."

He took a second wrap around the winch and started cranking.

"Now."

She pulled as though her life depended upon it, but of course there was very little load on the sheet as Jack was winching with two wraps so she had a confused look on her face as though she was preparing to lift 100 pounds that had turned out to be 10.

"I've got it, Angel," he took the tail and cleated it. The word "angel" was too strong, and he wondered if he'd be reprimanded for letting it slip. She said nothing.

The boat had heeled more, and now it had taken off.

"You can let that go," he said, "and just relax and keep your weight on the high side. The boat cannot flip over." And Jack joined her on the high side. This was what he had been waiting for, and he was correct. As usual, she stayed quiet, but now that the hurly-burly of the turn was over, the boat was being pulled by the wind, boat speed had tripled, the rig had hardened, and the wind was fresh in their faces not sweaty and behind them. The gentle vacuum pulled them. Jack had loved this feeling his entire life. His father had adored it. Her giant head of hair blew in his face, but he could finally see her neck and wanted to give her a big smooch and some little bites. She lit up as she sat there for five minutes or so. He had been correct; she felt it. He would not ruin it with speech. With the sails cleated, he steered a fine line. The gentle vacuum sucked her in.

"Oh, Jack it's so romantic, so wonderful," she said finally as they beam reached in moderate breeze.

"Romantic?"

"You know, like the Romantic period, like Beethoven, Ravel, like that."

"So wonderful. To be pulled by the wind," he tried to play it cool, but again struggled.

"I get it. What an indescribable feeling. Thank you, Jack."

"I'm not doing anything," he grinned.

"I wouldn't be here but for you." Again, the intermittent command of the English language both confused and elated Jack.

"I had a feeling you'd like it," and he put his left arm around her without touching her while he steered with his right arm.

And so they sailed for four hours. Always Jack had had a recognized fear of not talking to his dates. Always he felt the need to put on airs; to say something however stupid or awkward; and it usually was stupid or awkward. But not with Jen. She said nothing for most of the four hours; just sat and smiled; and had a ball. Jack felt no pressure, no pretensions. He could sit with this woman in silence and be comfortable. She smiled and smiled and smiled. He smiled back. She fished in her bags from time to time for nonsense: a blanket (it was near 90), a hat better suited for the Kentucky Derby (it flopped off and only Jack's reflexes kept it on board); two different sets of sun glasses; pillows little and medium; etc. Jack had planned to ask her if there was another set of panties in there, but the timing was never good enough to pull it off.

When they checked the boat back in, Jen said, "No more, Cleopatra."

"You see, don't you? It's a skill sport. Some muscles, but mostly touch, feel, perception, anticipation."

"I get it. I want to learn. You're so patient and sweet with me."

"You can hug an old man if you want." He smiled at her.

"Oh Rip," she laughed and punched him in the shoulder instead, just enough to both elate and confuse Jack beyond any comprehension. They sat in the cockpit for twenty minutes and he taught her the basic vocabulary, points of sail, and the names of the main lines. Was this really happening, Jack wondered?

They checked out and went to the car. "Next time, I'll teach you the most important thing of all," he said.

"Oh good, does it have more fancy words?"

"No."

"Well, what is it?"

"How not to get your ass kicked or die," said Jack.

"Whoa."

"Yeah, today was easy; a perfect starter day for Jennifer James Fairfield of the North. Things are not always like that. You must learn to respect the elements or believe me they will kick your ass and could even kill you."

"Give me an example."

"Remember when you were holding the line?" said Jack. "That's called 'tailing'; it's when one sailor helps another."

"Sure."

"You were surprised at how little tension you felt, weren't you?"

"Very much."

"Did you figure it out?" said Jack.

"Sure. Most of the tension was on the little circle thing. What's it called?"

"The winch, wench."

"Yeah, the winch," she said, the little dig going over her head.

"Exactly."

"So?" she said.

"So what if you got confused, or the line tangled, or the boat pitched, and there was big puff of wind, or the communication with the captain was faulty, and you got a finger, or your hand, of even an ankle or leg in that line when it came tight?"

"Big pain," she said.

"Could be much worse. Could easily tear a finger right off, break your leg or ankle. You could be yanked forward and have the winch handle smash you in the face, rip your eyeball out. All these things could happen, and other horrible things and they would happen in seconds or less depending upon conditions. Remember: always respect the elements or they can hurt you bad or even kill you."

"Will you protect me, Rip?" She did like to play the Blanche DuBois thing, Jack thought.

"Yes, but there may be nothing I can do. Your best protection is right in your noggin. Knowledge is king. Anticipation is queen. Let's fill it up together."

"Noggin?" she mocked

"You like to play dumb?"

No audible response but again the big smile. Jack observed the smile. It was a little too pat, a little too producible. Every woman could muster a cutesy face, he knew that; but Jen's smile seemed under a little too much control, a little contrived, maybe a lot. The Eagles old hit "Lyin' Eyes" went through his mind. He doubted she'd taken his little lecture seriously.

She Ubered away, and it was over. Jack paid and went home. They were allegedly just friends, but she hadn't even offered to split the bill. Other than talk and play in her bags, she hadn't done anything all day.

Chapter Seven

TWO JOBS NOW

After the Sunday sail, she didn't communicate. Six long days went by. June 2018 went slowly. Jack loved communication and very much wanted to communicate, but he was extremely confused. But for him, Jen had been *added* to his schedule; nothing had been removed. The Kowalski case got hotter, and Jack was having a blast getting ready. He'd told the client that if he wanted a 110% effort, he'd better pay his bills. Jack hadn't had the balls to say this kind of thing before, but he was older now. For once, the client actually appreciated the situation and put $150,000 on retainer for the trial. "I want blood," he said. Jack liked the guy and rejoined, "You mean you want *his* blood." Jack dug in. After twenty years, he had a great client, plenty of money, and an arrogant asshole to battle. Perfect, he thought. Meanwhile, Jack kept up his tennis and scheduled some offshore fishing as well. The more he worked, the more he needed to blow off steam.

And so, he lay in his living room at 8:47 p.m. when his pinger went off. He'd been thinking about Jen just then after his long day and longer week. What to do with this woman?

How could this woman be twenty-eight? What was she doing with him? Why would she go six days without communicating? Was she waiting for him?

It was a text from Jen: "Hey, Rip. I loved the sail. Music at my place, Wednesday at 7?"

Jack thought. It was Friday night at 9. Did she have a date? Did she think he had a date? If she didn't have a date, then why wait until next Wednesday? Why waste the weekend? Why not come over right now and rub her uvula across his aching, bulbous, purple mushroom while persistently fighting for air until he geysered off like Zeus? God you're a loser, he thought as he dreamed of the uppity coquette from up North finding herself with his Southern fried *weinershnitzel* stuffed down her throat. He imagined a Greek chorus in blue jeans and cowboy hats, spitting tobacco juice: "Oh the Southern Cock! The Sweat! The Stink! The Horror!"

Oh, Jack, you are so irrational, he thought. What to do with this crazy bitch? He poured himself another double and sat down to think. Be rational, he thought. Figure it out. That had been one of his first boss's mantras; figure it out, he would say all the time. Well, it had only been six months since he met her. He hadn't told anyone about her and had no third-party input. That was bad. He couldn't tell anyone within his family because they would tell everyone else; plus, the age difference would be silently or maybe not so silently disapproved of by the women. They'd all start texting each other, and it would be a shitshow. Wait a minute, there was his older sister, Jenny; she could keep a secret. Now that he did the math, his sister had a nephew that was a year or two older than Jen! That's right, Jack's nephew Ben was a little older than

Jen! Fuck! He put Jenny on the back burner for now; he didn't know how she might react.

He thought of the guys at the office. There were two senior partners, Larry and Steve. He was close with both, but they'd been married for thirty-plus years. Plus, Jen was a lawyer, which eventually would come out. There was Bill. Bill was about forty. He was on his second wife, and had a bad divorce, which he never mentioned. But Jack knew he had been hurt by it. Bill was one of Jack's many married friends who frequently joked at the horrible sex life he had. Of course, it wasn't funny at all, but Bill could make it funny. Bill could make capital punishment funny. But what could Bill tell him? What advice would be forthcoming? Of course, Jack could not tell any of the women in the law firm about Jen as he did not trust any of them to keep their mouths shut and most would disapprove anyway. He was close with his assistant Karen, but she would probably blab after a while.

Jack decided he would ask Lonnie, his tennis friend. There was no downside to asking Lonnie, and he could be objective. They had no mutual friends, and Lonnie would keep his mouth shut. She had neither confirmed nor denied a boyfriend. That really irritated Jack. But she had also just moved to a new place from out of state. Probably, Jack was her only friend. Maybe she thought telling him no sex would kill the friendship? But that didn't make any sense. She would know that he would expect her to say that given their extreme age difference. Or maybe *if* she had made it clear early that reasoning would be obtained. But she'd fucked up, suddenly four months had gone by; they'd done quite a bit together; amazingly, she liked him way more than she ever thought possible and wanted to keep the sex option open? Jack thought this was highly unlikely, but still his lawyer's mind could not say it was impossible, could not even say it was close to impossible. It was *possible.* Jack played pros and cons. It was a regular habit of his. Pros: potential musical friend—possible lover. Jack thought about number one awhile. He didn't need a sailing buddy or a tennis buddy or, what a minute, backgammon? He supposed he could find a backgammon buddy, but she must get big points for that. So, Pros: potential musical and backgammon friend—possible lover. But there was another one, Jack thought: fine arts companion. Sure, Jack could go with a woman in his family or alone as he had many times. Jack decided it was better to go with Jen as a friend. Cons: poor communicator; doesn't pay any money—cocktease. These all bothered Jack, especially the poor communicator part. The money was related to the cocktease. If she wanted to keep it friends, then cough up the cash. Anyway, Jack was tired, but it was clear the pros outweighed the cons. He'd lay this all out for Lonnie.

"Confirmed. I'll be there," he texted her back. He'd wanted to call her or send her a lengthy text vomiting everywhere. In his youth, he had repeatedly done so. Always be honest, his mother had told him, a horrible piece of advice guaranteed to lead to excessive masturbation. He hated coy, and she was coy, shit super coy. But he was forty-eight now. Geez that was old. He'd put up with it for now.

Wednesday at seven came, and Jack had practiced. But so had Jen. She was better than him; it now became clear on their sixth time playing together. She took off. Their routine had solidified, and they agreed on virtually everything. They practiced the following in this order:

1. Ave Maria, Schubert
2. The Swan, Saint-Saëns

3. Meditation, Massenet
4. Divertimento, K 135, second movement, Mozart
5. Air, Bach
6. Red River Valley, traditional
7. Minuet 2, Bach
8. Theme from Love Story
9. In the Bleak Midwinter, Holst
10. The romance from *Eine Kleine Nachtmusik*, Mozart

Again, Jack was in heaven. He'd played violin off and on since he was fifteen, but very rarely had anyone to play with. He'd never completely given up, but surely months and years had gone by while his violin moldered in its case. Now, somehow, he was playing with a beautiful woman twenty years younger who was a marvelous cellist.

They finished the romance from Mozart and looked at each other. Again, the silence which did not bother Jack. The gaze became pensive, and Jack resolved to match her silence. He knew from his career as a lawyer that he could stare people down, but he would stare her up with love, carry her up, up, up with his eyes. He thought of David Crosby's "Carry Me" and the old Joe Cocker/Jennifer Warren duet "Love Lift Us Up." He wanted to lift her up; he wanted to be lifted up with her. He felt like a four-year-old.

He lowered his violin without breaking eye contact. She kept looking at him and rested the upper neck and scroll along the long patch of white flesh from her left temple down to her third button. She'd worn a baby blue blouse tonight; midnight jeans again. Jack refused to speak. It occurred to him that her not speaking could be turned into a weakness. He'd match her! Let the tension build. But he was also mad with the most positive feelings he'd ever had. He softened his face and felt a little moisture in his eyes. She had no sardonic grin that he'd seen yet, but she did have a cat that ate the canary grin. She held his gaze and tried it now, but it was tentative, unsure, exploratory. Jack had been right. For all her life, she'd been getting away with *responding* only. But now there were no words to which to respond, only Jack's mien which he softened even more into utter contentment. She blushed hard. Jack could see the crimson flush down from her face, along that white neck, and down to her chest. His cock kicked. She was busted, broke his gaze, and looked toward the open door in the second bedroom cum music studio; the light hit her, and Jack saw little beads of sweat on her face. He knew she knew he knew she was busted. Again, she returned his gaze with a look he'd never seen before: exposed, unsure, vulnerable. Jack knew the status quo needed to be restored but not now. He gently milked the moment.

"Fantastic," he said slowly, finally breaking his eyes. "Really, you are so good, miles better than the first time we played."

She tried to speak but choked up, gulped, and tried to fake a cough. They both knew she was faking it. "Thanks. You too."

"I need to practice a lot; you're leaving me in your wake."

"Wake? Like a boat?" she smiled.

"Funeral? What's 'wake' for clouds?"

"Huh?"

"Sorry for the cliché, but that's where you just took me. Up, up, up."

"Too kind," she managed in a soft panic. "Water?"

The spell was broken, and they made their way to the kitchen. The harsh lights confirmed she had been sweating;

the dark hair at her temples was pressed in sweat. Her blush dissipated and seemed to whiten her skin even more. As usual, she kept her distance. As usual, she neither confirmed nor denied any sexual attraction. Jen was back. But Jack had pierced the veil, and he knew she knew. She'd run to the harsh light of the kitchen and that drink of water. He knew that. What to do? He'd never seen her be clumsy in any way, but now she turned and dropped the Evian bottle trying to get it back in the fridge. It was plastic so it didn't break, but she bent over in her midnight jeans in that harsh light, giving Jack a look at everything. And did he take that look. He had wanted it for some time. The sublime panty lines were asymmetrical, the left buttock wide encircled out on the hip, the right straight up her crack to the small of her back. Maybe she'd been squeezing and grinding while they'd been playing, Jack fantasized. Jack had studied panty lines unendingly in his long, lonely life. He doubted he was alone.

She turned back and busted him ogling her, but he played it cool as though what else did she think he'd be looking at? His cock kicked again. No. It was just like in the music room. He needed to get things back to normal.

"What a klutz I am," she attempted, roughing up her hair in exasperation. Like all girls, she knew if she showed her ass, men would look. It wasn't like Jack had done anything. She'd fumbled the water bottle, and she'd bent over right in front of him. What *else* would he look at?

"Ridiculous. Your playing was sublime. Fuck the water bottle."

"'Fuck the water bottle?' How tasteful, Jack," but after briefly trying her Northern rebuke, she couldn't look at him without laughing.

"It doesn't deserve you. Now, let me go. I don't deserve you either. I need to practice more," said Jack.

"Not true. You're getting better, Rip." Jen was back; the other girl glimpsed then gone.

There was no touching, and so he left.

Chapter Eight

PROSTRATE PROSTATE PREPARATION

Now, he decided, she needed a good fucking. It was July 2018. Entertain what euphemisms you will— "have," "take," "make love," "rogering" or the most ridiculed by Jack of all "sleep with"—it all came down to sex. She was a Westerner. She was well-read and well-educated, all of it in the Judeo-Christian tradition. The best sex was always in books, and Jen was a reader like him. He remembered being only thirteen or fourteen and being given a copy of Hemingway's short stories by his mother of all people. There was Up in Michigan right there, and Big Jim's cock driving into Liz's confused trough on the old planks down by the lake. As a boy, Jack had gotten a tremendous erection reading it, and it was still one of his favorites. He'd wondered if his mother even knew about it. Every movie based on a book led Jack to getting the book: they always had way more sex than the movie. Stephen King was available for teens, and he had all kinds of sex in his books. Jack read them all. No one said shit. Just don't mention it in conversation or sit in a theater or living room and tell everyone what's missing from the book. That never bothered Jack.

Jen was from the next generation, but nothing had changed. She was just like him. She probably had Paglia's *Sexual Personae* on her curricula somewhere, if not a summer reading list, or some feminist told her or whatever. Jack didn't care. He'd read it and couldn't agree more; there was more sex going on than anyone wanted to admit. Certainly, and without doubt, the females were much more inclined to not admit it, and Jennifer James Fairfield was no exception.

Jack was back at work at 7:00 a.m. on Thursday, and these thoughts consumed him through the weekend. But so did the Kowalski case. They were only two weeks out, and there was no settlement in sight. But Jack had learned over the years not to go 100% into the case until the very end. As a young lawyer, he was 100% in a month out or more. It was too long. He couldn't sustain it. So, he worked hard on the Kowalski case, but still kept his outside stuff going, including tennis. There was a big hearing on Monday, and Jack thought he had a decent chance of kicking Big Firm Asshole in the nuts with the cranky old judge.

On Sunday with Lonnie, after Jack had pounded him 6-4, 6-1, Jack started talking.

"I need to confide in you, Lonnie."

"Almighty Jack needs to confide in me? Wow, this must be good."

"I've been seeing this girl," said Jack.

"And what? She beats you at tennis and you want to commit suicide?"

"No, but that's funny—I met her here."

"Wow. Have I seen her?"

"I doubt it," said Jack.

"So, she's smarter than you and you want to commit suicide?"

"Hah. No, well actually I'm not sure about that."

"What's her name?"

"Jen," said Jack.

"Doesn't narrow the field tremendously, does it?"

"I'm about to," said Jack.

"Well?"

"She's twenty-eight."

"Holy Shit, Congrats man. What are you fifty now?"

"Forty-eight."

"Holy Shit. You look terrible." They smiled at each other. "Does she know how much money you certainly don't have?"

They both laughed. He'd known Lonnie for over fifteen years, and the relationship was 90% tennis. One of the reasons Jack loved tennis was that there was little social aspect to the game. You showed up; you played; you left. Sure, if you wanted to, you could stick around and socialize but by no means was it expected. It wasn't like golf where you might get stuck sitting in a golf cart for four hours with a guy who wouldn't shut up.

To this day, he still didn't really know what Lonnie did for a living, only that it was computer related. He knew very little about Lonnie's family, and he knew very little about Lonnie himself. He couldn't even guess what books Lonnie might have read. They'd literally never had a beer together or a meal or shot pool or anything. He knew that Lonnie was a tennis nut, and a fitness nut and that's all he needed to know. Lonnie had a New Year's Eve Party every year, and Jack never went.

"I hate social events," he'd tell Lonnie.

"Why?"

"Just always have."

But Lonnie didn't care. He thought it was odd as lawyers were generally known for being gregarious, but so what? Jack was his loyal tennis nut, and he was Jack's. Once, he'd moved to Ohio for eighteen months, and when he returned, Jack had eagerly resumed the relationship like nothing had happened. They loved tennis. That was all they needed.

"Probably. She's a lawyer, too."

"Oh fuck, incest. Isn't there a law against that or something?" But it soon dawned on Lonnie that, other than deaths in the family, they really had never confided in each other for anything. So, something important was up. Jack, normally a bit of a know it all, had come to him for help.

"Well?" Lonnie asked.

"She won't make clear to me whether she wants to have sex or not. She neither mentions a boy friend nor indicates there isn't one. On our first what you'd call 'date,' she'd said, 'just friends' but since then, she hasn't said anything similar."

"Did she touch you?" Lonnie asked.

"Not really. Handshakes. A shoulder punch or two."

"Did you touch her?" asked Lonnie.

"Same, not really."

"Is she hot?"

"Very, but not as hot as she thinks she is," chuckled Jack.

"Fuck. So, you can't figure out what a hot twenty-eight-year-old would be doing with an old geezer?"

"That's it," said Jack.

"You sure it isn't money?"

"She's a rich girl from Virginia. Family goes way back. Father is loaded. She's already making decent money at twenty-eight. I guess they're all gold diggers but that makes no sense to me. Plus, if she were then she must know you've got to fuck for the money, right?"

"You've given this some thought, huh?" said Lonnie.

Jack shook his head. Lonnie toweled off again. There was no one waiting for the court. Old Jack, he thought, met him when he was thirty-four and he never got married or ever told me about a girl. Now he's forty-eight and all fucked up. Funny guy; sick sense of humor. Certainly, his brusqueness would turn off a decent percentage of girls, but so what? That still left a big chunk. He was a tall, athletic, decent guy with an excellent job. There should be no problem. And Jack was always decisive. Now, Lonnie looked over at his old tennis nutcase and could see Jack was lost. He couldn't make a decision. He'd lost his confidence. If he didn't like social events that would certainly kill off potential females. Twenty-eight? So this was the lottery for Jack, once in a lifetime.

"Has she been to your house?" Lonnie said.

"No."

"Have you been to hers?"

"Her apartment, yes, eight times," said Jack.

"Well, if she invites you to her apartment, that's panties off, at least when I was in the game."

"She plays cello, and you know I play the violin. So we've been playing music together at her apartment," said Jack.

"Holy shit! The cello. You two play classical music together, looking into each other's eyes at her apartment? Man, if that ain't pink panties, what is?"

"Well, what do you mean? It's either her place or mine. We're not going to rent a place for amateur music practice."

"Hmm. These are unusual circumstances," Lonnie agreed.

"*Super very unusual,* and I took it that since she never mentioned coming to my place, then it means she wanted to control the situation a little more by playing at her place."

"Hmm. Yeah, I see your point. It would be more sexual if she came to your place, possibly. Who knows, you might rape her . . . ," said Lonnie. They chuckled together. "A cello player? Man, that is rare. Is she good?"

"Very."

"Fuck. I'm getting a hard on; don't tell my wife."

They laughed. There was no one waiting for the court. Lonnie thought some more. A blue blood cellist from up North? Jack liked to play redneck, sometimes loudly, but no one who knew him fell for it. He was well read and could be extremely articulate and engaging. Twenty-eight? Lonnie tried to remember what a twenty-eight-year-old ass looked like. Other than porn, he couldn't think of any images. And a classy, smart, twenty-eight-year-old from old money up North. Wow. Jack really stepped into some shit.

"Why don't you just bring it out on the table," said Lonnie.

"I have a feeling that will backfire in the negative."

"Why?"

"I can't explain it. She's very spoiled and doesn't seem to regret it. She likes . . . artifice is the right word," said Jack.

"Artifice? So?"

"Well, it's like the dick has to be fully robed and slide in without its ugliness being seen. Some kinda Wizard of Oz 'behind the curtain' dick or some shit," said Jack.

"Ha. Jesus, you are a sick dog, Jack," Lonnie said laughing. "Who the fuck is going to see it?"

"I know. It's stupid. Also, the subject has sort of come up, and she doesn't want to be explicit."

"How?" said Lonnie.

"Well, we've had a few moments where we locked eyes, and I know my eyes told her I wanted her, and she did not accept but neither did she look away."

"Oh fuck. What is this, *The Scarlett Letter* or something?" said Lonnie.

"You mean *Lady Chatterley's Lover*?"

"Say what?"

Jack laughed. He had a feeling Lonnie wouldn't be familiar.

"I mean what century are we in with this girl?" Lonnie said.

"Exactly. And she's a Millennial. Who doesn't want to move on from Queen Victoria more than a Millennial?" asked Jack.

"Totally agree. All they do is fuck around on their phones. And they've got a million dating apps."

"Exactly. She's way out there. Now what do I do?" asked Jack.

"Let me ask my wife."

"Seriously?" Jack had only met Lonnie's wife twice, for about two minutes each time, in all the time they'd known each other.

"Ok. Do you know any younger girls?" asked Jack.

"Yeah, but not well enough to ask them."

"Funny. Me too."

"Play Tuesday night?" said Lonnie

"Fuck yeah, mutherfucker. I'm going to go home and do one hundred sit-ups. Big Jack is beasting."

"Pussy. I'll do one-hundred miles on the stationary bike just for you."

They chuckled at their middle-aged bullshit and left.

Despite the enormous exertion and the certainty of a giant work week ahead of him, Jack's chronic obstructive sleep apnea got the best of him. All Sunday night, he tossed and turned thinking of Jen, running permutations through his head, wondering if she ever thought of him. But he knew she must be thinking of him; they'd bonded the last time on some level. But now, nothing. No communication. How could she be so detached, under control, that she didn't even call or text? When he slept, he slept shallowly dreaming of vampires killing one another. If Jen wore the right makeup, she could pass for a vampire, but she wasn't in the dreams. They bit Jack on the neck over and over and kept killing him. Then he dreamed of refrigerators at the bottom of lakes; every time he opened one his mother's dead body was in it with the light on and her smiling clownishly at him. He kept waking up, sweating, and dreading the next dream. There was drool on his pillow. Jen was in none of them. None of them were happy.

Jack was a body snatcher on Monday, but put his head down, guzzled coffee, and remained productive. The big hearing was at 10:00, and Jack got up at 3:00 a.m. He'd done this about one thousand times in his career. There were a bunch of motions scheduled, but Jack knew if he could just win one of them, things were going to go his way. Specifically, half of Big Firm's claim was "consequential damages," and there was some good law that they were barred. Such an order would be unappealable, so Big Dickhead would have to go through trial and face the possibility of resurrecting the issue on appeal. Tough spot. A lot could go wrong for Big Arrogant Asshole.

Sure enough, Jack played it cool while the cranky old judge ruled against him on lesser issues. He hated losing, but he wanted the judge's energy on the one issue. Sure enough, the judge put her finger right on the issue which Jack had laid out for her in his papers. "I don't see a response," she said, or "what is your response?" or "tell me why I shouldn't bar the damages." Larry stammered and struggled and most of the questions were obvious. That irritated the judge. "Mr. Friedman I'm asking you questions right out of Mr. Forester's brief; there's nothing new here; your response." Jack felt like shit, but he was going to ass rape Friedman! The judge ruled in his favor, and Jack had an order ready. Friedman had won three motions prior to the big one but had no orders ready. So, Jack eliminated any chance Friedman had to water down the ruling outside the judge's presence by negotiating the language in the order. To the contrary, the judge complimented Jack on his order, which was highly specific, and Friedman, jack off to the end, had faux agreed on the record with the court reporter typing away. Some appeal! Jack thought. Jack got back to the office and was worshipped. Karen had an absurd Hawaiian lei ready for him. Larry and Steve knew exactly what had happened. Jack felt like shit, but Jack felt great.

Jen knew about the Kowalski case, and the big hearing on Monday. But she attempted no communication. Jack was hurt. He didn't know whether to tell her or not. He was afraid.

On Tuesday she texted: "Music Wednesday, after work tomorrow at 7?"

"Confirmed." He was pissed now. But he couldn't make a good argument as to why he should be. She had not done a single thing wrong. In fact, if she only wanted to be friends, then Jack had to agree her behavior was close to impeccable. But Jack had long ago gone through the post-law school period where instinct and common sense leave the truly studious for a period of time. Jack had been one of those for sure, actually one of the worst, but it had worn off some. His instinct had returned. The more he'd practiced in the real world, the sharper it got. No, he'd seen humans at their worst, and his instinct had proven him correct. The issue boiled down to the fact that Jen could easily make the situation asexual if she wanted but didn't.

He worked a full day, took his clothes with him, and got to the courts early. He warmed up a little, and then Lonnie showed right on time. What a lucky guy I am, Jack thought, to have a steady partner like Lonnie. Jack beat him 6-3, 6-2.

"Man, you were a buzz saw tonight, Jack," said Lonnie.

"That's funny. I feel like death warmed over."

"You kept coming at me with consistency off both sides; nowhere to run."

"Thanks, bud," Jack said.

"Well, bad news—the wife says 'probably no go.'"

"Shit," said Jack.

"Yeah. She said without the financial angle; it just doesn't make sense. Your dick isn't big enough."

"You didn't tell me your wife thinks about my dick, Lonnie?" They laughed.

"Yeah. She says the music angle is the only one that makes any sense at all."

"Hmm. That's not good."

"However, I did tell her your 'Dick in Shining Armor' take on the whole thing."

"You mean, don't mention it and pretend it's not ugly?" asked Jack.

"Yes."

"And?"

"I used the word 'formal' a lot. She'd never understand it in Jack speak," said Lonnie.

"And?"

"Well, she said if you want to make a fool of yourself go all the way formal with her and see if it works. You know, give her what she wants."

"What the hell does that mean?" said Jack.

"I don't know either."

"Chicks. They never have to do anything on dates," Jack lamented.

"True. She could never get in another girl's pants."

"Thanks for trying."

Jack went home, and he was more confused than ever. But Lonnie had given him a solid match, and he'd worked all day. His brain was jelly, his body mush. Once in a while, Jack defeated his chronic obstructive sleep apnea, and tonight was such an occasion. Jack slept great. He did not dream of Jen, but he woke up with a big erection, and he knew he had had it much of the night. His balls felt nice and tight. He was a realist. The thing with Jen had to come to a head sooner or later. He had the trial coming, and he was booked with her for the next music session. If she wanted to play games, what could he do?

Wednesday came and Jen greeted him warmly or at least warmly for Jen. His mother had always told him that women dress up for men they're interested in, but the older he got the more he realized his mother was wrong. Pay close attention, she'd told him. He didn't need to be told that; but the fact was these Millennials were just a distinct species. Jack didn't know that he agreed or he just rarely met anyone who was interested in him. Plus, the slut level was elevated across the board. His own nieces wore bathing suits that made their grandmothers gasp, so the dress up for the man thing was tenuous to nonexistent.

Jen wore white shorts, sandals, and a purple blouse with long sleeves. What skin she'd revealed, her legs, seemed matched by that which she'd covered, her arms. Jack smelled perfume. If she'd worn some before, it would have been minimal. Jack couldn't recall any at all. What to make of this? Inconclusive as usual, Jack thought, as they had tea in the kitchen. He got aggressive and wandered into the living room. He'd never had a look around, and she'd never invited him to. The second bedroom, the kitchen and the bathroom were all he'd seen. She seemed a bit miffed, but he resolved to take a quick tour before they started playing. What was she going to do, tackle him?

There were books: T. S. Eliot; Collected Essays of the Transcendentalist Movement; Simone De Beauvoir, Oscar Wilde, and several oversized art books. She had the normal, no stereo TV set up which Jack would have been afraid to touch had she asked him. And then, there were four framed photos, two of her family, one of Jen at undergraduate graduation, and a small one that said "Lakepointe Regional Chess Club." There, seven boys and men and Jen with short hair seated around a single chess board, with a tiny, little, gold cup that they'd evidently won.

"Oh, I can't wait," Jack said ostentatiously gesturing.

"Ha. My father got that framed for me. I was the only girl in the club."

"I see. Nice hair, huh?" Jack deadpanned.

"Bastard."

"I mean on this guy here." Jack grinned at her.

"Bastard."

"And the little trophy?"

"Oh, let me remember. It was like third place in the Virginia regionals or something like that," she said.

"And you led the team, of course."

"No. I was the lowest ranked player, but my father was immensely proud that I had a ranking at all. He told my Mom I had balls." Jen was all smiles. "Your favorite intensifier."

"You don't mean I'm rubbing off on you. Oh Jeez, too many puns, I'm sorry," Jack straight faced.

"What the heck did you just say?"

"Nothing," Jack tested her. "Sorry. You mean 'cause all the players were male."

"95%," she cut her eyes at him, "but also because our own club had no other girls in it. My dad told everyone. It was so embarrassing."

"Was he in the club?"

"No, he was . . . is a talented player, but he was working so hard he just couldn't devote the time. There were tournaments, weekly matches. It was a bit of a commitment," she said.

"And this photo?"

"It came in the mail to our house because I was an official team member, and we did win this little trophy so everyone in the club got a copy of the photo," she beamed. Jack thought: all Millennials get a lot of trophies.

"And your what . . . fifteen with a bob?" asked Jack.

"Seventeen. Bastard, that's not a bob," she huffed, "But you see there were two boys younger than me, here and here, or maybe about the same age. Then grown-up men. It didn't matter. There were so few players; we were all in the one club. My mom opened the mail and just went wild. 'Jen, and her men,' she laughed when she showed it to my father. He had it framed and put it right in the living room, told everyone when they came over 'Look at my girl.' And then when I went off to college, he gave it to me."

"Did you keep playing?" Jack could see one of the boys had longer hair than Jen, but he decided he'd run the joke out.

"I mean not really. I was only mediocre, and when I got to college I went once and it was all men at the college club, so I kinda faded out."

"Sucks being surrounded by men, huh?" said Jack softly.

"I didn't mean that. It was just . . ."

"Yes?"

"I mean, I just wasn't that good," she had some defense in her eyes, but Jack knew when he was winning.

"Sooooo, therefore, thus, ergo, you stayed in the club to get practice and get better?" He reversed the whole thing on her.

"Well," she looked at him but claimed some privilege with which he was unfamiliar, "no, but I mean who cares anyway?" He'd seen her claim that privilege before.

Of course, it was a *non sequitur*. For regular women, Jack found such very annoying. When he was little, he couldn't believe they could hold their own nonsense in their head; as he aged, he wondered if they knew their own nonsense. For Jen, the *lawyer*, trained presumably in objective rational thinking, it surely must be impossible to think like this. Jack kept looking at her, and she tried her big smile. He did not smile back. What was it with that smile, he thought? Did she give the same one to those she admired and those she held in contempt? He knew the answer was yes. Is that the smile she'd have administering the lethal injection to the mass murderer? He could see her sticking the needle in with that smile, "Here you go, honey," the condemned being the only man she'd call "honey" in her entire life. He let it go as she dropped her eyes from his. Geez, Jack, you hardly know her.

"Well I do. I played very little as a kid. Would you mind killing me someday?" Jack grinned at her.

She had swung around next to Jack as they had discussed the picture but had positioned herself precisely where it was unclear whether anything sexual was going on. She could have easily touched his shoulder, or thrown an arm around him, or mock bumped into him, or any of the dozens of ways women can break the ice. Or, she could have just called from the kitchen; there would be no way to mistake this photo for another. But no. She'd elected to torture him instead. When she did not answer his question, she could have turned toward him but instead moved away just a little. The perfume was in his nose, and Jack was pissed. Why all the bullshit with this woman? If she did want him, her sex drive had to be infinitesimal. She knew darn well he wanted her but elected to remain unsatisfied or unspoken. Why?

"Let's play," she moved off, not answering his question. Jack talked himself off his ledge. You're just friends, Jack thought, don't be a fool.

They played and again it got a little better. As Jack had been floundering with his violin off and on for thirty years, he was glad there was some improvement. He'd had dark periods where no improvement of any kind seemed to occur. In fact, sometimes it seemed regression was extant. The few partners he'd had over the years were fleeting. Mrs. Gillespie, his first teacher as a junior in high school, had played duets with him for about two years, but Jack was just starting. They only played simple stuff. In college, Jack found no one and months went by when he did not play at all. In law school, for one summer semester, there was Bruce from England who played cello/violin duets. It was only three months or so and he was gone. Then, Jack started his career and worked extremely long hours. Very briefly, he'd tried playing with the community orchestra, but they were too good for him and the schedule was set in stone, to which Jack could not commit. That was it.

He could see Jen was getting better quickly. Jack could see she had an old level from childhood she knew she could get back to and she was. Jack liked that she didn't let on that she was better than him; she didn't want him to practice that much; she liked being better than him. She was competitive, wanted to be in charge, and did not like vulnerability, especially in the presence of some hideous Southerner. Where they might go from there, Jack didn't know. Jack struggled to get the sex out of his mind, but Jen's white legs and white neck didn't help.

The time flew by. Jack's hand went way out, and they shook goodnight. Another pattern was starting. At the point of departure, Jen never got blabby, emotional, or giggly. No, she was instead formal, almost like she reverted to being a ten-year-old saying good night to her parent's friends in old Virginia, the kids in the *Sound of Music* formally saying goodnight, friendly, but pretty stiff, and after playing music with Jack and Jack alone, the only little difference was a set of shiny, penetrating, even daring eyes that said "you'll lose control before I do" or something like that, egging him on, Lucy waiting with the football, not quite a bitch.

After the hearing, Jack had told his client, Ed, that the phone might ring. He needed to have his numbers ready and process any settlement offers decisively. Sure enough, Friedman called, and bloviated war stories about Cambridge, Boston, New York, and Baltimore. Jack sucked him off while he gave him the air finger the whole time. Friedman's client was better at math than Friedman, figured out there was no way to "win" after the consequential damages ruling, and started folding. Jack advised his client to be firm but not rub it in their face. Ed listened. The case settled very favorably. Jack felt great. "Another Big Firm Bites the Dust" he sang at the office.

Eventually, he told Jen. "Nice work," she said and nothing more.

Chapter Nine

COLD-BLOODED KILLER

It was August 2018, and the big, heavy, massive, ripe Florida heat was omnipresent. Jack couldn't take a piss outside in the night anymore—heat, humidity, bugs. But it didn't matter. Tonight, for the first time in his life, he would be a cold-blooded killer, and they don't piss outside. He was old now and tired of her bullshit. Just like his first girlfriend thirty-eight years before, after chapel, behind the storage shed, what could have been the sweetest little kiss, had been dragged into a big pile of bullshit. Like all of them, Jennifer had been playing a lot of games, never making clear whether he was in or out, whether he had a chance or not, whether she wanted to hold and be held, whether she wanted deep, long kisses or whether the lovely curls of her hair would caress his scrotum while she dove down, his hand on her nape, deeper and deeper to gorge on his meat. No, instead—bullshit. Plus, it would have been easy for her to make her intentions clear. Instead—bullshit. She'd been playing with him, having a ball at his expense. But she didn't realize he was old now. He wanted the sex; there was plenty of fire in the furnace; but it didn't consume him like from fifteen to thirty-five, or even thirty-six to forty, still less forty-one to God knows what he was now. His best orgasms were behind him; he knew that. He would roll the bitch into a ball, and if she showed any weakness, he'd whisper "Leda" after he'd unclenched into her sopping trough. No romance at all, he resolved.

A cold-blooded killer would follow all the preposterous conventions, even kick them up a notch. So, he booked an appointment the evening before the *Pirates of Penzance* for a full manicure and facial. He would not follow the rules laid down by his mother which had proven so relentlessly unsuccessful. Respect? Whatever. Chivalry? Tons of it, but not because of respect. Restraint? Negative. Spontaneousness? Might as well piss in the wind. Even his father had said stupid shit to him when he was a young man, like "It's not the clothes, son; it's the man." What a crock of shit that proved to be. Women loved superficial bullshit.

He felt like a super douche walking into Winter Springs Hair and Nails, but then, remembering he was a different person, laughed his way through the entire two hours. Manicure? Check. Facial? Check. While the women worked on him, he listened carefully to their bullshit, and goodness was there a lot, and practiced his own.

One had been married for over twenty years, the other was twice divorced, had sundry kids whom she massively overrated, and was now on boyfriend number whatever. He listened carefully while neither said anything good about any man, except ones they couldn't have, for the full two hours. It was just like at the office when he sat in the library rather than his office. The library had been Jack's favorite room in the law firm for twenty years. At the beginning of his career, it had been a bustling place, but then the horrible electronic era arrived which Jack detested, and the Millennials came with it. They were never in the library, and other than old Larry and old Steve rarely making an appearance, old Jack had the place to himself. Jack had sat on tree stands for more than one thousand hours in his life, and he liked being quiet for long periods of time.

The girls in the kitchen cut loose a little when they didn't think anyone could hear, but he could hear perfectly in the library. After a few preliminaries, the tones would change and then it was time to run down the men. At the manicure, he let his ears wander off to some of the other stations which he could hear. Other than a couple of gay guys who worked there, it was all women. It seemed like every conversation was the same as he expected, but that didn't bother him. Tonight, he was a cold-blooded killer, so these were his benevolent instructors.

"Anything else repulsive you see?" He asked them both after the facial.

"Huh?"

"Big date tomorrow," explained Jack.

"Oh, that's sweet." This would normally irritate him, but not tonight. He would practice his bullshit instead. He certainly needed practice.

"Anything else?"

"How are the brows and ears?" said Kiki, the one who had done the manicure to Kirsten the one who had done the facial.

"Oh, well . . . Not too bad." Tonight, he knew this was code for "beastly." Geez, could they decide for themselves when to take a shit?

"Let's clean it up," he said.

Relieved, Kirsten set to work tweezing and yanking prodigiously. "When did Kristen become Kirsten?" he thought. "And who was the dumbshit who thought that was clever?" But he reminded himself: Instructors.

"Any tips?" he asked.

"Huh?"

"The date," he said.

"Where are you going?"

He was nearly an idiot but filtered out *The Pirates of Penzance* and went with "Theater."

"Oh God, what a man. Dinner too?"

He nodded.

"Coat and tie?"

"Just coat," said Jack.

"Oh God. Night cap?"

"Hadn't thought about it," said Jack, even though he had.

"Oh God," she laughed to Kiki, "another one who hasn't thought about the nightcap."

Kiki laughed back: "Imbeciles all."

He imagined it was the biggest word in her vocabulary. She'd learned it from a TV show and had been using it for years. After all, she was in the business of running down men. Instructors, he thought.

"Any suggestions?" Jack asked.

"Champagne."

"Where?" said Jack.

"Close to her place." They laughed.

"What kind?" asked Jack, only because he assumed they couldn't name any.

"Not cheap." They laughed again.

"Am I hurting you?" asked Kirsten.

"Yes, but keep going."

"Oh God, what a man."

"Anything else on the date?" said Jack. He liked emphasizing the word "date."

"Make sure you do most of the talking." Their zeal was evident in this remark. So, there it was, he thought: my life in a sentence. But instead of becoming depressed, he marveled at the trio's new production rate.

"Anything else?" said Jack.

"Well, what kind of girl is she?"

"Normal."

"Oh God, wrong answer. Kiki, did you hear that?"

"Imbeciles all."

"How old is she?" asked Kirsten.

"I don't know, thirty-fiveish." Jack shocked himself with how easily he lied; the treatment was working.

"Oh God. Kiki, did you hear that?"

"Where were all the classy older guys when I was young and beautiful?" Kiki said.

"You're still young and beautiful," he salved.

"Oh God, that's terrible; stop it." They loved it. This simple pile of horseshit delivered with Eddie Haskell sincerity was his first step of pantloadhood. He noted the use of the word "older" which he knew from the office was a benevolent substitution for "old." So, they didn't think he was too old to fuck a thirty-five-year-old? Great instructors, he thought.

There was the normal period of silence while they mused and smiled on the greatest gobs of horseshit they had experienced. They never grew tired of these memories. Their hands worked as though on autopilot. Kirsten seemed particularly determined and assiduously plucked and scrubbed his face of the decades of disgustingness hence unattended. He did not make his normal mistake of trying to fill the silence. Instead, he watched Kirsten who smiled at him periodically. He could tell she had more to say.

"Anything else?" he said after a while.

The ice had been broken between the three now, and the two girls did not hesitate.

"Well, the neck. Kiki what do you think?"

"Oh God, for sure. Sasquatch."

"Trim?" he asked.

"Waxing would be better."

"Let's do it," he said without hesitation. He'd never been waxed before and figured it was something gay guys did. But he would listen to his instructors. Fuck it, I'm a stroke off, too.

Kirsten heated the wax and disappeared into the back with Kiki. There was a lot of excited women noises, frantic panties rummaging through the memories of yesteryears while the dork waited on the operating table. He strained to listen because he knew they were talking about him. But he couldn't hear. When they came back, at least one of them had smoked a cigarette. Kirsten washed her hands and asked if he was ready.

It took nearly twenty minutes, and Kirsten had a ball. She showed him the long hairs on the sticky paper that she yanked out of his neck. She asked Kiki to put a cold towel on ice. He could see it was *their* date now. Kirsten finished the ripping and pulling and then applied the cold towel to close the pores and alleviate the sting. He could see her hands and her focus in the mirror. She cared. He had started an erection when she asked whether he wanted any cucumber lotion.

"I'm in your hands," he said, a complete cheeseball line which he could tell had worked as she applied the lotion. It did smell like cucumbers. He started another erection, but then she was done. Maybe the joke from Animal House? No, keep the cloak on the dick, he thought.

He paid and tipped them both generously. It was 9:45 p.m. He was a full blown, urban coxcomb, waxed, asshole now.

"Anything else?" He wanted to call them "grasshoppers," but something had changed now. He was smart. They weren't women. They didn't have souls. They weren't individuals. No, they were laboratory rats hitting food pellets, and Goddamnit, it was his job to put them out dipped in as much horseshit as possible.

"You're ready, Jack. Just make all the decisions and don't ask her what she wants too much." Wow. He walked out a predator.

The next day he had a normal day at work and cut out an hour early. He had the schedule laid out in his head, and it was all business:

5:30	Meet for dinner. She would Uber.
7:00	Leave for concert
7:30	Champagne (optional)
7:45	Take seats
10:15	Offer nightcap
11:00	Her apartment (preferable) or his house
11:30	Clean sex or clean no

Everything he had always done, he would either not do or do the opposite. He knew she'd either say yes (he'd ball her brains out) or no (he'd have a friend who was female) or no (she'd end it all). By this twisted reasoning, he convinced himself the odds were in his favor, and his confidence soared.

As he weighed the odds, he thought she had to be at least a little horny, unless she was lying about the no-boyfriend issue. He reasoned that she had no reason to lie, so there really was no boyfriend. Thus, she had to be at least a little horny. But he'd questioned over the years whether girls really did get horny? How come there were no songs sung by women about how horny they were? What major fictional character who was a female ever got horny and in what play/novel/story? Maybe Joni Mitchell got close, but even she pulled punches, euphemized, "loved me so naughty?" very vague. In the female mind, "naughty" constituted a continuum between "looked at me funny" to "stuffed a cayenne-peppered eggplant up my ass, and not the Japanese kind." Hmmm, Jack mused, not a bad subject for future research, tentative title "Is There a Female Equivalent to Zeppelin's 'The Lemon Song?'" Jack slapped himself sober. Forget these theoreticals and get back to work.

What to do if she was a little drunk? The answer was crystal clear in his mind: fuck her but no exotics. He recalled with agony how he'd played this wrong over the decades by "being a gentleman." What stupid shit that had been. There had been Cathy at sophomore retreat; sixteen with big knockers and four beers in her. She'd been flirting with him all spring semester but of course had mixed in several tons of bullshit. She was a very nice girl from a very nice family. But mid-summer, they'd all been at the Lutheran retreat, and someone had smuggled some beer in. There were quite a few chaperons around, but they had been on their best behavior all week. It was Saturday night, and they'd cut loose a little themselves. Jack could see the police level going down. Meanwhile, there was Florida woods all around, and a midnight curfew. Cathy had probably never had a beer in her life, and now she'd had four, and her hands started to wander all over his shoulders, after he'd secured her for a walk. Her lips were nearly as loose as her hands as they kissed aggressively. He had a giant, aching boner which kept poking her as they grappled; he was sure the tip was leaking. She loved it, but he knew she'd never do anything without the beer. He had no blanket (not stupid because why would he need a blanket in July?); the chaperones would have been suspicious; no condoms (stupid), and no plan. Plus, there was a bench on the trail. Geez, at a minimum he could have fingered her, and at a maximum sat her down and throttled her for the twenty seconds it would have taken to spray her tonsils. (He found out the following week that his buddy, Jimmy, had done just that with Liz the same night only a few hundred yards away.)

Instead, he was the dumbshit who had said: "Hey, Cathy, maybe we shouldn't because you've been drinking."

"Ok. I always knew you were a decent guy."

And then he'd walked her back. They even made curfew. What a dumbshit he was. Loser. Cathy had paid him back the following week by telling him what a gentleman he was and how they'd always be friends. She then lost her virginity (not confirmed, but likely) and fucked one other guy before she graduated. Neither of them was Jack.

In college, most of the girls had lost their virginity and were on boyfriend number three through ten. Plus, all of them were drinking and smoking pot, if not more. He could remember three drug/alcohol opportunities: Lisa, Kathy, and Trish. He fumbled them all on the altar of "gentlemanliness," while his friends banged every bitch in site and often never gave them the time of day again. None of the three ever had sex with him after the fact. Trish had been particularly torturesome as she had passed out at his apartment. Eight hours later, he made her coffee, initiated the sex now that she was sober, and she declined. "I'm sorry," she said. Sorry for *what?* He thought. So, she was horny eight hours earlier, but not horny now? The word started to irritate him.

In the twenty years he had been practicing law, there had been seven other drunken opportunities he had squandered. He remembered each with vivid regret. Of those, one had subsequently become his girlfriend. So, I'm one for eleven, he thought, getting dressed. Not tonight, he thought, if Jennifer plays games, she's getting the cock first and the apology second. His mind was purified of all indecision.

He arrived before her and instantly decided to wait for her in the bar. He would not be the lapdog waiting in the foyer for the queen. Instead, he'd be the stud out for the night in the bar. He ordered club soda and positioned himself so he could see the foyer but also place the piano, the column, and the hanging flowers in his line of sight. He'd watch her come in, check out the clothes, but then turn away so that she'd have to approach him from the side. Geez, he thought, so this is what woman want? 100% horseshit. So, this is how the guys who get the pussy operate? 100% horseshit. But tonight, for the first time, he was one of those guys.

The preposterous ruse worked perfectly. She came dressed in an auburn cocktail dress with black trim and high heels, the famous hair a huge, foreboding, gold medal winner. The dress was just barely long enough, and the heels were just barely low enough not to be slutty. He could tell she'd be tugging at that hemline all night especially since they'd be sitting next to one another thus jacking it up quite a bit with her womanly hips. Hmm, he thought, classy with a teaspoon of slut. His mind remained pellucid. She approached exactly as planned, and he played it perfectly—greeting her warmly but with no physical contact, complimenting her appearance but only briefly (as though he had been on countless dates with chicks of her caliber) and gently encouraging her to have the drink brought to the table rather than wait at the bar. He was all velvet suave, utterly unauthentic, devoid of sincerity. The drink trick would keep the evening on schedule, and remove her from the presence of the jackals—although it was early there were already four or five in the area playing it cool, polishing their acts, never experiencing a drop of love or consideration for the women they were going to fuck.

Dinner went perfectly. She asked very few stupid questions (he briefly recalled why he liked her so much but banished it out of his mind) and so he had little concern to follow Kirsten and Kiki's advice. Cologne was another area he had screwed up over the decades. His father never wore any, and it smelled gay to Jack. End of story. Surely no woman of substance would want her man to smell gay. Even if he was wrong, surely it was a minor point. Wrong, wrong, wrong, Kirsten and Kiki had instructed. He obeyed, even making them spell out a specific acceptable cologne which he had bought at his lunch break earlier that day. The lady who sold it to him tried to suggest alternatives. Obviously, she too had given it a lot of thought. Ah, *Variation on a Theme of Cloaking the Penis* by Forester, he smiled at her. He squashed the sales lady quietly but instantly; the plan would be followed.

He even had the sequence clear in his mind. Either Jennifer would say nothing about the cologne in which case he would ignore it completely. Or she'd compliment it in which case he'd quickly acknowledge the compliment (as though he'd been wearing cologne his whole life) and move the conversation to how beautiful she looked that evening. God, I'm a loser, he thought as he went over these details. As it happened, the latter occurred and with some enthusiasm. He flinched not a bit and joked that she should do her hair up for tennis. She loved it, though he sensed awkwardness on his use of the word "do." Too 'eighties' he worried, but only for a second. After all, she knew he was a geezer, and here she was.

Dinner went perfectly as far as he could tell, and soon they were at the theater. He had not touched her at all, and when she climbed into his truck after dinner, the distance between the bucket seats was the Grand Canyon. Being the predator asshole which he had recently become, he knew some form of contact must occur. Without asking her (thank you, Kirsten and Kiki), he elected to valet and very briefly touched her shoulder in orientation to the building. Absurd of course, but she at least did not hate it. He'd monitored her alcohol during dinner and decided to discourage the champagne. She'd had an Old Fashioned (only drank 3/4s) and a glass of pinot noir (only drank 1/2), so she certainly wasn't drunk. However, they were a touch behind schedule, and he enjoyed the moments before a performance where there was quiet with a slight buzz in the audience. So, when his perfunctory offer of champagne was declined, he eagerly directed her toward their seats without asking her opinion on anything. He had gotten great seats. He wondered where the actors were right now. Did they smoke a big joint before a performance like Led Zeppelin? He chuckled aloud. "What?" she said and gave him a shoulder punch. He had thought about it for months and this was the first time she'd touched him in a while, but his mind was purer than Mengele's. "Oh, just the anticipation." Pure spankoff response. Remember: never tell the truth.

God, how did men go through their whole lives like this? He was only 90 minutes in and wanted to make a full confession. But again, he stuck to his plan which was to stay quiet or lie. He'd checked, and there was no intermission. He figured there would be some kind of bathroom gambit which he resolved to decline. Were women's bladders really that small or was it all a bunch of bullshit? Now that he was a killer, he figured the latter. Urinate? Might as well. Any stains on my dress? Unruly pubic hair? Little blood where I shaved too close and now only tiny panties to cover? Farting? Oh God what choice do I have? Early dinner shit? Oh God. Oh God. I'm wearing a thong with minimal asshole coverage how am I going to safely shit? Might have to use an entire roll of toilet paper as an insurance policy. I mean there were only eight billion cute little apes on the planet; surely, we each deserved one roll of toilet paper per shit—well at least the girls . . . He could hear her mind all too clearly. His conscience was cleaner than white linen still in the wrapper.

He'd seen the *Pirates of Penzance* three times before, and once again it was great. The actors were having a blast as the script was so good. The sets were over the top, exaggerated, the costumes preposterous. The audience laughed and laughed, and Jen and Jack laughed with them.

He could see she loved it, and now it was over. There might be a bathroom situation now, so he would roll with the punches. But she didn't say a word, the theater was small, and they were outside in only ten minutes. He put his game face on in those ten minutes. Either she would suggest they go to her apartment which would be immediately but not excitedly accepted. Or she would suggest they go to his house which would be immediately but not excitedly accepted. Or she would suggest they go for a nightcap which would be immediately but not excitedly accepted. If she vacillated (likely) he would suggest a nightcap but not offer to take her home. To Fuck or Not to Fuck, that was the question.

"Well, did you like it?" he asked.

"It was lovely. Thanks so much for taking me." There was a tinge of finality to the comment, but he was undeterred.

"Would you like a nightcap or shall I take you home?" Jack asked.

"How about that game of chess you promised me?"

"Ok. Sounds great. The night is young and so are you." Total stroke! He'd practiced saying "great" too enthusiastically, and of course it worked.

Too easy, he thought as he drove her to her apartment. She smelled great. She looked great. She was both smart and clever. She was twenty years younger than him. Tighten up, Dumbshit, Jack thought. He purged all romance from his mind and refined his intercourse plan. He had the condoms in his sport jacket as well as his phone and keys. Only his wallet was in his pants, and he could drop those without any awkwardness. He had to piss, but she hadn't in hours. Of course, he thought, she'd have to run to the bathroom first when they got there. That would give him time to move a single condom to his pants (three would show), sit down for chess and plan the attack. He'd piss after her, but now, at forty-eight, he wasn't pissing, he was "using the restroom." For decades, Jack had mocked this massacre of the English language by asking defecators how their "rest" had been? Were there any blankets or pillows in the "rest" room? But now, he was a certified asshole.

Sure enough, upon arrival she excused herself, and he very quietly tore one of the condoms off and put it in his pants. For a few seconds, he ran through in his mind all the fumbles of his life. Five or six had cost him sex which was there for the taking. Five or six more had diminished or ruined the experience. Not tonight, Killer, he thought. He would keep his coat on until invited to remove it, have a single condom discretely prepared, and then commence what had at this point turned into a military situation.

She took forever, which he interpreted as good. Cleaning that slot up, huh? Expelling those unfeminine farts? Mmm Hmm. If she only wanted to play chess, there'd be no need for elaborate primping would there? Don't try to get in the female mind, Dumbshit, he thought. Tighten up. She came out with an "all yours" but disappeared into what he presumed was her bedroom (he'd never been in there after all this time) without him getting a look. But he didn't get distracted trying to figure that out. He was a killer. He sat down to urinate so he could direct the stream against the side of the bowl rather than have it sound like there was a camel in her bathroom. His cock was like an inflated fire hose, but so big it needed additional stimulation to actually go North. He took his coat off to check the sweat level on his pits: not too bad. He splashed his face with cold water and toweled off meticulously. He checked the condom: a slight ring mark in the harsh light, but once he got into normal light it would be invisible. Unfortunately, he didn't know which side of her he'd end up on so that presented a problem. If they were sitting next to each other, she might touch the condom while they were making out, and it could

131

be a turnoff. Dumbfuck, he thought, where is your head? If she's got her hand on your leg, it's a go so who cares at that point? His lax thinking alarmed him, and he took a hard look in the mirror. Time to kill.

"Over here, Jack," she called as he walked into the living room. The board was all set up, the light subdued, and she'd done a little something to look vampy.

"Want a drink, Jack?"

"Sure. Whatever you're having and some water if it's not too much trouble." He had this planned as well. Lots of water equals big erection.

She brought the four glasses, and they started playing. Whether she was a poor player or nervous he did not know, but she lost the first game in about four minutes. "Whoops a checkmate," he said.

"Bastard."

"Correction. Heartless bastard."

She laughed, and they started another game. He quickly realized the mood was going in the wrong direction, if in fact there was going to be sex. There had always been competition between them, and she was no drunk floozy destined to giggle until spread eagled and pinned. She'd been on the fucking chess team, however long ago it was. Now, he'd beaten her in under five minutes, and there was unpleasant tension in the room. He looked around for a stereo. Dumbshit, he thought, when's the last time you saw a Millennial with a stereo. Plus, he'd been there before and knew there wasn't one, so what was wrong with his brain?

Then, he got lucky and saw a lovely print of Rembrandt's *The Night Watch* on the wall. It reminded him how she'd never invited him into this room before, and he'd only barged in the one time. The print wasn't as big as the original, which he knew was enormous but still huge and brilliant. There's a reason you're together, he thought, remember why.

"One of my favorites," he said pointing at it. "Was that here before?"

"Really? What else? And no, I got it about a month ago."

"Oh, the Wyeth with the woman on her side; *The Last Supper* by Da Vinci—"

"Did you think I didn't know who painted *The Last Supper*?" She laughed.

He was going to make the bacon, lettuce, and tomato joke from *Trading Places*, but she may not get it. C'mon, Killer, he thought, tighten up.

"Sorry. I just have never seen anyone with a big vibrant print of *The Night Watch*," he said. Whether it was using the word "print" or knowing the title or something else, he scored a bullseye as she gave a big smile and looked directly at him.

"Care for a better look?"

"Sure."

"Ok. Sorry, gotta pee again."

He said nothing, but when she left, he drained his water and quickly filled another glass to take to the couch. He picked the left side thus forcing her to sit to the right and making her decision easy for her. She was out quickly and sat a perfect four feet from him—any farther and clearly, they were only friends. Any closer and clearly, they were lovers. He was pissed but didn't let it shake his confidence. So, you had a perfect opportunity to clarify the situation, and you intentionally fostered confusion, he thought? Another episode of Torture Poor Jack. Hmm, well, your problem tonight, Jennifer, is that

I'm forty-eight and don't care. He finished his second glass of water.

She had changed into white shorts and a navy Cornell Law sweatshirt, but he hadn't been able to see her that well by the chess board. There was more light over by the Rembrandt, and when she said "music" and went over to whatever Millennials use to play music, she bent over and give him an excellent butt shot. Whatever went through her mind, in his it was intentional, but all doubts about his plan were now gone. He moved one foot to the right but intentionally gave off a look like he either hadn't seen the butt shot or it wasn't that great. He remembered this tactic had made her angry months ago when she'd bent over in the kitchen. Games and nonsense, so this is what it takes to be successful with chicks is about? Geez, no wonder you're a loser, Forester.

He held his smile when he could see it worked; she was irked. She'd picked Cat Stevens. Where has this woman been all my life? He thought. His arm was on the couch behind her, and he let his hand fall *pianissimo legato* onto her shoulder; a softer touch was not possible. She turned; they closed the ground on the couch and had an incredibly soft kiss. Then, a very long hug. He'd wanted to hold her for so long, he hated releasing the embrace. The kissing became more intense. He remembered his plan: don't speak unless you must.

"I like a lot of kissing," she said after ten minutes.

"More," he said.

After another ten minutes, she said "I thought you'd never touch me, Jack."

He was so on his game; he'd anticipated a preposterous remark of this nature. She deserved a punch in the mouth for this purified bullshit. In his youth, he would have responded with vigor, but tonight there would be a different vigor. He let the annoying errata slide write off and said instead:

"I haven't yet, Jen. Are there any prints in the bedroom?" More bullshit! Came the female chorus. More! More! We must have more bullshit!

"Yes." And she held his hand, and they went into the bedroom. Cornell Law came right off, and interestingly she had no bra underneath. Bitch planned it, he thought. He worked her nipples while standing, and his hand found the button and zipper on her shorts. Off they came, but she did have panties on. His mind was as clear as bell.

"I'll meet you in bed," he said motioning to the fact that he still had all his clothes on. She slid away and pulled the sheets back, while he undressed. He put the condom on before he got in bed with her and was annoyed to find she had not taken her panties off. The last little rampart of nonsense, he thought? Why on Earth would she leave those on? Now, still, one last time, just before the apogee, she still, yet, still, yet millimeters away, reserved the right to kick him down the mountain should he panty-fumble at the very end.

Oh well, back to the nipples, he thought. She responded well. After a while, he hooked his index finger into one side of her panties and started to pull. He hoped she'd help him with the other side, and she did. After a little wrangling, they succumbed and ended up on the bed. He kissed her and pushed the panties off the side of the bed as he didn't want them to get in the way. The way Jack's life had gone, if not kicked off, those panties would have somehow gotten horseshoed around his cock or his hand or something and fucked the whole thing up.

Now to finger or not to finger? He had it all planned. If she pushed him away, he'd stop. If she did nothing, he'd continue. She pushed him away but said "Kiss me, Jack," which threw him off for a split-second, but he simply complied and went back to work. He often thought of how the first sex with a woman was not good. In fact, he'd never had good first sex. There was too much tension, too much awkwardness, too much ignorance. Like the rest, he figured her pussy would be very tight and she would be very tense. Absolutely everything had to be a fucking hassle. He would be too horny, frustrated that the pussy would not yield, and then *staccato and fortissimo.* When she finally yielded, he'd be far too late in his cycle, come quickly, and start off on a disappointment. If the woman was one who could climax during intercourse, she had no chance. A lose-lose. But not tonight. The old, big-hearted Jack, Mr. Loving and Sincere, the fucking loser, was gone. The new, heartless, military Jack was born, popping out of the uterus fully cologned and forty-eight; just in time to go back in.

He got between her legs and hoped she would guide him.

"Do you have a condom?" she said.

"I'm wearing one." Despite all the foreplay, she had not put her hand anywhere near his dick, an all too common occurrence.

"I like a lot of kissing," she said.

"I'm in sexual agony."

He hoped she would grant formal permission in some way, but she didn't. But as he kissed her again, her hand did make its way and guided him to her labia. With the condom on he couldn't feel much, but knew a gentle push was in order. He sunk in one inch. Now is when he would not repeat the mistakes of the past. He kept kissing her while making the tiniest thrusts; he knew her natural juices needed invitation. He sunk in another inch; now the entire bulbous head of his cock was in her. More kissing, and he felt more lubrication. He sunk in another inch, and she writhed under him.

"Are you okay?" he said.

"So good. Go slow."

His confidence soared. He kept to his gentle thrusting, and she lubricated more. More kissing.

"Deeper?" he said.

"Yes."

He sunk in another inch or so, and she writhed again. Her legs had been open with knees bent, but now she straightened them into a gymnast's flying V. He sunk deeper into her pussy. Now there was full lubrication. His plan was flawless, and for once being an old man was an advantage. Although he could feel his kettle simmering it was far from a boil. Jen was either having a marvelous time or faking it very impressively.

Without asking permission, he drove into her all the way, balls deep. She gasped and sucked in a huge breath of air. His scrotum, which was not covered with plastic, tapped on her perineum. He could feel the juices stick to his scrotum as he pulled back, little droplets of female ooze. He held his thrust while kissing her on the neck for a full thirty seconds and then stopped.

"Can you come?" said Jack.

"Oh yes. I'm going to for sure."

He was shocked. Iterations of women he'd never made orgasm or for whom it was difficult ran through him, but he kicked them out of his mind.

"Come Jennifer. I want you to come."

"Drive your cock into me."

He complied with long deep but unhurried strokes. She came in just a couple of minutes. And then he made yet another brilliant decision: he stopped again. His kettle had been kicking at him, and she had come. Hit the brakes, he thought.

"Did you come?" said Jack.

"Oh yes. Oh Jack."

"I like a lot of kissing, you sweet angel from heaven."

She laughed a little between her gasps for air.

"Come again," said Jack.

"Don't you need to come?"

"Later," he forced himself to make eye contact. She looked at him in slight confusion. The age difference what else?

She clawed his back and wrapped her legs all the way around him. He was under control and felt like her pussy had pushed him out a little during the rest. He went back to his small thrusting and within twenty seconds was back in her all the way. She splayed her legs wide again, and he drove into her more rapidly.

Three "Ohs" followed each louder than the first, and she came again. He paused again.

"Wrap your legs around me."

"You like that?" she said sucking air. He'd forgotten he'd been on top of her the whole time.

"Am I too fat?" said Jack.

"No."

"Do you want to get on top?"

"No."

"Are you okay?" whispered Jack.

"Fantastic. I always thought you'd be sweet. Now you come, Jack."

His heart melted. It had been years since any woman had said anything so nice to him. But he was still a killer as he started thrusting into her.

"Come again," he said.

"I can't. Never mind. You come."

He continued thrusting and put her out of his mind. She was at the bottom of the ocean now, and his hoary cock reached all the way down with ease. It was Leda and the Swan, and she was going to get the gyre. It was the Dick of Moby Dick. Now his scrotum started to slap against her perineum and tingle and bubbly bounce while his shaft got thicker and thicker. He felt the massive kick in his prostate building and decided to go for an early pinch. Trying to get cute and letting the semen creep up the urethra a little before the pinch was not an option. He hadn't had sex in years and couldn't even believe he was doing as good as he was; no need to take chances on a late pinch. His kettle was boiling, and as soon as it breached the valve and he knew his agony would end in strands of grisly goo, he applied a full pinch clinch immediately. The column of boiling jism was past the valve but only halfway up the length of his tightened cock. In vain, he applied the full python to the surging, darting, bobbing column of jism.

The column was split at his crotch and went down in two mighty forks to his toenails; all along the route was agony, heartbreak. There it pulsed and scrubbed out of every crack and crevice in his toes all the rotten rejected jism that had accumulated over the decades. Robin from kindergarten was dissolved in jism under the oak tree where she'd denied him and broke his little heart for the first time. Mary from middle school was expunged as she gawked at him, due to her unskilled stroking of his shorts as though he were a carnival animal, big, silver dollar leak in his corduroys. The kisses from Tanya in junior high which had made him leak (merely a quarter this time) into his shorts were scrubbed clean. The crusading column pulled and jostled his ankle bones. Banished were Pam and Angela from tenth grade who teased him, alone, at Angela's house at midnight, erect, bowed, balls trembling for relief which was denied by both after being promised by both, both laughing at him, mocking. He'd never had a threesome in his entire life. The jism tore his tight calves apart lengthwise and there too mined and extracted the shamed semen of yesteryear. Leah to whom he had lost his virginity but who then cooly rationed his sex was evaporated forever. Jack's patella, ACL, MCL and everything else whirred and hummed in reorganization—like paint can shakers at the hardware store— as the mighty forks achingly yanked, pulled and realigned the wear and tear of decades of male-hood. The many tennis tournaments he might have won had some women wanted to heal him after the first round of matches with explosive hot sex and the deepest of sleeps were more distant than Pluto. Instead, he'd drank too much beer and gone to bed alone, unsatisfied, unwanted. Now, the hamstrings, the tightest part of his body, were subject to the forked column; they were kneaded and pulled and kneaded again; they were beaten like piano wire with soft furious mallets. The graves of the endless bitches who'd rejected him were filled with Satan's diarrhea, immersing and gargling them to suffocate and die again and again. For once, he would giggle at them as they gurgled and gasped. The tiny python was no match for forty-eight years and as it lost its grip and yielded to a far superior power, he was somehow outside his body watching himself spasm into an unknown female. Finally, there would be redemption.

Jack ejaculated. He came in one long glorious strand; three big "kick and squirts" followed; he thought the much smaller fourth was the finish. He lay heaving on top of her and came back to earth, this spot, the hollow of her neck, his spent engorgement impossibly deep in her. He kissed her neck worried that his cock was so far in her, the head might poke her in the Adams' apple near where he was kissing.

"Thank you so much. I've wanted you for so long," said Jack.

"Poor baby," she said. "Just rest."

And then his prostate kicked unexpectedly, and he pumped into her one last time, anus aching.

"Oh, I'm sorry, Jen."

"Huh?" She sounded confused.

He was run over by a Fed Ex truck and did not feel sexy laying on her like a giant sack of potatoes. As he went to pull out of her, she said very softly "Don't forget about the condom."

And he had. Horrible condom memories flashed through his head, but Killer had one more moment of clarity. He felt for it imagining he would have to pull a garbage bag with three gallons of Bar B Q sauce out of her. He could see the inventor of the condom, some kind of engineer no doubt, calculating the force and quantity of the average ejaculation, dectupling it, and designing the condom accordingly. Dectupling won't be enough, he smiled to himself. His estimation was slightly off, but he successfully held onto the condom as he pulled his whole life out and checked to make sure there had been no problems.

"All safe, Jen," he said and lay next to her on his back. No parts of their bodies were touching at all now, and he reached and found her hand which he held, while he took massive breaths, wondered why he couldn't feel his feet, wondered why he couldn't feel his legs, wondered why his back was more relaxed then he could ever remember it being, and wondered why he was listed as a 6'3" man but felt like a 6'6" tube of Jello—boneless, inert, stretched, racked, not an ache or pain to be found.

She didn't say anything, and he remembered his promise not to say anything unless prompted. He didn't know about her sex history, but in his mind there was nowhere to go but down from where they were. She'd either come twice or lied about it. He'd come harder than he thought a man of his age ever could. Shut the fuck up, brother, he thought, and let it ride.

Her phone pinged in the kitchen. "Oh, that's my, mom," she said. They looked at each other and laughed for a solid ten seconds.

"She'll get suspicious if I don't text or call within thirty minutes." He had a quip ready but now was not the time.

"We both have to work tomorrow."

"That's right. It's Thursday."

"Ten more minutes with the old man, and then you can kick him out?

"You're not old, Jack," she said.

"Ten minutes?"

"Fifteen," she smiled and ran her hand across his chest in circles.

He wanted to pour his heart out, but Killer was still around. Just be cool, he thought. Kiss her, and then give one or two compliments and leave. Don't tell her she just saved what's left of your life. So, he did, but they had worked up a tremendous sweat and now it all dried as the A/C ran; there was some bad breath on the kisses and he moved to her neck and nuzzled and licked. She seemed very content, and they both got incredibly quiet. He remembered one of the first things that had attracted him to her was the simple fact they could be quiet together with no tension. It happened again, and then there was another ping.

"Better take care of your mother while I get dressed," he said, sitting erect on the edge of the bed. He noticed his back didn't hurt as it always did.

"I've always wanted to see your back."

He laughed. "Pretty terrifying, huh?"

By the time he was dressed, she had on a robe, the most expensive one Jack had ever seen, and was in the kitchen checking her phone. It was her mother as predicted. He gave her a big hug and left. He went home and collapsed in a heap. His chronic obstructive sleep apnea was as weak as his python and succumbed to the much greater force of his fatigue. Jack slept at the bottom of the ocean from which he had just risen.

Chapter Ten

WHY DID WE WASTE ALL THAT TIME?

With the dam breached, things flowed quickly. It was late August 2018, the month with no end. It seemed like all of the things that had brought them together were rolled in a ball and submerged in a pool of hot sex. Jack was in his urologist's office in less than a week. He hadn't needed any Viagra after *The Pirates of Penzance*, but he was smarter now, more cautious. How could it possibly hurt to have it around if necessary? Even better, his urologist prescribed testosterone injections, including the first one on the spot. Jack did not take it personally at all. What a lucky son of a bitch I am, he thought. Although he was honest to the point of fault and although he would not lie to Jen if directly and unequivocally confronted, in the meantime he would keep her entirely in the dark, avoid the subject, and even engage in some minor fraud if warranted. Jack was told his prostate was normal, and the late "kick" was deferred to a future appointment.

She seemed sexually satisfied but never said so. In fact, she never really said anything about Jack that was nice. If she did, it was a very quick, unadorned, unemotional "check the box" comment, such as "you played better tonight," "great French toast, Jack" or "that's nice; thank you." Jack didn't know what to do. Before they'd had sex, she'd been a low volume communicator; after sex, nothing had changed in that area.

They were at her apartment sitting in the extremely expensive chaise lounge that she had, and Jack asked her if she was happy. She closed *The Great Gatsby*, putting it on the end table and looked at him from a foot away.

"My last boyfriend said he didn't want to kiss more than nine times per session."

"You're joking," said Jack.

"Verbatim."

"Geez. I'll make up for him!" said Jack.

"You noticed?"

"I listen, Jennifer," Jack said. "You told me you liked a lot of kissing the first time we did it."

"Yes and you do, so I am happy. But you haven't taken me on a fancy trip."

"So? It's only been a few weeks," Jack said. He knew "fancy" really meant expensive. But he said, "No objection. What'd you have in mind?"

"Well, you like to use the word 'balls' a lot."

"You love that don't you?" Jack tickled her neck.

"No! Big balls. Balls of steel. Funnier than balls. Ballsy. Expensive as balls." She sing-songed her way through a few more with great derision.

"Gosh, you've got balls." He said, nibbling on her ear lobe. "Balls, balls, balls," he whispered. He flipped her over and ground his chin into her starting with her shoulders and moving down to her butt. The chaise was like a bathtub; she couldn't get out. "Balls, balls, there were some very big balls."

She started to laugh uncontrollably, and when he got to her butt, she bucked him off and rolled back on her side.

"And what's one of your favorite balls, Jack?"

He looked at her, signaling he needed another hint. "I like a lot of kissing."

"No. You've got that covered, Rip."

"Hint, hint, hinty hint," Jack said and got on top of her and went to work with his chin while he gave her hamstring a hard squeeze. She screamed and tried to play defense while they mock wrestled on the chaise. "You'll hurt my super expensive chaise from UpNorth.com if you don't submit," Jack snickered in her ear. She laughed and laughed.

"What time of year is it, Jack?"

"Is that my hint?" asked Jack.

"Affirmative."

"Ah, *hotter* than balls," nodded Jack.

"Exactly. Let's go north."

"Done. Where and what's the schedule?" said Jack.

"Jack, you bastard. We're only just talking about it now."

"Say 'bastard' affectionately?"

"No."

"Please."

"No," she moused.

"Well, say something nice to me," said Jack.

"What? No. Weirdo."

She laughed, and he rolled her back and kept working his chin into her back and telling her how sexy she was. In ten minutes, they decided on fly fishing. In ten more minutes, they had the schedule planned. Labor Day weekend; what else? Where has this woman been all my life? He thought. But Jack was hurt that she didn't say anything nice to him.

"How much money are you putting in?" asked Jack.

"Nothing, you got sex, and you're the man."

She'd said this for the first time only days after they'd first had sex, and Jack took note. Of course, it made no sense, and she must know it made no sense. He wanted to say "actually you owe me some sex then" as he had been paying for months before they had sex but that would probably just piss her off. He'd let it slide before, and he let it slide again. She was going to dump him anyway, he reasoned.

They flew to Montana, spent a lovely long weekend at a five-star lodge, and flew back. $6,000 in round numbers. She paid none of it. They got back and went to work.

She was working very hard to climb the ladder, and he was working very hard to stay on the very same ladder. He knew exactly what she was going through though the profession had taken yet another step down, maybe two. He remembered his first boss saddened at the decline and that was over twenty years ago. No doubt it was much worse now—brokers masquerading as lawyers and clients stupid enough to go along, probably because they were doing the same thing in their business. Poor Jen, he thought.

In any event, he had always been a scheduler and now the schedule practically filled itself. They would see each other several times per week, sometimes sleep over, and look for long weekends. He figured she would ditch him shortly, and that was perfectly normal. What in hell did she want with a forty-eight-year-old anyway? They had lots of sex, and she orgasmed very easily. He didn't even feel like he was doing anything special. He created a rule where she had to tell him she'd been kissed enough before he'd stop. "Mr. Considerate" or "Mr. Thoughtful" she'd throw at him once a week or two, but to his ears it sounded observational, neutral, lacking in any affection. He alternated between Viagra and Cialis as instructed, and soon started waking up feeling like he didn't need anything. She was a morning person. He was a morning person. She liked sex in the morning, and so did he. Once he tried without any pill, and it was no problem. He explained matter-of-factly to her that his erection would always be stronger in the morning, and she rolled her eyes. "Mr. Consideration," she laughed. His urologist said it was a good sign; he only used the pills in the evening.

Six weeks went by, and she hadn't ditched him. On the other hand, she had never become emotional about him. He went through his check list. Music? Impossible, but double check. Movies? Even more impossible, but check. What kind of twenty-eight-year-old wanted to watch *Gone with the Wind*? Food? Check. He had always been a good cook, and he pulled out all the stops for her. She said no man had ever made anything but scrambled eggs for her. Fine arts? Check. She promised to take him to the opera for the first time, but it had to be up North. Certainly, no woman had ever promised him that. Tennis? Sort of a check. She was somewhat athletic, but even at forty-eight he could beat her easily. If he played down to her, she got pissed. He remembered Lynn and resolved to steer her toward female competition.

Jack noticed she did not appear to have any friends. No one called or texted except her mother, her father, and work. He had not even been present when her brother called, if he ever had. Jack asked Elan to update the social media search, but it still came back nothing. If she was hiding, she was hiding good, but Jack also felt guilty at thinking ill of her with zero supporting evidence. He'd sat right next to her for hours with her phone on the table right next to them, and she never hid anything. Same with her laptop, she'd sit with it open right in front of him for hours.

Jack noticed she had no interest in law. He had told her about the Kowalski case for months, but she had never asked a single question. When it settled very favorably, she shrugged. She never brought up any recent appellate opinion though every week dozens were published. Very rarely, she would ask his advice on a case, but it was usually a "Southern etiquette" question framed as a legal issue, like: "How many breaks do you give them in a deposition?"

She rarely finished a meal or a drink, and she left her partially filled dishes all over. When hunting season started, she complained about how much time it took, but he countered that her shopping trips were usually longer. "Truce," she said but her eyes said otherwise. Jack knew to watch the "time together" issue, but otherwise he let everything roll and said nothing.

But one problem arose pretty quickly; they had no one to tell. They were both lawyers, and the legal community was pretty small. Sure, no one would actually do anything, but there would be some frowns at them being together, most would be at Jack's expense. Family? Jen told him straightaway her parents would be mortified. That left her brother. The problem was not that he would object, but that Jen didn't trust him to keep his mouth shut. Also, what was to be gained from telling him? He lived in Virginia, so it wasn't like they'd have dinner together. Jen had some friends from law school, but they were all in different states. And they were all on social media. Jack had been astonished when Jen told him she didn't use social media. He was in open rebellion against it. "We don't need any help being anthropocentric!" Jack would scream at anyone who would listen. She thought it was "stupid." He didn't tell her he had Elan look her up. Plus, again, what was to be gained by her telling friends in other states?

Jack told Jen that he had lost his father a few years prior, and his mother would have both burst into tears and told the entire planet. She had been trying to get Jack married forever. Jack had been close to his older sister, Jenny, as a child, and thought Jen would probably like her, but Jenny was thrice divorced with five kids. The oldest was older than Jen by a year or two. Again, what was the upside to telling her? Jen was not amused that Jack had not told her that his sister shared her name and gave him some hard eyes about it. Jack had a joke ready— "I didn't want to tell you that you're like fucking my sister!"—but he decided Jen wouldn't laugh. She had her fake smile which she used all the time, Jack observed. She had some other smiles Jack hadn't figured out. She had a little laugh which was always accompanied by her putting her hand over her mouth like it wasn't ladylike to laugh. And then, once a week maybe, Jack could get her to really laugh. Five minutes later, she'd be taciturn, unable to believe this ancient teddy bear from Orlando had gotten her to lose control. Jack thought he would call his sister eventually, but what was the rush?

Jack had a baby brother, Jerry. Again, Jack had been close to Jerry until Jerry met his wife, fifteen years ago. Other than Thanksgiving and Christmas, they basically didn't see each other. Also, Jerry had a ten and a twelve-year-old and a wife, Tabitha. What on earth would they say about the age difference? Nothing good.

And so it evolved that Jen and Jack didn't tell anyone. They were both kind of secret anyway. When they went out, they had a plan if they were noticed. If it was one of Jack's friends, Jack would say Jen was his cousin from Illinois. If it was someone who knew Jen, she'd say Jack was her cousin from Illinois. If it was obvious the Illinois story wouldn't work, they'd say they were just friends. But months had gone by, and they hadn't been busted yet. Lonnie knew. If Jen told anyone, she never told Jack. And it didn't seem to matter. They went out in public all the time but never seemed to run into anyone. The fact that they never saw anyone out and about only seemed to further the proposition that they belonged together. They called themselves the "preposterous pair." Someday, somewhere, someone would bust them. So be it.

Their routine was refined. She got a little pissed when he started hunting in late September—bow season, he loved it. She'd seen deer in Jack's yard, and he explained it all to her. But she didn't understand and bitched a little about the time. Jack reminded her she'd said she didn't want a "skinny jeans" guy. Jack killed a doe for meat, and she loved the venison. So Jack let it roll off, but he kept the "shopping" and "venison" arguments ready because he knew she would probably bitch a little more. Big deal. He was happier than he'd ever been. He couldn't tell how happy Jen was.

Chapter Eleven

WHEN ARE YOU GOING TO TELL YOUR PARENTS?

October came. Jen seemed to think October meant cool temperatures and colored leaves. But, as usual it didn't really cool down, just a teaser for days here and there. It readily roared into the high 80s with high humidity all month, but Jack's house got nicer. It was in the country and the mornings were cool. He'd bring her coffee or breakfast on the patio. He filled up the hot tub, and she loved it.

She said she had to go home for Thanksgiving, and did not invite Jack. That really hurt his feelings, but he let it slide. They were going to the Met in New York City for the opera in mid-October, Jen's old stomping grounds. They had a great time in New York City and saw *Rigoletto*. Jen did her hair for three hours instead of the normal two and dressed flamboyantly. Ironically, since everyone else was dressed up too, there was no gawking at them. They got more looks at "T & G's Hardware" near Jack's house. Jen had even been called "Jack's babe" or "Jack's girly" by some of the employees who'd known Jack forever; this drove Jen insane as she had instructed Jack never to call her "honey," "sweetheart," "babe" or anything else prosaic. It was a big huff.

Jack struggled with the operatic singing style but still enjoyed it. She stuck him with the bill for the entire three-day weekend: about 7,000. Jack knew generally they could have driven to the opera in Tampa, Florida, for a couple hundred bucks, but she wanted him to see her old haunts. She thought it was cute or something to stick Jack with the bill. Jack looked at her a long time waiting for the relationship to mature. No audible response. Oh well, Jack thought, she's going to dump you anyway so just roll with it.

It was 8:38 p.m., and they had had sex after work, and then a small dinner which Jack had made. It was a couple days after getting back from New York on Sunday night. They were at Jack's house. After they had had sex the first time, she eagerly went to Jack's house. He had told her he lived in the country, and was surprised when she said, "I hope I can't see your neighbors." Jen seemed very urban to Jack. All her stories involved an urban environment. She knew he was an outdoors guy, but it didn't mean anything to her. Jack feared she wouldn't like it.

The first time she saw it she said: "I thought there would be a castle and a moat."

But she liked it except for all the taxidermy, and it was small. She knew what hunting and fishing were, but only in the abstract. She couldn't believe it the first time she went to Jack's house. But apparently, without explanation, she'd resigned herself to it, and they were gradually spending more time at Jack's house and less at her apartment.

"When are you going to tell your parents?" Jack asked. It had started to bother him.

At first, he wasn't having sex with her, so she couldn't tell him what to do. Now, they had been having sex for about three months, and he had scheduled a few things without her permission. Jack had never cared what any girlfriend had done, and Jen was no exception. He encouraged her always, dictated to her never. She surveyed the living room while his question hung: seven bucks, two turkeys, a dozen ducks, a bass, a sailfish, and a tuna; otherwise, countless knick-knacks and memorabilia. Jack thought it would be funny to have Jen put her opera outfit on and photograph her in Jack's living room with the title: *I've finally arrived* or, *If you can make it here, you can make it anywhere*. But he didn't have enough confidence to make the request.

"I don't know," she said.

"You're hurting me."

"No. It's not you. It's me," she said.

"How do you think it makes me feel that you won't tell your parents?"

"Well, you haven't told your mother?"

"Do you want me to?"

"No," she said.

"Exactly. I will if you want me to."

"Sorry. You're right." She'd told him the taxidermy was unbearable, but he'd parried that she must agree her apartment in the city must be much more "unbearable." Jack was fond of ironic hyperbole, but not serious hyperbole. She loved the lake. She loved the sunrise. She loved the kitchen where Jack waited on her. She loved the patio. The taxidermy wasn't "unbearable" any more than her posh-cum-shitty apartment in downtown shit city was "unbearable." She loved Jack's bedroom; it had only one mount, a buck over the headboard.

The only problem was when they had sex, she frequently couldn't avoid looking at it.

The living room was oversized as Jack had knocked down two walls and absorbed a small room he deemed worthless. It had a wonderful masonry fireplace. He made her many fires, and she loved them all.

Jack couldn't believe she had the balls to complain about the taxidermy. Of course, he had only mounted the most cherished of the animals he had killed. She had no clue how much work hunting was, how hard Jack had pursued these game animals. Also, usually she had been very circumspect about topics of which she had no knowledge, but now she wanted to speak without having a clue?

The silence lingered while Jack recalled her running down his mounts, seeming to think it was some sort of *decorating* decision. He'd let it pass for weeks now, knowing the issue would soon have to be resolved, planning on how to best resolve it, wondering why the onus was on him to fix it, hurt that it seemed every problem was his to solve. He never complained about her apartment, which resembled a clothing warehouse more than anything else. Plus, it was right in downtown Orlando, a real shithole.

"Well?" he said. Jen's mother called or texted her almost every day. Jack recalled *Terms of Endearment* and Debra Winger and Shirley MacLaine joking at how much their phone bills were going to be when the Debra Winger character moved away as they had to talk every day. Otherwise, he'd never heard of such a thing. Jack had lots of women in his family and never could recall anyone talking every single day. Still, Jack thought, with women it wouldn't be totally unprecedented. Jen's father called or texted at least weekly. As the time had gone by, Jack had noticed she'd been in Orlando for months now yet seemed to have no friends. She certainly was an odd bird, Jack thought. But shit, Jack thought, I'm the odd bird, so how can I possibly think of her as odd? Even better, Jack had initially thought, *that means I get Jen all to myself*. Never could he remember that she had cancelled or rescheduled anything, except work, to avoid Jack. Or maybe, she was keeping him in the dark, but that didn't bother Jack.

"I've been thinking about how to tell them," she said.

At first, Jack had translated this—"I'll be dumping you soon, so the problem will go away." Now, they'd made it through the break-in period, at least what he thought it was. As far as Jack could tell, she seemed happy. He was happier than he'd ever been in his life. What to do with this ridiculous position she'd taken? Well, Jack reasoned, one or both of the parents were bound to visit sooner or later, that would push the issue to the front, and so best to do nothing.

They had been on the couch in the living room this whole time. Jack thinking. Jen reading *Anna Karenina* and wearing his Regan/Bush 1984 shirt. After the sex started, she'd gone straight to bare feet, and there they were. A jock his whole life, Jack silently suspected that even at twenty-eight Jen's feet were hurt by the absurd heels she wore almost every day. Jack couldn't believe any Millennial had read "*Anna Karenina*," they all had ten-second attention spans, but to be with one who did bordered on the fantastical. Also, he loved her feet, and decided it was time for some wrestling.

"Am I going to have to gore you again, *Mein Liebchen*?" Jack lifted his eyebrows at her.

"Oh, weirdo time." Apparently, Jen's upbringing had been a little on the reserved Protestant side. Not Jack's. Jack's English father was affectionate, and Jack's mother and relatives were all earthy Slavs of some sort. Jack had been cuffed, hugged, tussled, and wrestled and beat up his whole life. He couldn't keep his hands off Jen.

"That's right," Jack was crazy-voiced and started to twist her toes until she screamed and writhed. He worked his way up to her calves and squeezed them hard until she squealed. Now, he mock-rammed his forehead and chin into her back as she rolled onto her stomach, the book hitting the floor. Jack made pig noises and squeezed the hamstrings again. "Squeal like a pig."

But for once she missed the allusion. "Weirdo," she laughed and shrieked.

He picked her up, sat back down, flipped her over and spanked her butt. "Here's my little rich girl, my coquette, my debutante, my uppityness, my prissy little wonderful big head of raven hair!" He drum-rolled on her butt.

"Raven is a cliché! No!" she shrieked.

"Oh, my dark, piggy head of hair? Rigoletto!"

"What? Rigoletto is the father, not the lover," she corrected him, something he knew she loved to do, particularly if the topic was utterly inconsequential.

"You said don't say 'raven,' so that's my synonym, smarty panties, and there's lots of incest in opera, right?" and he slithered out from under her and burrowed in longwise beside her and dug his chin into her shoulder.

"Pig hair? Incest?" she said.

"Well, you asked for it. Most girls would be elated with 'raven'?"

"Bastard. Weirdo." She wriggled next to him.

He got under her now, and rolled her on top, longwise.

"Big hug for Weirdo, please," he whispered in her ear, hugging her and stroking her hair.

"Oh, Rip, you're just . . ."

"Huggie. Huggie. Huggie. Huggie," he did crescendos and decrescendos. She muffle-laughed in his shirt and allowed herself to be hugged. He held her tight and resolved to hide his pain from her. He loved squeezing her ass and did so now. What was wrong with him? It had only been months? Did he have leprosy? Did he smell bad? A lisp? Uneducated? Indebted? A criminal? Wife beater? Dead beat? No, he was forty-eight, and that was worse. It hurt him, but he resolved to play the percentages and try not to let it show. What was a little pain? What was a minor delay? The parents would show eventually. He had her now and nibbled and gummed her extra white goose flesh. She did not get off him for twenty minutes.

"What about kids?" Jack said.

"What about them?"

"You haven't said anything about kids."

"Neither have you," she retorted.

"I'm not a nubile female."

"Nubile means 'marriageable' not 'fertile,'" said Jen.

Jack looked over at her. She smiled. "Thank you for correcting me. I'm not a fertile female either."

"I don't want kids," she said.

"Why not?"

"I just . . . The future doesn't seem bright. You can't even spank your kids anymore."

"Say what?" said Jack.

"You know what I mean. Music is dead. Movies suck. Skinny jeans. Everyone hates each other," she lamented.

Jack looked at her. It was the longest speech she'd ever given. Wearing his Reagan/Bush 1984 shirt, Jack had to agree: Jen would never have a USA like 1984, not even close.

"Did your parents hit you and your brother?" asked Jack.

"Hell yes; spanked us both when we deserved it. Now these parents all coddle their little puppies."

"Me too. Do they know you don't want kids?" Jack thought: Jen is extremely coddled?

"Yes. There was a massive fight by Fairfield standards. My mother didn't speak to me for two weeks," she said.

"Wow. I understand."

"How?" she said.

"You're smart, talented, beautiful, tall, elegant, ambitious— a huge winner, not the kind of genes the species ought to throw in the garbage."

"You're sweet, Rip. I'm just more like my father."

"But he *also* wants you to have kids, Jen," Jack responded.

"You're right," she did a big hair tussle, "You're right. I'm just too selfish, and the idea that I'm going to take orders from my own kids is just so backwards. I mean I see these girls my age *catering* to their kids and it's just embarrassing and wrong."

Jack flinched at the candor from her.

"Well," he said after a while, "I must concur in your gloomy assessment." He interlaced their fingers. He was very depressed that apparently the world would have no more Jennifer James Fairfields.

The pleasant version of the silence came, and they said nothing. Jack thought of when he was twenty-eight and his generation of women. He couldn't remember any of them giving the world such a rotten report card. Delay kids? Sure, there were some of those at twenty-eight. Never have kids at all? He couldn't think of one. At twenty-nine, his own sister already had a decade of disasters behind her, yet she had remained optimistic and was in fact still optimistic. Yet, here was Jen, with the world by the balls as far as Jack could see, ready to give up on the USA. He held her closer while the black cloud hung over them. Jen turned back into Jen, and she said nothing more.

Jen went home for Thanksgiving. She left on Wednesday morning and came home on Sunday evening. Jack waited for her text or call, but she never did. Finally, on Friday afternoon he texted her: "I give thanks for Jennifer," with red hearts.

A few hours later, she replied: "Sorry, busy, ditto," with a thumbs up.

That was it, until Sunday after midnight: "Delayed flight; call you tomorrow."

Chapter Twelve

THE OTHER JENNIFER

Jack discussed the "I won't tell my parents" thing with Lonnie, and they both agreed there was nothing to do. She couldn't be forced, and it wouldn't do any good to try. Plus, she might dump him, and the whole thing backfire. But Jack was a lawyer, and he decided he needed a woman's point of view in addition to Lonnie's.

There was only one to call: his sister, Jennifer. The oldest of the three Forester kids, Jenny had missed the wisdom of Ronald Reagan and tried to relive the '60s. After graduating high school Salutatorian, and getting a full ride to University of Florida, she promptly fucked up and got pregnant her freshman year at UF. Unwilling to abort, she had the child and dragged the family through a horrible time. In particular, Jenny had always been the apple of their father Melvin's eye, and one of the very few times Jack ever saw his father cry was when Jenny had come home pregnant with no husband and no boyfriend even. Jack's mother was similarly destroyed.

Who could have guessed that this was only the beginning of Jenny's saga. Over the next twenty-five years, she racked up five children with four other men, three of whom married her, all ending in divorce. Now, fifty-three, Jenny lived in Nashville and was a songwriter and record producer—the ones with real talent while the pretty boys and girls get all the attention. She had reconciled with Jack's parents after a lengthy period of mutual banishment. "We don't know what to say to you, our dearest and only daughter," Melvin had said at the time, "We are at a loss." No one knew exactly where Jenny's kids were or where her exes were. Jack's mother asked periodically but couldn't keep track of it all. Sometimes, Jenny didn't seem to know herself.

Jack had worshipped his older sister all through childhood, and been kicked in the ass by his father a thousand times: "Why can't you be as good as Jenny? Why don't you work harder?" Jenny excelled at math and science, but really excelled at the arts. She could do it all. As Jack grew up, he figured out he only had one slight edge on Jenny: he was funnier. Jenny was not funny, and like a lot of talented people she took herself a little too seriously. But that was it, and Jenny sang Jack's praises all through grade school and high school to everyone whether they wanted to listen or not. Unfortunately, the pregnancy at eighteen and ensuing twenty-five-year roller coaster had separated them, and things would never get back to where they had been. But Jack still remembered his youth and loved his sister. She was one of the only females in his life that had ever stood up for him.

"Look at little Jackie play basketball like a pro," she had said when Jack led the junior high school team to the regional championship.

"Look at my stud, little brother," she said when Jack hit puberty and grew nearly a foot in two years.

"Look at the soft hands on my little brother," she said when Jack started playing violin.

No one ever listened to her, but Jack remembered her tireless advocacy for him. She had had a phenomenal life, but Jack still respected her and trusted her to keep her mouth shut. So, he called her.

"Hello."

"Jenny, it's your brother, Jack."

"OMG, my brother. How are you?" said Jenny.

"Ok. But I need some help from the Salutatorian."

"Ha. You always remember that. What's up?" asked Jenny.

"It's a woman."

"Lord. *Your* woman?" she said.

"Yeah."

"Jack has a girlfriend? The confirmed bachelor? The loner? This must be some sparkling shit," she laughed.

"Sort of. I need help. I wouldn't call you if I didn't need it."

"Ok. Of course," she said.

"Please confidential. No social media. Nothing. Absolute dead end."

"Ok. Ok. My gosh, what's up?"

"She's twenty-eight."

She laughed. "What else?"

"Another lawyer, from Virginia, wealthy family, very good looking, plays the cello . . ." Jack's voice trailed off.

"Wow, my brother. And the question?" she said.

"She won't tell her parents about us."

"How long have you been together?" she asked.

"Pre-sex 10 months, post-sex 4 months."

"Well, how blunt do you want me to be?" she said.

"Very."

"I know you've always had trouble with women, Jack. I know that. I remember you crying in your room in junior high and high school and trying to take it like a man. And I don't want to hurt you, but unless there's something I don't know about, it'll never work. She's a gold digger or just playing along for fun or worse. I mean you are fifty; if she won't tell her parents, it couldn't be clearer that she doesn't care about you. Hell, even if she *did* introduce you to her parents, I'd still be suspicious."

"No good news, huh," Jack said.

"I mean I don't know her, but just from the sidelines of basic human nature, it's a loser. Older man, younger woman, I mean you're the reader. It's a cliché of history. Sorry."

"No. I know you're telling me straight, Jenny," but Jack choked up.

"Oh, I'm sorry, little Jack. I'm sorry. That hurt like shit, didn't it?"

Jack struggled to speak.

"I'm sorry, my little brother."

"I know. Thank you, Jenny," Jack recovered. It wasn't as though her answers surprised him. "Enough about me, how are you doing? How are the kids?"

"Doing fine, Jack. Kids are just fine. I didn't mean to hurt you. You know all I've been through with men, so I'm not the best to ask. Terribly cynical at this point, you know . . .

"Anyway . . . so you've been playing your violin. Should we resurrect Minuet 1?" Jack had forgotten. But when he'd taken the violin up at fifteen, Jenny had already been a star pianist. Even as he struggled, she'd insisted that they play one piece together, and it was Bach Minuet 1.

"Possibly, but I have a feeling you're right," said Jack. "Can't get a break, I guess? I asked for it. I'm glad you're doing well. Will I see you for the holidays? And yes, I will dig up Minuet 1. That'd be lovely, Sis."

"Yes, I'd like that. Let me call mom and confirm my excommunication is still in abeyance," Jenny laughed.

"Thanks, Jenny. I love you."

"I love you too, little Jack."

Chapter Thirteen

THE LOVE HE THOUGHT HE'D NEVER FIND

The holidays were coming. Without admitting it, Jen had started to like staying at Jack's. He had seen Jen's closets at her apartment and quipped: "Since there are two-hundred outfits here, why not leave ten of them at my place?"

"Oh good," Jen said, "then I can get ten more for here."

The two closets in the two bedrooms in the unit occupied by one woman probably had enough room for fifty outfits. The rest were in piles everywhere. Jack didn't understand it. On most subjects, Jen could be, indeed demanded others be, substantive in their response. Not clothes. Jack let it roll off. Anyway, what did it concern Jack? He was the dowdy forty-eight-year-old who dressed like nothing. Complain about a twenty-eight-year-old woman having too many clothes? Dude, get real, he thought.

In any event, she had moved the ten outfits over and more. She complained that he didn't have enough closet space. He had moved 90% of his wardrobe into the laundry room and presented her with all of the closet in the master bedroom. She radiated happiness. They had no set schedule, but for a normal workweek with a normal weekend, she would typically spend three nights at his house, and he might stay one-two nights "in the city" he called it at her place. He never complained about her apartment, and knew she loved it. Why take air out of her balloon? Conversely, she continued the general put down of his house while spending more and more time there. It seemed the more she was there, the more she saw fit to complain: unbearable bathroom, non-matching kitchen, warehouse living room, no guest room, no dining room, hillbilly neighbors, etc. It became what she appeared to think was a running joke. Jack said little, but he was hurt.

He never thought it was Versailles. But he did think it was a nice piece of property with a decent house on it. The house was admittedly old and small for the lot, 2,000 square feet, but the whole point of life was to get the fuck out of the house in Jack's mind. In any event, the quiet was nice, and it was only two of them. What more room did they need? Jack had spent a little money on the kitchen as he loved to cook, and why didn't she appreciate it? Jack knew the one bathroom was the number one complaint as it had been ridiculed over the years, so he thought a win-win was in order.

"Why don't we remodel your bathroom?" he asked her one morning after they had had sex and she had complained about it, knocking over and clanging her endless lotions, potions, cans, and jars and on and on. Jack had set up a little TV table in the bathroom because the counter tops were so small. Normally graceful, Jen hated it and never seemed to stop knocking stuff over. Jack suspected she might be doing it on purpose.

"Oh yes," she screamed over the most expensive hair dryer Jack had ever seen. She loved when he said "your" bathroom.

In fact, Jack had been showering outside, which made it her bathroom. But he didn't care. He liked showering outside, and he liked making her happy.

"What do you want to do?" he said.

"Oh God. The vanity, the shelves, the tile, and the fixtures. Everything."

"Cool. What about the toilet?" he said.

"Girls don't poop."

"Shower?"

"Heeeelll, yes," she mocked him.

"Ok. You present a budget and a plan. I'll pay," he said.

"Deal." She got more excited than he'd ever seen her get about sex with him.

But she couldn't make it happen. Instead, she brought him a series of questions and issues to decide. Why? He couldn't figure it out. This, that, and the other, but he didn't care. The goal had been to make *her* happy, but somehow, he'd been sucked into it.

"Should we hire a professional?" she said after weeks of stasis.

"Honey, Baby, Fucking Andy Griffith, are you kidding me?" Jack was aghast. "We're in Geneva, Florida, not Geneva, Switzerland. No one will ever see or care about this. I did it for you. I mean let's just get it done."

"I hate 'honey' and 'baby' and bullshit. I can't fix it."

It was the first real argument they had had. He was not attracted to Jen for the first time. He'd never seen this side of her. And over what? A fucking bathroom?

"Well, I'm *paying* and I'm doing this for *you*."

"I knew you'd say that."

"And your retort, mademoiselle?"

"I just can't find anything I like," she said, but Jack could see, out of nowhere, she was serious. This was serious. This stupid bathroom had become a problem. Her eyes were hard, her brow knitted. Jack tried to remain rational, tried to solve the problem. He had a house. It was nice. She wanted to change it. He said yes to her. Now, it was his problem. Huh?

"Ok, ok," he said, "Let's give it a week so we can deliberate."

No audible response—her favorite. Jen hung her head. It was the first time Jack ever saw her lacking in confidence. The issue was so inconsequential, Jack could not conceive of anyone becoming so despondent over such a nonissue. And from a girl whose apartment had bums and freaks of all kinds lingering everywhere in the neighborhood.

She left and did not communicate for several days. Jack stewed. The holidays were coming and now this. She created the problem; he offered to pay to fix it to her tastes; and now this was his problem? Fucking women. He recalled his mother and sister laughing at the bathroom over the years, chiding him, busting his balls. Now Jen was giving him silent treatment. Jack's mother had given him this treatment in his youth, and he hated it. What did it solve? In Jack's mind, nothing. Now a Millennial was doing it to him, his Millennial, the one he loved. Jack struggled to remain rational. He had given her a $10,000 budget which he had told her was more than his most expensive shotgun. She didn't get it. Certainly, the house was a tear down, and this $10,000 would go down the toilet one day. The bathroom couldn't be more than 10 x 10. It seemed to him $10,000 was more than it deserved.

She was gone. He missed her more than he thought possible. He felt the divide increasing. Now she didn't communicate, and he didn't know what to say if he was the one to reach out. "Thanks for fucking us over, wanna start anew?" he thought of as a text he'd sent her. Yeah, that's a great idea, Jack. Dumbfuck. He went and smelled her clothes in his closet; they killed him. He saw her coffee cups in the dishwasher, tiny monuments to her superiority, Cornell, Waldorf Astoria, La Scala, Prague. Her bathroom looked like half of Bloomingdale's was in it.

He felt her slipping away, just as he had felt other girlfriends slip away, just as his never-happened marriage had slipped away, his never-conceived children had slipped away, his 30s, his 40s, loveless decades of silent suffering, every asshole on the planet telling him to "stay positive" or some such nonsense, all of it sliding downhill at him like a dumpster, while he shriveled at the bottom of the hill waiting to take the hit. Jack had seen and smelled many dead animals; some of them he'd killed; many more had died naturally in their own neighborhoods into which they'd been born, never left, and died. That was the worst smell in the woods, a carcass usually being mercilessly eaten by vultures, pecked in death, and the smell. He imagined he was that carcass; he knew someday he *would* be that carcass. And now he'd lose Jennifer James Fairfield over a shitty, fucking bathroom in a 1940s house in what was left of rural Florida. Might as well draft my own obituary, Jack thought, not that anyone would read it.

Jack kept going to work of course, and he lied when several people had asked him what was wrong. Even his new friend, Gretch, had busted him in the kitchen, but he'd lied to her as well. What was he going to do, tell a sixteen-year-old-girl what a fucking loser he was? He was surprised she'd noticed, and his lawyer's mind told him he must look really bad for her to pick up on it. He cancelled a match with Lonnie. He declined an invitation to an offshore fishing tournament. He tried to practice his violin, but of course that only drove the stake in deeper; every note was Jen vibrating against his chest. He mowed the lawn. He cleaned the house in the evenings. He read *The Death of Ivan Illych* again. He'd forgotten the part about the corpse smelling in the opening scene. He'd first read it in college, and felt terrible for Illych, his whole life a fraud—a fake, his family and friends circling his corpse thinking what they could do for themselves. Was there really redemption in the end as argued by Jack's creative writing instructor at the time? Jack would search again to find it as he had read it fifteen times in his life; he never really had. If anything, the redemption was religious, surely Illych's wife never came to him in his pitiable end, nor did his daughter. There was no outpouring of love or forgiveness, much less absolution; they wanted him dead as soon as he turned into a nuisance. Illych just died alone with his nurse and was left to rot in the woods like all the animals Jack had smelled over the years.

Shit, Jack thought, I'm worse than Illych; I don't even have a wife or daughter. What a loser I am, Jack thought. How did things get so bad? How could he have worked as hard as he had and ended up with nothing? Jack cried and hugged Jen's pillow. She'd put some flowery pillowcase on it, and now Jack hugged it and cried every night and early in the morning. A few of her millions of lotions and potions had embedded themselves in the material, and Jack breathed it in, one little dagger for each nostril hair. She was gone, like all the others, except he'd never had feelings like this for any of the others and there hadn't been many. True, he was sad when they left, but in other ways he was relieved; no longer did he have to pretend.

Jack drank an entire bottle of Wild Turkey over five straight days, plus a case of Budweiser cans; this aggravated his sleep apnea. He got no sleep. He ate pre-made sandwiches from "T & G's Hardware" and chips. He woke up and cried and felt like shit and went to work, came home, drank too much, passed out, and woke up one hundred times a night with his apneas. They would kill him, these apneas. He would kill himself. After all, neither the apneas nor the drinking were external forces; they were in Jack.

There was no communication from Jen. If there was one thing Jack hated about Jen from the beginning it was the lack of communication, the never ending "read my mind" bullshit. Sure, at the beginning of what might end up being a relationship, some of this was to be expected. Girls kept their guard up, etc. But they'd been having sex for months; they'd spent days and weeks and months together. When was she going to realize that she needed to clock in and get to work on this relationship? Would she ever *solve* a problem? Yet, here again, as always, Jack had to do everything. Deep down he knew that even though she'd created the problem with the bathroom, she'd just sit on her ass and do nothing. Jack even supposed she'd turned the whole thing around in her head and it was somehow all Jack's fault. "I think of a man, and then I take away reason and accountability," Jack recalled from *As Good as It Gets*. The timing of the line in the movie was funny, but the more Jack thought about it the more unfunny it got; it was terrifying actually. Because he'd never had a relationship last more than eighteen months, Jack wondered if things *ever* progressed. Could you be with a woman for thirty years and still be dealing with this? It couldn't be, could it? Jack thought of his own parents, happily married for fifty-three years before his father had died. In Jack's youth, they'd have one fight per year, lasting about twenty minutes, and that was it. Jack's father would slam the back door, go for a walk, and within the hour they'd be in each other's arms on the couch, laughing, watching *Kojak,* or *Charlie's Angels.* Jack remembered the look on his mother's face when that door slammed once a year, a look of weakness and fear, head down, murmuring. What if Melvin, Jack's father, did not come back? Boy, Jack thought, that look does not even exist anymore in the USA. Would Jen even miss him for ten minutes if they broke up?

Jack also remembered his grandparents. He had spent a lot of time with both sets. Once his mother had even shipped him off for the entire summer to his maternal grandparents' cottage in Michigan. There was no pretense of equality and much less preening and primping by the women. Shit, his maternal grandmother literally still had a "Sunday dress". These people had lived through the Great Depression. They knew of living with no plumbing or electricity. Nobody got divorced. They were happy to have a bathroom, never mind what it looked like. Of course, his mother was a little more spoiled, but Jack recalled his father not caring about anything his mother had ever done to the house. Anything over $1,000, she'd come and get the budget approved and Jack never recalled his father saying no. If the money was realistic, he didn't care. Like Jack, his father always thought the point of life was to get out of the house. Now, two measly generations later, and a spoiled rich girl from Virginia named Jen had turned his stupid, shitty, little bathroom into a constitutional crisis, the financial score in the relationship being something like Jack:

$25,000; Jen: $430. Bitterly, Jack laughed for the first time in days as he lay in bed drunk and depressed, ruminating, and weepy, Illych on his nightstand, wasting away.

Jack woke up feeling like shit again. His apneas had tortured him all night, and his gut was burning with Wild Turkey. He also was sure he'd either thrown up or drooled in the night as his throat was raw and painful. This had happened about one-hundred times before. He went to work and resolved to try and be rational. By his lunch break, he told Gretch to slap him, and she wouldn't do it, but didn't flinch either. "Larry," Jack nearly yelled down the hall, "your daughter won't slap me even though I deserve it. What's wrong with this kid?"

"Give him a slap, Gretchen!" Gretch ran out of the kitchen.

Back in his office with his sixth cup of coffee, a whiskey/coffee/white bread/chicken salad/Doritos acid bath eating his guts up, Jack's mind had distilled the issue as follows: either (1) waste another $5,000 getting Jen a consultant or (2) withdraw the offer or (3) stand pat on the offer or (4) do nothing and wait and see what she did. And what did he want? He wanted Jen back. She was the girl he'd never thought he'd meet, the one he'd given up hope of ever finding. If so, which option gave the highest likelihood of getting Jen back? Clearly (1). It was in fact, in her manufactured hysteria, the one she'd suggested. How could she possibly hold it against him? All the other options assumed a rational, grown-up, mature Jen who gave ten cents about the relationship, and Jack didn't like that bet. His mind now clear for the first time in days, Jack resolved to schedule a phone call rather than text or call unexpectedly. He wanted to hear the timbre in her voice, and he wanted her to have time to prepare for the call.

"May I call you at noon?" Jack texted her the next morning, Friday, 8:11 a.m.

"Ok." She texted back in fifteen minutes. Jack relapsed instantly and sucked in air. She'd given the worst possible response. Two letters. Not "I'd like that" or "I miss you" or "Perfect" or anything at all. "Ok." That was it. Jack got his third cup of coffee and went back to work. His gut churned barbed wire.

"Hello Jennifer," he said at noon.

"Are you ok? Your voice sounds funny."

"Sorry, a little cold I guess," Jack lied.

"Oh." Then nothing.

"I want to clear the air with you," he said.

"Ok."

"I'm sorry for the tussle over the bathroom," he offered.

"Tussle? Me too."

"It's the first time since I met you that I had negative thoughts about you."

"Sorry," but she didn't elaborate and it didn't make any sense. Sorry for what?

"I miss you, Jen, miss you a lot," said Jack, "and I want to fix the situation."

"Ok."

"Ok?" Jack thought. Who answers, "I miss you" with "ok"? Tears came to his eyes.

"I was wondering," Jack stammered and paused as he walked his plank.

"Are you okay?"

"Sorry, some congestion over here," Jack managed. "I was wondering if you'd like to get the consultant and fix the bathroom." His voice was weak and trailed off. He was sure she was going to dump him.

"Oh, that's nice. Yes, that sounds nice." This was the Jen who had not communicated in seven days?

"Ok. How would you like to proceed?" he said.

"Well, I'll find one and go over it with you."

"Ok." There was a long pause. Did he have to ask her whether she gave a shit about him? She'd had hours to plan for this call, and she was just going to let him twist in the wind?

"Well," he choked again, "I guess I'll wait to hear from you?"

"Oh, you sound terrible, Jack. How have you been?" she said.

"I just told you I missed you terribly. How do you think I've been?"

"Oh," but he heard her voice break a little. Still, after a long pause which she didn't fill, he humiliatingly said, "Did you miss me?"

"Of course." She said. Jack was filled with rage. *"Of course?"* How could she be so insensitive? Was she joking? Jack struggled to control himself. Did she have no idea who he was at all? Could she not see how weak he was *"Of course???"*

"When may I see you?" Jack finally managed.

"Tonight, Jack?"

Jack was stunned.

"Ok." Jack didn't ask what time or even where. He was wiped out, at the end of his rope, spent, gut-shot.

"I'll come to your house after work about seven," Jen said. "I want to take some photos for the consultant anyway."

"Ok," Jack mumbled, and they hung up. At least the consultant was important to her. Jack felt like shit. Why did he agree to see her tonight? Wait a minute, he was millimeters from losing her. Jack went into the law firm's bathroom and splashed his face with water. It was 12:10 p.m. How could he possibly get it together by 7? He told Karen he felt like shit and had to go home, but she reminded him of a 3:30 teleconference with Kowalski. As with all things legal, the joy had been sucked out of the win when the general contractor started reneging on his payments. The client was going downhill. He couldn't reschedule it, and it went way beyond the thirty minutes, the client and his project manager spraying him with new details of new jobs the general contractor had gotten. They had plenty of money so why didn't they pay?

He drove home by 5:30 and did thirty minutes treading water in the lake. He drank a lot of water and sat on the back patio trying to get more fresh air. But it was a December humidity wave, and there was no air to breathe. He went in and tried to get ready to see Jen. What was he going to do? He had nothing planned to eat? Would she want to have sex? Could he get an erection? Would she be cold? He toweled off and lay in bed worrying. The week of misery hit him. Jack passed out.

She knocked on the door at 7:17. Jack panicked but threw some shorts on and a T-shirt and answered the door. For some reason, she had never asked for a key, or it would have been even worse.

"Hey," she started, but then she looked at him, "Oh Jack, what's wrong?"

"Nothing. I'm sorry."

"You look terrible. Did you go to the doctor?" she said walking in and putting her hand on his forehead. "Come into the kitchen," she said. Jack was terribly embarrassed. In his whole life, he had never felt so weak and frail. He could not meet her eyes in the kitchen as she examined him. Finally, she manually pulled his chin up so she could look into his eyes. Their eyes met and Jack started crying. Could she not *see* anything?

"Are you sick? Did something happen?" Jen said, as he laid his head on her shoulder and cried. Finally, she put her arms around him and held him. "What is it?" He tried to gather himself, but the week had beaten him. He couldn't meet her eyes again. He knew he must smell like the lake or sweat or shit or all of them. "I missed you," is all he could manage. She must have finally figured it out because she squeezed him in their hug. He leaked for a couple of more minutes before he could gather himself. "I'm sorry," he said.

"Come to the couch," she said. And they laid longwise like they used to, and she held him and gave him little kisses. "You had a bad moment, that's all," she said. "Just take a deep breath," and she hugged and squeezed him. After a while, she got him some more water and looked in the fridge.

"What have you been eating all week?" she asked.

"I don't know."

She knew that was an answer Jack never gave, and she looked in the liquor cabinet. It was empty.

"Have you been drinking?" she said.

"Not today. Come back please."

She got back on the couch with him and held him again. "I missed you," he said again.

"How about a pizza and some sweet tea?" she said.

He nodded in assent. It was 7:37. She left and brought the pizza and sweet tea back. They ate.

"Let's go to bed," Jen said. It was only 8:45.

"It's so early," Jack said weakly.

"You haven't slept all week, have you? And you've been drinking and working yourself to death, haven't you?" He didn't protest. "C'mon, Rip. You'll be all right," and she led him to the bedroom.

"Oh, these sheets smell terrible." She looked at him, and was about to ask what happened, but his refusal to meet her eyes told her everything. He was ashamed. No one had a steadier gaze when he wanted than Jack, but now he could not look at her.

They changed the sheets and pillowcases, and Jack fell into bed. She took off all her clothes and got in bed with him. She rolled him over on his side where he had told her the sleep apnea doctors said it was best. He strapped on his mask and turned on the CPAP. She ran her hands on his shoulders and neck and gave him little kisses. She "shhsshhed" in his ear. He needed all these things. Jack was asleep in three minutes.

Jack slept well for hours, but his apneas kicked him awake at 4:11 a.m. It had been years since he had been able to sleep through the night completely, so he didn't despair; 4:11 was good. He felt decent, not great. Jen was fast asleep. He could only see a giant head of dark hair. She was the quietest sleeper Jack had ever slept with. He leaned over, as he had done before, within inches of her head and listened. He could only hear the faintest of breathing noises. His heart was filled with wild emotions, but he had gathered himself enough in the night to get back to work.

He slipped out of bed. He knew the hall to the kitchen was quiet, but not the kitchen. So, he gently closed the bedroom door behind him. He went down to the kitchen and drank three big glasses of water. He walked out the front door and urinated in the open air. It was cooler than before but still extremely humid, no relief even in December. He went to the bathroom, and very quietly brushed his teeth for a long time; he got the tongue scrapper out and went to work there as well. He swished his death week all out with too much mouthwash, nearly gagging, but, afraid to wake Jen, controlled it. He washed his hands and his face for five full minutes. Now, he had a problem. His dick pills were in the bedroom in his top dresser drawer. Last night had only been a blur for him, but he knew it must have been horrible for Jen. At twenty-eight, she'd never seen such a wretch as him. She was usually willing in the morning, and so was he, but he couldn't afford to take a chance. He turned off all the lights and crept back into the bedroom, lifted the drawer while pulling it out so there would be no scraping noise, relaxed his trustworthy hand to the corner of the drawer, felt the top of one of the bottles, picked it up and slipped out and closed the door again. In the kitchen, he could see it was the Cialis—good, the slower acting of the dick pills. He took one and drank his fourth glass of water. On top of the horrible week he'd been through, his urologist had told him that lots of water both made his dick bigger and created semen. What to do with the bottle? He hadn't heard a sound from the bedroom and assumed Jen was still out. He wouldn't fumble now. He put the bottle in the top shelf of the cupboard with the spices in it. She'd never look there; plus, he would just put it back in a day or two where it belonged. He told himself to try one more leak and went outside again. To his surprise, quite a bit more urine came out. He closed the front door, turned off all the lights, and catfooted back into bed. The big head of hair hadn't moved at all. It was 4:27. Jack had no trouble falling back asleep.

Chapter Fourteen

BAD NEWS: I LOVE YOU

The lake by the house was mostly to the East. The master bedroom was entirely to the East. In December, the sun moved to the South, and the sunrises was less direct but still spectacular, coming from the corner of the lake rather than straight across. They were both morning people, and Jen had to admit the mornings were spectacular. Today was no different, and when Jack awoke it was 6: 41 and Saturday. He could sense that she was already awake, and he reached over with his left hand and touched her very softly on the arm. "Oh, I gotta pee," she whispered. "Me too." There was enough light to see her very white shoulders, butt and legs go out the bedroom door. She left it open and a little more light came in from the hall. He went off the front porch again, prodigiously, while she used the bathroom she hated. He beat her back to bed.

Jack was flooded with emotions, and his dick was flooded with blood. He'd masturbated only twice all week as he hoped he would die, and now he had a massive erection. She came back, got in bed, and looked over at him in the gently increasing light. "Jack is back?" she said, and he nodded and pulled her in and held her and squeezed her butt and legs. She kissed him on the neck and ears and head, and he pythoned her very tight until she gasped a little and then he relaxed a touch and did it again—little hug repetitions of her delicious flesh. As always, she did not perform fellatio.

After a few minutes, he rubbed his hard on against her leg, and she gave him a sweet smile—a different smile then the one he'd become suspicious of. "What's this?" she mocked. Her lovely left cello hand went down and stroked his balls, the tips of her nails softly digging into his scrotum, strokes of an inch and a half or less. Jack moaned, but she kept eye contact, and ran her finger tips up his urethra super lightly to the tip. She felt his huge drop of precum, and her eyes widened. "What's *this*?" She mocked him again and kissed him on the neck. Please, Jack thought, now go down and suck the length of me until I fire into the back of your throat. A Millennial who didn't give blowjobs? I guess some problems cross all generations. But she didn't. She kept stroking him and rubbing her face against his and finally threw her leg over him.

Jack was in agony and knew his biggest danger was coming too quickly. More light was present, and Jen lowered herself. Usually, she had to work it in, but now she was soaking wet, and she slid down all the way, throwing her head back in ecstasy. "Hohm," they said simultaneously. Jack could see her long, white face, her long, white neck, and her big, white breasts. The nipples were erect, and he started sucking the left one while she gently bucked on him. She came in five minutes and threw her head back.

"Stop, please." Jack said

"Oh, why? Are you okay?"

"I don't want to come. Stop," said Jack.

"Ok." And she kept his cock inside her but stopped moving.

"Kiss me," Jack said.

"I didn't brush my teeth."

"Well, just hold me then," said Jack.

And they held each other for a few minutes while she stayed on top of him, cock inside.

"You're so sweet, my old Rip," she said.

"I thought you said I am not old?"

"I meant familiar." She snicker kissed him.

"I missed you so much," he said.

"It was only a week."

"I missed you so much. Come again for me. Really hard."

"Mmm," she said.

"Hit me on the chest."

"What?" she laughed.

"Ride me and come and just hit me on the chest."

She didn't say anything but gave him a confused look as she got to work. It took longer this time, but old Jack had control of his erection. She kept rocking on his cock, and he took her hands and put them on his chest, which made her taller in her cockseat. Again, he enjoyed the glory of her whiteness from the increased angle. She started making little "ohs" and pressed down on his chest. And then she fingered her clit and went off like a firecracker. Jack felt juices drip down his shaft and onto his balls.

She finally stopped, and he held her in again. "How come you didn't hit me?" he whispered in her ear, but she just hung her head temporarily exhausted. He kept kissing her neck and finally she got off his cock and laid next to him.

"Thank you," she said. "Oh, I made a mess, didn't I?"

"Not a mess," Jack said to her.

She laid back her head on the pillow almost like she was going to pass out, but of course she knew he hadn't come yet. After a few minutes, she reached over and started stroking his balls again.

"You must be in pain," she said.

"Bad news: I love you," Jack said.

He hit the bullseye, but she only shook her head "yes"; whether that meant recognition or reciprocity Jack did not know. She didn't respond audibly just kissed him on the neck and stroked his balls, her left cello hand masterful in its touch.

"How do you want me?" she said after a minute or so.

"How do you want me?" he said.

"Oh Jack, Jack, Jack. You're so considerate."

"I want you to come again," he said.

"Well, missionary always makes me come, but how about you?"

It was obvious that she was not going to tell him she loved him, so Jack moved on.

"Ok," and he rolled her over into missionary. Her hand led him in and he sank balls deep.

"Hohm," she said. He loved the way she was able to start everything over.

"Come for me, Jen."

Again, she orgasmed in five minutes her legs flying V'd. He stopped again, while they panted. "So beautiful," he said to her as he held her.

She gripped him fiercely and nuzzled and then pulled back and looked at him. "You still haven't come."

"See, there is an advantage to having a boyfriend who's old."

"You're not old, Jack."

He rolled his eyes and kissed her on the neck while he held himself off her. "Can you come again?" he said.

"I'm done. You need to come." He still had his cock in her.

"Do you want me to?" he asked.

"Of course."

Ouch. The same words that had hurt Jack so much, which he had not told her of course. But this time, they at least made sense. Jack started to thrust, and he felt like he was twenty-five again. He had several gears in him, and he kept shifting higher. Jen nodded her head in the affirmative as he silently checked whether she was okay. And then Jack slowed and said, "Wrap your legs around me please," and she did and he ejaculated, his whole body spasming into her.

"Are you ok?" she said, "I've never seen any man come like that."

He was going to make a joke "Well, how many men have you seen come?" but decided against it.

"Sorry. I'm just old that's all," he said.

"Are you ok? Did you hurt yourself?"

"No, no. I'm great; just totally gone, like a train ran over me," he said.

"Hmm."

"What about you? You came three times," Jack said.

"Not like that, I didn't."

"Well, tell me," Jack said, pulling up his files on how many times he'd talked to women about their orgasms. He couldn't think of any as he lay wasted.

"Really?" she asked.

"It's only the most important thing in the world."

She laughed. "You're out there, Rip."

"C'mon, tell me," he said.

"Well, it's like a little pulse, a throb, a constant, and then it gets more intense, but sort of stays the same character, and then more intense, and then finally kinda gets out of control for ten or twenty seconds. And then it kinda starts all over."

Jack was happy. It was one of the longest soliloquies she'd ever given. Laconic Jen finally cut loose a little.

"Where does all his happen?" he said.

"In my clitoris."

"Does it radiate?"

"Not really," she said.

"How much?

"Maybe a tennis ball," she said. He could not tell whether or how much she had thought about it.

"Oh, so very localized to your clit?"

"Yes, you must have heard this before?" she said.

"Are you kidding? Trying to get a woman to talk about sex is like pulling wisdom teeth without anesthesia."

She laughed. "Really."

"Oh yeah. How about you girls? Do you talk about sex with each other?" Jack asked.

"Not in detail, just maybe whether you're having any or not."

"Now, that sounds realistic. How does it start back up again, so quick?" Jack asked.

"I don't know. You guys are spent, aren't you?"

"It's a one-way street, yes; and then we kinda have to recreate the world again after we've destroyed it."

She laughed. "Rip, you're on a roll."

"Sounds like more of a circle for you?" he inquired.

"Interesting. I can't believe a man is saying this to me. Yeah, after I climax, it doesn't go away, kinda keeps ticking just at a much lower intensity."

"How does it start?" Jack asked.

"Well, for me it's mental."

"Mental?" said Jack.

"Yeah, like you always ask me why I come so quick; well, it's because way before you actually touch anything, my brain is turned on and wants to come. So, I'm like 50% there before we even start. And then just putting your hands on me, things escalate rapidly so by the time you get to my clitoris, I'm just already there so to speak."

"Wow. True of all women?" asked Jack.

"I don't know. This is the most in-depth discussion I've ever had with anyone."

"What a privilege for me; the feeling is mutual. So then how come you can't come indefinitely? If it's a loop?" said Jack.

"Well, I can't explain it but the clitoris kinda gets over stimulated or too intense."

"Hmm. What about your vagina?" he said.

"What about it?"

"Does it make you come?"

"No," she said. "It feels great when you penetrate me and thrust into me, but it's kind of ancillary, subservient to the clitoris. Also, it's more mental than you might think."

"What do you mean?" he asked.

"Well, I'm *giving* myself to you; you're *having* me, and I want you to have me in my mind. So, it adds to the mental aspect greatly even though it also feels incredible."

"So you would never come without your clitoris?" Jack concluded.

"Oh, that's for sure."

"Sounds like a good country song, 'Oh, I'll never come without my clitoris, just don't be stupid, Mr. Irritus,'" Jack sang.

"Gosh, you are messed up, Rip."

"Hey, just trying to spread some joy and information to the population," he said.

"Now, you tell me."

"What?"

"The male orgasm."

"Oh, *that*. Well, how many times have you discussed it in detail with anyone?"

"Sounds like a deposition."

"Thank you for the compliment. And?"

Jen rolled her eyes and looked up at the ceiling. It was 8:44, and the room was a little lighter still. "Never," she said finally.

"Never?! What about all your boyfriends?"

"No. They just enjoyed themselves and never felt a need to explain."

"Did you ask?"

"No; didn't seem I don't know *important* to anything."

"Girls?"

"Oh, never. Again, they either don't discuss it at all or hide behind euphemisms and then change the subject."

"Shoes and stuff?"

She laughed.

"Mom and Dad?"

"Oh, Lord no."

"Hmm. Read any books, articles?"

"Sometimes *Cosmo* will have something fairly graphic but it's usually about technique, not what actually happens."

"Really? What did you learn?" Jack asked.

"I can't tell you that, Jack. You're the enemy. At least in *Cosmo*, boys are usually impliedly presented as the enemy."

"Bummer," he said. "We never do that to you." After a pause, "So? What'd you learn," Jack asked.

"Darn, you're persistent," but she smiled at him in approval.

"Well," she said. "One article said girls don't know what to do with the balls, they seem so fragile and awkward and kind of weird. Yet, they must be the source of great stimulation, right? So, one of the things I remembered was that there's a little strip of flesh in the scrotum between the two testicles and I'm to take my fingernail or nails and gently flick it up and down waiting for sounds of approval."

"Gosh, that's the most beautiful thing I've ever heard, and you do it, you minx!"

"I do, and it works doesn't it?" she asked.

"Oh Gawd yeah," Jack Southernized softly. But he also thought, wouldn't the same magazine have an article on fellatio and how it's to be performed both skillfully and on a regular basis? And wouldn't she have read that too? He'd pick up a copy of Cosmo next time he was at "T & G's" and do a little research.

She got up and opened one of the three blinds. Florida came through big. "Want some water?" and she didn't wait for an answer and came back with two glasses.

"Well, I'm ready now," she demanded

"The male orgasm?"

"Yes. You've been pushing me off, deferring and deflecting."

"So negative; you mean inquiring and learning?"

"Proceed Forester," she said.

"Well, it's much more physical, based on what you're telling me. Our balls make semen every day or every other day or whatever they do they make it regularly. So that semen causes tension, pressure, in a pleasant way, but still, it is not an optional pressure."

"So you get horny for your girl?" she asked.

"Interesting. Well, no, see we get horny for *a* girl. The semen doesn't discriminate. It wants to get shot."

"Oh, so that's why you're all dog sluts," she said.

"Yeah, that's pretty much it."

"So your brain doesn't tell your balls 'I'm horny,' your balls tell your brain you're horny?" she said.

"Worse or better, depending upon your attitude. Our balls tell our entire body we're horny. The brain is important, ironically, in controlling the rage, not so much as creating it. But then if we're actually going to have sex then the brain goes the other way and turns into a, how did your highness put it, 'dog slut' itself."

"Then why do they say men are so visual?" she said.

"Well that's horseshit; that's like saying people are hungry or something; of course, we're visual; women are visual; everyone is visual; we're going to see females virtually every day of our lives, but that's hardly the creation of the sex drive; that happened at night when we slept and our balls created the pressure."

"Hmm. Well as much as a female can, I get it. So then, tell me about the orgasm. I thought you were going to die just now."

"So did I, but I wanted to." They laughed together.

"Well," said Jack, "since we're essentially always horny, the brain has sort of a governor on it that says 'it ain't going to happen' or 'holy shit, it's going to happen.' So, when we get the second signal, then everything intensifies and it's kind of like boiling a pot of water. How slowly can you control the boil before it happens? And that's where men get in trouble and prematurely ejaculate because the system is not completely under control. Or young men just come in thirty seconds, not prematurely but because their bodies are too strong for their minds. It's not like my brain saying to my right arm 'pick up the glass of water on the nightstand and dump it over Jen's head so you can kiss it off.' Right? I mean I can do that ninety-nine out of one hundred times. Angry jism has a mind of its own."

"Rip the Poet," she said. "Keep going; no one has ever told me this before."

"Me either; like I said just getting women to have sex is a lifetime chore, much less discussing it in detail with them. So, the semen starts to come to a boil as the stimulation increases, and the brain wants to delay the boil as long as possible because it's paradoxical; the more pressure the better until it becomes unbearable and must be released."

"My, my Aristotle." They laughed together.

"Did he ever write about this? Anyway, so eventually the semen gets hotter and hotter, and there is a seal or a gasket or something in the anatomy." Jack reached over and held her arm up.

"So if the semen is in here," he continued, "your elbow, and your hand is the tip of the penis, then somewhere at the bottom here, the bottom third or so, there is a seal or gasket or something and that's stage one. Once the semen gets past the gasket, then the man is toast, he's going to come. So, the first battle is to keep the semen from breaching the gasket. That's when I tell you to stop, or I stop. Then, the second battle is there is a muscle, tendon, something above the gasket that a man can use as a clamp, just like you squeezing your hand around a hose except not that precise, and the second battle is after the semen breaches the gasket and starts climbing up the urethra to the promised land how long until you apply the clamp, the later the better provided you don't lose control, and then how long can you hold the clamp before the pressure overwhelms you." Jack shook her arm.

"See," he said, "This is your penis shaking because it has a long column of jism in it that is above the gasket, and your clamping it. The further up the tip you got it before clamping the more ecstasy you're going to enjoy because then the column of jism is longer and starts darting and surging within the length of the urethra. And then, it's just unbearable and the clamp fails, and the semen is shot."

"Sounds wonderful. And what is that aftereffect you have sometimes; you didn't have it this morning."

"What?" he said.

"Sometimes you act like you've finished coming, and then you thrust into me like you didn't even mean it."

"Oh yeah. I'm sorry; that's old age, Jen. So, my prostate pump is supposed to fully clean the system of all the semen when the ejaculation finally comes, and young men don't even think about that. But as a man gets older, there must be some deterioration of either the pump or the reservoir of where the semen is located because I pump out 90 percent when I ejaculate, and then I think I'm done, but that last 10 percent absolutely has to go and so I get that delayed kick, which isn't really pleasurable, it kind of hurts."

Jack stopped talking and started kissing her arm *cum* penis that he was using as a model.

"Thanks, Jack. No one has ever described anything like that to me."

"Thank you, too. I have wondered about the female orgasm all my life."

"Really?" she asked.

"Of course, we all do. Lack of communication will kill any relationship, especially male/female relationships. So, yours is localized, isn't it?"

"Yes, and yours?" she asked.

"Oh no, not at all. It goes all the way down both legs to the toenails, and all the way up the spine into the neck."

"Is that why your neck is so tight when you come?" she said.

"You noticed?"

"Oh, it's like steel, it scares me, like your head would break off cleanly, in one piece."

Jen burrowed into his chest, and they lay there. It was 9:55. Jack was pleased that it seemed a new plateau of communication between them had been reached. They spent the weekend together, and she never mentioned that he'd said he loved her. She used her eyes to tell him that she recognized he had said he loved her but that was it. Jack did not know what to do.

Chapter Fifteen

CANNOT THOUST TWEEZE WITH LOVE?

The holidays came and went. She visited her family, turned twenty-nine, and it was January of 2019. Though Jack had to initiate the conversation, she had been remarkably clear about the holidays and her birthday: there would be no gifts; the new bathroom was more than enough. She got nothing for Jack. He had some great family time, and some excellent duck hunting over the holidays, and he had the Kowalski collection hearing teed up for January. Jack figured they had the money and would cough it up or a sizable chunk anyway. Everything had to be shitty in the practice of the law, so why not turn this win into a tooth-pulling situation? Every lawyer likes to have something big in January the only time of the year they mail it in is Christmas to New Years. All things considered, Jack was looking forward to the new year.

She sat with him in the chair in his living room, and leaned over, without looking in his eyes, and said "I love you too, Jack." It was the first sentence of this conversation, after work. Jack's heart twitched and thumped, but when she pulled away and he looked into her eyes, she only gave him the stock smile, the one he no longer trusted. The timbre was wrong too. He looked into her eyes, but he didn't see anything. "I love you, too," he said. He was hoping she might say something else, so he just hugged her. But she never did, and they moved on. Jack pondered the sincerity level, but who would say they loved someone when they didn't? It made no sense. She'd taken weeks, so it certainly didn't get blurted out. On the contrary, if anything she'd planned it. But why so little emotion?

And more on that smile. It was the first one she'd flashed at him on the tennis courts. The problem was he'd seen her use it a lot now. He'd seen her use the same smile on people she held in contempt: the clerks at the gas station near Jack's house, waiters and waitresses at restaurants they'd been to. Even at the University Club, she'd given that smile and then dismissed some middle weight developers, guys with way more money than Jack, as "rapacious rubes." Jack didn't trust that smile. Very rarely, he'd seen other smiles from her, but now when she said "I love you," they didn't show up. Well, Jack thought, it was early. What was he going to do, ask for a different smile? Accuse her of being dishonest?

The bathroom remodel made Jen happier than Jack ever did. The consultant was a gay guy from Connecticut named Trey. Jack could see that Trey and Jen had hit it off right away with a lot of Northern nonsense. Also, he gave a flat fee for his services of $2,500, which in effect increased the budget to $12,500. Short of gold, Trey said, it was a small bathroom and the budget was huge. Jen could get anything she wanted. But Trey wasn't stupid, and he knew who was paying the bills, so he discreetly kept Jack informed.

The old bathroom had been garish, with cinnamon colored tile, the original bathtub from the '40s, an old window that was terribly small, and some old, shitty cabinets. Jack saw the original design and called Trey privately. "The only thing I want, but don't tell her I said it," Jack said, "Is the biggest window you think is reasonable for the space, and one that can be opened in the winter—you know, not fixed." Trey figured it out, suggested it to Jen as his own idea, and she loved it.

The bathroom faced North, so it got no direct sunlight. However, the new large window lightened the entire room. Jen had thrown the tub out and put in only a shower. The new tile was white marble with black and grey veining, big pieces 2 x 2, and Trey had picked out some gold trim that was not garish. Again, the room was lightened. There was only a small group of cabinets, but Trey had picked out a blond maple wood, and they looked very good. As the finisher, Trey and Jen had picked out a high-end vanity with black top and a big mirror doubling as a medicine cabinet. The black top was the only dark thing in the entire room, and it easily handled it. Jack had to admit the plumbing and electrical fixtures were also quite nice. As usual, Trey blew the budget by $2,500 and wanted another $500 for himself. Jack grumbled *pro forma* but paid and it was over. Even though Trey said the budget was huge, Jack knew from his job, they'd find a way to exceed it. In any event, it was a dramatic improvement. Somehow it did not look overly feminine, and when the time came Jack would lie easily to whomever might inquire. Jen loved it. It was her baby, and she had delivered.

This had all taken two months, which Jack considered miraculously fast. During the two months, still no one really knew about Jack and Jen. She had not told her parents about

Jack, and that continued to hurt Jack a lot. Her parents had not visited, and that precluded Jack's plan. Jen acted like it wasn't a problem when she knew it was. Jen had not told any of her law school friends, but the more time Jack spent with her, the more she didn't really have any friends, law school or otherwise. He couldn't recall a single time any old friend of hers had ever called, as she sat on the couch at either her place or his and chewed the fat about the old days. Who was this woman? The Millennial who didn't communicate? The nice girl with no friends? She didn't seem to care either. The stores in Jack's neighborhood were filled with lower class people, and Jen had shit on all of them, thinking Jack must think similarly. "We're all God's creatures," he said to her, and she rolled her eyes as though his comment was unbearable. "They told me there was a lot of stupid people in Florida," she'd say. Even if she thought it, why would she say it? And why to him? Jack despised laziness because it was within one's control, but he never held anyone in contempt for lack of talent or circumstances.

She'd also taken a decent sized dump on his record collection, but Jack had turned that into a positive. First, no one had a record collection anymore, so eventually she came around to agreeing it was quaint. Second, of the two hundred odd albums Jack had, she'd sniffed at half. Again, Jack thought, why would she tell me that? But she loved Van Morrison, Cat Stevens, Bob Dylan, and most of the classical. So, they ended up making another connection, and she even said the living room—previously dismissed as a "warehouse with a fireplace"—wasn't terrible." Jack let it all roll off and focused on the good. What kind of Millennial likes Cat Stevens?! Most of them wouldn't even know who Cat Stevens was. It was amazing. Jack had a big laundry room, carpeted, but it was full of what Jen called "shit," so they played music in the living room which "wasn't terrible." The lake Jack lived on was just big enough for a small sailboat, and they surfed the net and discussed whether they should get one. Jack had never met any woman ever with an interest in sailing, so again this was a huge positive to him. There were five or six sailing books in Jack's little library, and Jen read all of them. Where would Jack find such a woman again?

Movies? Check. She hated all the new stuff, and wanted to watch old classics: *The Sting; The Sound of Music; Love Story; A River Runs Through It; Out of Africa; Amadeus*, etc. Again, it was just too easy, too remarkable. They could spend an entire evening together without a moment's awkwardness. She was very well-read and liked to show it off.

Sex? She never sucked his cock. He had attempted to go down on her soon after the sex had started, but she pushed him off with a glare and said, "not my thing." So, it wasn't a lack of reciprocity. It had been eight months since they had been having sex, and she had never sucked his cock. What kind of a woman doesn't suck her man's cock? Jack thought. But based on his life experiences he would have to say quite a few. But the issue needed to be phrased more precisely: What kind of a woman doesn't suck her man's cock at the initial stages of the relationship at least? Jack thought the answer must be a very low percentage of women. He made a mental note to ask the married guys who confessed they weren't getting any now, whether they had been getting any early on. Jack dwelled on these details at length. He very much wanted his cock deep throated for several centuries, and she knew that he did, so didn't that mean she was intentionally denying him? It's not like he was expecting her to stick a hot dog up his ass, pull it out, and then put it on a bun and say "Mmm, good," while she ate it wild-eyed with manic pleasure. No, just a conventional blow job would do. The girl who claimed to have read every book in the library would not perform fellatio but said she would?

Otherwise, sexually things seemed good, which amazed Jack since he was so old. They had sex two to seven times per week, depending upon how often they saw each other. Jen orgasmed very easily, and that solved most of the problems Jack had experienced over the course of his life. Women who struggled to orgasm were a terrible thing. It always made Jack feel like shit, and yet they were the ones not having the orgasms so they must feel like shit. But then some of them would say it didn't matter to them that they weren't orgasming which made no sense to Jack. These conversations over the decades had been some of the worst Jack had ever had; he didn't recall ever solving any of these problems. But that was gone with Jen because she came so easily. Jack felt extremely positive about the whole thing. He had had few sexual problems and went to his urologist regularly. He never told Jen. She hadn't found his pills, or if she had she hadn't let on.

One morning after the sex had been great and the sun very bright, they lay together in Jack's bedroom. Jack felt better than he had in his whole life. She had continued to say, "I love you," but he noticed it was only in response to when he said "I love you." The timbre continued to be wrong. But it was early, so he let it roll. One day, he hoped, things would break. She pulled the shade open, the same one she always did, the third one furthest from the bed so the light would be oblique, the same one Jack had pulled open for the same reason for years before he'd met her. What were the odds of that? He wondered.

She got back on top of him and looked him in the eyes. Now, she'd finally open up, he thought. But her face broke and she said, "Oh Jack, no no."

"What is it?"

"Oh God," she said, "look at them with this light, right on your nose and brow and, my God, even your ears." She got up and went to the bathroom and came back with something in her hand: tweezers.

"I'm sorry," he said.

"It's such an old guy thing," and the words were out. Jack winced.

"I'm sorry," she tried.

"Hold still," she said, and she tweezed hairs out of the top of his nose. "Look at them, how long, my God," she said yanking. "There, no, turn to the right . . . Oh a bunch more," and she yanked out another group. Jack felt terrible. She finished and went to his brow, tweezing away. It hurt more than the nose. Then she went to the ears, but it didn't work. "Gosh, these are like *cables* or something," as she tried to pull a couple out.

"Why didn't you say something before?" he said.

"Well," it was the stern dismissive Jen, "It's so embarrassing. I just thought you would get to them eventually." She could see he was hurt. "I'm sorry."

"Are you?" he said.

"Sure, I am."

"Why couldn't you just say there's a problem and then fix it with kindness, you know love," he said.

"Well, I'm sorry," and she kissed him on the nose. "You look fine now."

Jack felt like shit. What kind of woman kicks her man in the face over minor grooming? It wasn't like he didn't take a shower or wear deodorant. "An old guy thing?" Why would she say that? He *was* old so it made no sense; and it was hurtful for no reason. She knew he was self-conscious about the age difference. Everywhere they went people gawked at them, and usually him. Why hurt him over nothing? Why not say "I love you and want to help you with a little problem?" or just anything. And why continue like he was a tarantula? Never in his life had anyone even mentioned his nose hairs. And I look "fine" not "good?" What was she doing with me anyway? He never knew. He couldn't remember a single compliment she'd ever given him, direct or indirect. Now he was hurt and turned away from her. He didn't want her to see him leak tears. Why would she hurt him so casually? Obviously, the hair had been there all along, and she had months to think about it.

He got up so she wouldn't see him crying and managed "Coffee?"

"Sure," she said.

He made the coffee, but he didn't bring it to her as he often did. He could not deliver love so why coffee? He cried in the shower alone with his coffee and his new nose.

Chapter Sixteen

THE UNSUCKED DEAD

It was 6:25 a.m. February 2019. Jack waited for his cock to be sucked by Jennifer. He was very tired of waiting. It appeared he'd been waiting for his cock to be sucked his whole life. But this was different. They were thirteen months in altogether and seven months post sex. She was his redeemer. Things would be different this time. He would finally be loved relentlessly.

She was in her new bathroom doing her hair, a preposterous procedure that took two hours on a standard workday. At first, he didn't believe it. He supposed it had been only one hour in the old bathroom she couldn't wait to get out of, but she *loved* the new bathroom. He thought she was only testing him. But no, it was real. It was every day. The hair dryer was very loud and very on. There was no mistaking what was going on. Worse, she had a habit of doing her hair naked or with only panties on. At first, he was excited thinking it was some odd form of foreplay. But nothing ever happened and most of the time they'd already had sex anyway. If they hadn't, she never made a move. What was the point of walking around naked doing one's hair?

It was 6:31 a.m. Jack surveyed his cock-sucked history—a very depressing field of defeat and depression compelling suicide by any objective observer was his assessment. The world was filled with unsucked miserable men, and he was one of them. There were tens of millions more poorly sucked or infrequently sucked or reluctantly sucked or suffering from combinations of these unsucked miseries. Soldiers can live in a ditch for a year for women, but women can't suck their men for 15 minutes three times a week. What a wonderful world it *could* be.

Jack drifted off and became a psychiatrist dispensing prescriptions. Each said, "suck cock fifteen minutes min. three x week; return for counseling only if needed." The line of couples was a thousand miles long—always a confused woman and an unsucked man; always the same script; and, if the script were followed, 90 percent did not return for further counseling. But the script was rarely followed. Dr. Forester would gently explain to the woman. It doesn't matter whether you want to do it or not, though that would be a bonus, you've got to do it anyway. Just like he has to go to war and get killed so you can stay home and bake brownies. It's a task that you must perform, just like he has to do a million things for you that he doesn't want to. It's food. If you don't feed him, he starves to death. In Jack's morning fantasy, all the women experience an epiphany and a cavalcade of cocksucking ensues, all are healed, all are absolved. Her hairdryer brought him back.

It was 6:37 a.m., and Jack's erection had gone down some as he dwelled upon the most important thing in the world. Plato and Socrates were light weights. No, it was Jack who put his finger on the real issue. T. S. Eliot had not really rolled the universe into a ball. Prufrock was clearly unsucked but forearm hair? Shit. John Updike had come closer. Today's lesson, Professor Jack announced, *The Overwhelming Importance of Constant, Eager and Skillful Cocksucking to the Happiness of the Species or, Alternatively, Getting Some Is a Lot Better than Getting None.* The US Tour sold out in five minutes.

Of the thirteen women Jack had had sex with, four had never sucked his cock at all. Jen was five. Ruby had told him "It's gross." The other three had just told him: "Take it or leave it; I don't suck." Two of the three couldn't bring themselves to use the word "cock" and said "weiner" or "thingy." Also, Jack had heard "icky" a lot. These were not the greatest memories of Jack's life. The remainder of his erection deflated, but Jen kept flashing him in and out of her new bathroom. She had on full, white panties this morning, not a thong. Jack was a fan; they kind of pulled and squeezed the buttocks making them more attractive, setting off the hips a little more. Thongs were great, but they erroneously assumed the butt cheeks didn't need any assistance to look their absolute best, a dubious assumption Jack mused as his erection started coming back. As usual, wherever Jen had gotten her panties, they must have cost a hundred dollars each.

It was 6:40. Jen stood and anointed the next ointment to her high-hat hair. She had her back to him. Typical. He could see her two hemispheres of heaven hanging heavenly in their silk hammocks. She had a solid B ass. If she worked out, she could move up to B+. His erection came back, and his tip pulsed a scosche of precum. Jen didn't even look and started singing Patsy Cline to herself.

They'd had sex that Jack thought was hot for seven months, but she did not suck his cock. Of course, Jen said nothing, so he didn't know if she thought the sex was hot or not. Worse, she *said* she would suck his cock but never did. The cock was always too "icky" (first heard circa 1984) or some nonsense. Because his cock was easy for Jen to suck, Jack felt like shit. What kind of a woman says she will suck your cock but then has ample opportunity and does not? Again, zero explanation.

It was 6:47 a.m. Jack's erection remained solid, and he loitered with stupid optimism. Jen looked very sexy, and he hoped she'd drop something so she had to bend over, and he would get a look, preferably a long one, at her labia pooched in panties. Mmmm, so wonderful and so important, Jack dreamed. Why did it need to be an accident? Why not on purpose? He cupped his balls and thought back and rated the other nightmares:

Sheila, Tammy, Lynn and Susie: 5 minutes tops and mostly hand and only on request

Linda 1, Linda 2, Mitzy: 15 minutes! Mostly hand but not always, and sometimes *sua sponte!*

Jack laughed out loud.

"What's so funny?" Jen clicked the hairdryer off. Jack worried the thing would damage her cello ears he loved so much.

"Nothing absolutely," Jack said.

Tina: cum in mouth but only if requested; prevalent as fore play.

But he'd only been with Tina for three months, and then she was gone with the wind. She was one of the few girls who dumped him only for geography—as far as he knew anyway. She'd moved to Oregon and said she'd stay connected, but Jack knew it was bullshit when he first heard it. She'd also let him titty fuck her, but a lot of girls didn't have the equipment for that so you couldn't blame them. Though, Jack countered to himself, wouldn't the same ones who don't suck cock be unlikely to allow titty fucking? He attempted a syllogism on this but failed. In any event, delectable Tina was gone, and some other lucky man was getting sucked by her. What a sweet girl.

And that left Karen: the gold medal winner by far. She was so ugly that Jack could not believe he was ever with her to begin with. But she was the only woman Jack had ever been with who at least pretended that sex was the main attraction. The very first time they had sex, she had refused intercourse and insisted he cum in her mouth. Then, she did it again for weeks. And brother, what head did she give! She could have turned Schopenhauer into an optimist. Persistent, inquisitive, and always eager, she had given Jack the best cocksucks of his life by far. When she raised her face after swallowing him whole, he couldn't believe how ugly she was. Were her ugliness and desire to cocksuck related? He never knew. She repeatedly invited him, once when drunk commanded him, to cum in her mouth. Jack was eager to oblige. She asked how her cocksucks could be better, and Jack was shocked. He gleefully instructed her how to gently squeeze and stroke his balls without using them as a speed bag, how the hand was massively over utilized and should spend half its time squeezing his hamstrings or stroking and cupping balls, and how the back of the throat was the honey pie he wanted, all men wanted, deep throat all the way. What an angel, Jack recalled. If only she didn't talk about getting married every ten minutes. She too had moved away but when she came back, she sucked him one last time. They didn't even have intercourse. She just said she had to suck him. Mystified, Jack accepted the bonus. Jack resolved to do some math later, but he was sure that she had sucked him more than all of the others combined. Additionally, her zeal was by far the highest. But Dr. Jack returned to his unsucked men, stretched farther than the eye could see—endless, hopeless, miserable, good guys who tried their best and would die unsucked. Jack couldn't think of anything worse while he stroked his boner.

It was 6:59 a.m.

Jack went to get his second cup of coffee. His cock, though old, was very hard, thinking of Karen.

There was a pause in the hair dryer and Jack heard the spraying start. Geez. He loitered. She called through the doorway: "What are you doing?"

"Hoping."

"For what?" she said. "Ha ha. Help me?" She giggled, a rare occurrence for Jen who giggled perhaps twice a month. He imagined sounds other than giggling.

He figured he had to go so why not look good? He walked into the bathroom, which was fewer than twenty feet from where he'd been ruminating and dragged his precum tip over her ass.

"How can an old man help here?" he said.

"Oh gosh, what is that, Jack?"

"It's called 'precum'" and he dragged the "pre" out.

"Silly," she said.

"Silly? Whatever the antonyms of "silly' are, that's where we are."

"What do you mean?"

"Oh, Jen dear, I think you know."

"How does it look?" She motioned to her hair.

Defer or dare? Jack did a quick calculation, erring on the "at-least-some-sex" side.

"Lovely as always. How does he look?" Jack asked, motioning toward his erection.

"Useful," Jen laughed, but it was not an affectionate laugh, instead mocking.

"Well?" Now, finally, she would service him, lead him to the bed or the chair and lovingly deep throat him, hum a tune with his balls in her mouth, and with a wolf's eyes beg him to cum in her mouth.

"I mean later," she said, a *non sequitur* of course and a stupid one. She knew that he knew that it was stupid, so it could only hurt him, and it did. Again, Jack took the safe route and slunk off to his coffee. Jack felt rejected, confused, and shitty. Why wouldn't she satisfy him? Didn't she want to satisfy him? What kind of woman doesn't want to satisfy her man?

It was 7:07 a.m. "Ready," Jen said as though nothing had happened. Jack made her breakfast, and then they went to work.

Chapter Seventeen

POP GOES THE WEASEL

"Well, my dad busted me, so I told them everything," Jen said. It was Wednesday, March 2019. They were about to practice. Jack thought, so you didn't want to tell them even though you've been hurting me—hurting us—for months but because your dad busted you, you were forced to tell your parents about your boyfriend of whom you are apparently embarrassed?

"And?" Jack said.

"My mother went into orbit. My dad just listened." Jack had been waiting for this for months and months, and now the woman he loved, the woman who said she loved him, gave him two sentences.

"They said I should have told them sooner," she continued.

"What parent *wouldn't*?"

"Ok."

"And?" Jack said.

"Well, they want to meet you." One more sentence.

"How long was this conversation?"

"An hour and a half."

"And you've given me three sentences so far?"

"Oh, Jack, you don't understand."

"True. I'd like to," he said.

She softened, and her defiant tone (defiant against what? Whom?) turned diffident. "I'm sorry. What are we going to do?"

"We?" Jack knew what that meant. He got to solve her problem, but this one didn't phase him.

"I want to meet your parents. I've told you that from the beginning. What is the problem?"

"Where?"

"I don't care. Where is the greatest likelihood of success?"

"Well, I need to think about it," she said. As though she hadn't thought about it? This little, horrible sentence hurt Jack deeply, yet Jen appeared oblivious, her head down, tussling her hair (nearly all of her moods had an attendant tussle, this one downward, face covering), drawing a circle with her big toe, her beautiful cello hands tensed, crustacean-like, making another mutherfucking mountain of a another mole hill. Any lawyer could see, objectively, that the meeting had to occur, yet somehow Jen thought she could ignore it forever.

What are they going to do, Jack thought, shoot us? If they're as stiff as Jen, it would just be a bad weekend. And he'd heard enough to know, any ire would be directed at him, not their baby, their little girl, the shiny apple of their shiny eyes. Jack thought "I need to think about it" would turn into three weeks, so he decided to speak up.

"It's getting hot as balls; let's go up there," he said.

"Is there a sentence that comes out of your mouth that doesn't have 'balls' in it?"

"What are you, my mother?" he said.

"Are you going to tell my mother you like her balls?" Jen asked as she fluffed in from the kitchen to where Jack sat with his violin.

"Certainly not," Jack deadpanned, "only your father."

She hissed but it didn't work. He put his violin down, reached out his arms and pulled her down onto the couch with him. He grinned wildly and started dry humping her side and making monkey noises, "Ooooooooo; oooo-oo-ohohh; ah-balls." She tried to get away, but he tickled her, and she said "stop it" but couldn't get away. "Hi Mom," this is my boyfriend Balls, but I call him Big Balls!" he mocked her introduction to be. "Daddy, Daddy, my hero Big Balls is just the man for me." "'I can *see* that, 'rejoined Mr. Fairfield.'" And he chin-rubbed her all over and whispered gibberish until she calmed down. He chanted, "balls, balls, balls," in her ear and she had to smile reluctantly.

"I love you, Jennifer James."

"I love you too," but as usual it sounded singsong, not serious, not affectionate, certainly not genuine. Who was this Millennial who wanted to watch *Gone with the Wind*, but couldn't say "I love you?"

"You know I'll be on my best behavior," he said.

"I know."

"And you knew that before your little tizzy there."

"Yes."

"So why?"

No audible response. The same woman whose silence he adored could hurt him with silence. Whom did these blank spaces benefit? No one he could think of. Why did she do it? He couldn't imagine. She never explained. The air conditioner kicked on while he laid on the couch holding her. The ice machine tumbled out a rack in the kitchen, reverberating over the marble floor and into the living room. Jack had a poor angle, but he could still see her mien harden and chill. He'd seen that before, but he couldn't think of any circumstances she'd been in which called for it. It was like she was facing a midterm or final in school or a week in the county jail. Why assume the worst, Jack thought. Why not plan to at least try for success? They were probably googling him right now. Good. They'd see how old he was—the main problem as far as Jack knew—and get prepared. Geez. No one had cancer.

"Let's take a long weekend for Memorial Day, and go to the house of your girlhood," he said.

"That makes sense. Ok." There was something close to dread in her voice, and Jack worried she wouldn't follow up. He'd seen her commit to things before and then not follow up. Jack hated that in general, but when it came to the meeting with her parents, he was so far over it.

"Want me to get the plane tickets?" he said.

"Well, what's the schedule?"

"Memorial Day is always Monday." Jack checked his phone, saying, "I'm old enough to do pretty much anything I want in the office, so it's your schedule and your folks."

"Don't you have a fishing tournament or something?" Jen asked

"Fuck that. Let's go. I'm going to hook your mother. From what you told me, I have no chance with your father."

"Hook my mother, huh?"

"C'mon, Jennifer, she can't resist an old, harmless, fart like me. Wait until I give her the Deep South twang—"

"Oh God, don't."

"—and the old surfer stud routine."

"Oh. No."

"Well," Jack said, "I can pose as a landowner, you know, cotton belt stuff, slaves, any Virginian can relate, right?"

"No more joking."

"Well, what do you want me to do? What did you tell them about me? I'm forty-eight from Orlando, Florida. What the fuck?"

"Nothing, except your age and that you're a lawyer. I told you my dad busted me."

"Jen, you said the conversation was an hour and half. I've heard you get on the phone with your mom, and I don't think there's been a conversation less than thirty minutes."

"You're right, you're right. Don't beat me up."

"I never have, and I never will. Come here, lover." And he pulled her in a few inches from where she'd gravitated away from him.

"I'm sorry," she said.

"Is your brother going to be there?"

"Oh God. I hope not."

"He's not going to beat me up is he?" Jack started to chin her shoulders while she tried to wriggle free, squealing.

"Not at all," she said.

"Say something nice."

"I love it when you hold me, your hands," she said.

"See how easy."

Chapter Eighteen

ALWAYS RESPECT THE ELEMENTS

She'd come a long way with her sailing, and Jack suggested they rent a boat and go over to the Banana River for some more serious sailing. It was only mid-May, but the first days of the big heavy relentless heat had already arrived. Once they arrived, they didn't leave until mid-October. Jack knew that.

She had queried whether it was the Atlantic Ocean, and he said no but close, which was true. She'd learned the points of sail, basic boat trim, basic sail trim, and basic sailing vocabulary. When he said "head up" she no longer had to ask him what it meant. She knew. When he said they were on the windward shore, she knew. Her confidence increased, but she'd never been in a blow, let alone a big blow. Jack explained how wind volume like audio volume increased exponentially not merely in degrees. He didn't actually know if that were true, but it seemed the best way to explain it. She understood, but only in theory. Jack had been to the Banana River for nearly twenty years and had some spectacular failures over there.

The first was his Uncle Glenn from Michigan. A famous lover of freshwater and hater of salt water, he was not impressed when Jack explained the water in the Banana River was merely brackish, not salt. Uncle Glenn was impressed, however, when he was hurtled twenty feet off the boat in an afternoon gale-induced capsize. He came up spitting brackish water out his mouth and nose. It took Jack and him at least fifteen minutes to get the boat righted and under control after which Uncle Glenn, whose balls were advertised by Uncle Glenn as the world's biggest, announced: "I want off this boat." Jack had laughed at his uncle and said, "Turn the motor on whenever you like." Of course, the rented Hobie 16 had no motor and Uncle Glenn had to sail it another hour to get it back to the beach. During that hour, they capsized two more times. Uncle Glenn was sixty-six at the time and announced he was going to die as the boat rocketed along. "You can't die; I need you to steer, Uncle Glenn," Jack had needled him. Thankfully, the afternoon wind died off, and after mostly Jack had righted the old, rental Hobie 16—amazingly nothing had broken—for the third time, they had a lovely sail in to the beach. It was late in the afternoon, but the sun was still very high. Upon arriving on shore, Uncle Glenn shed forty years, and suddenly he was a twenty-six-year-old strutting on the beach like a horny rooster. Fuck Charles Atlas; he was the man.

He flirted with every girl on the beach, and some of them had even seen the wipe outs from afar. If so, Uncle Glenn assured them his cock was ten inches long with the diameter of a silver dollar and had two furry tennis balls sturdily attached and ready for duty. It was about the funniest thing Jack had ever seen, and he told everyone he thought a porno was going to be shot on site called *Grandpa Does the Girls*. It quickly became a family story and had only grown as the years had passed.

Then, years later, his buddy, Nick, also a type A guy, had gone to the Banana River with Jack. A natural athlete but having little experience or respect for sailing, Nick, too, had gotten his doors blown off. The old Hobie 16 was scuttled, so Jack rented a Johnson 18 this time, an obscure planning boat that Jack had only read about. The Johnson looked very hot and pissed off sitting on the beach. "No one will take her out," the rental guy had told Jack. So, Jack rented her, and she was very hot indeed. In the morning, Nick had floundered on the trapeze wire as Jack captained, but the boat was just itching to take off. Jack seemed to recall from the review that the Johnson 18 wasn't supposed to have a trapeze—but, what the hell—let's party. Jack felt the potential—like a guy on the bull before they opened the gate.

They took a break, and Jack had warned Nick the wind had a tendency to rise off the ocean in the afternoon and was Nick up for it? Nick dismissed the warning, said any retard could trapeze, and sure enough the wind kicked on. Well, they turned onto a beam reach, and the Johnson kicked off! It seemed to Jack that the bow rose a yard and the speed more than doubled in a matter of ten seconds. The rigging had that wonderful hum to it, one of Jack's all time favorite sounds.

While screaming along, Nick had trouble on the trapeze and the boat began to Dutch roll and kick and buck—the wake behind it spanned three crests. "Relax; hang on the wire with all your weight." Jack advised, but Nick kept lurching. "Come in," Jack ordered Nick, "we're out of control."

"FUCK THAT," Nick said, but it was clear to Jack that Nick would have gladly come in if he could have figured out how to get off the mechanical bull. But it was too late anyway; the boat dove hard to leeward in a puff and Nick was catapulted and raked against the shroud and spreader. He came up screaming "motherfucker!" near the tip of the mast. Again, Jack was sailing with someone who didn't know what to do, so Jack had to do most of the righting. But when Nick finally got on board, he had a 16-inch slice in his side and up his chest and was bleeding profusely. "Holy shit," Jack hollered, "don't panic, but you've got to go to a hospital." Nick looked down, realized what had happened, and for once followed Jack's orders all the way back to the beach with a gritty stoicism. It was the only time Jack had ever sailed with a steady stream of blood going into the cockpit, mixing with the water, and out the back. Thankfully, the cut was shallow, so they stitched Nick up easily. But it could have been different. It could have been death.

These and other events ran through Jack's mind as the day approached. "Always respect the elements," he had told Jen a million times, but she was still a virgin. Her knowledge was only theoretical. It was all set for Saturday, but the night before ran late for some reason and Jen had had two drinks. Jack rarely saw her even finish one drink. He'd uncharacteristically slept late, and when he awakened, she'd gone for a walk near Jack's house. It was steamy and hot in the morning, the prior day's thunderstorms percolating *up* into the air off the soaked land. Jen was sweating hard when she came back. He'd already packed everything, and they were going to the same spot he'd been using for twenty years. He'd told her a million times things were likely to get hairy, and safety was number one. He checked the forecast, and it was East winds at 5-10, but he didn't trust it. He'd seen the Banana River consistently turn on in the afternoon like a light switch regardless of the forecast.

They got there at 9:45, and it was very hot. There wasn't a cloud in the sky, and it was obvious there hadn't been all morning. The parking lot was too hot to walk barefoot. They walked over to the rental place that was attended by a young girl with a bikini on and a halter top that was still wet. She'd obviously just been in the water which was about thirty feet away. Jack waited and hoped that Jen would make clear he was her boyfriend and cut off the usual stares and glares. But no, typical Jen, she didn't help at all as the girl tried to figure out what the old man asking all the questions was doing with the girl who didn't say anything. Jack had suffered through this at least fifty times now, and it hurt him very much. He'd discussed it with Jen, told her how much it hurt him, and here again she let him twist in the wind. Why was it so hard to use the word "boyfriend" or "my man" or anything?

The decline in sailing in general had led to a decline in sailing options at the rental facility. Jack asked about the Johnson 18, but the girl didn't even know what it was. However, there was another Hobie 16. Jack decided that there was really no other boat worth renting. They had some sunfishes, and one small keel boat, and that was it. He had told Jen about the Uncle Glenn story, but she didn't ask if this was the same boat, and Jack saw no benefit in pointing it out to her. One thing about those Hobie 16's, there was no room for storage. It was just two sailors and a trampoline. Jack had anticipated this and transferred two ginger ales from the big cooler he'd packed to a small soft cooler, which he threaded through the trampoline and stitched up tight. Jen had been noticeably quiet all the way over to the Banana River. Jack always felt comfortable when she didn't say anything when in fact nothing needed to be said. He'd never had a similar feeling with any other woman. She'd also said virtually nothing while he finished rigging the boat when questions and comments would have been appreciated.

They were booked to see her parents in about two weeks, and Jen was too nervous. To Jack, it felt like she *wanted* it to be a disaster with her parents. She'd had two drinks the night before and a glass of wine—a heavy alcohol night for Jen but as usual she didn't actually finish any of the drinks. This trait was not limited to alcohol. He had never seen her finish a cup of coffee and rarely a glass of water. Frequently, half her meals were thrown away or eaten by Jack as leftovers. Her unfinished drinks were found by Jack all over his house. She never got any of them in the sink, let alone the dishwasher. Jack had eaten breakfast and packed them the big cooler for the day. He'd packed that big cooler more than two hundred times, and his father before him was also a big cooler packer. His uncles too. He'd been around cooler packers and packed coolers his whole life. She skipped breakfast, which was odd, but Jack didn't give it a moment's thought. She was in her twenties for goodness' sake, made of steel. He was more worried about her getting killed in the Banana River when it started to kick, buck and froth.

They set off heading east toward the Atlantic, a light breeze in their faces on a close reach. Jack skippered and Jen put the harness on for trapeze work. It was Jack's harness as he knew the rental place either wouldn't rent one at all or would give you a terrible one. The harness was too big for Jen, but he'd adjusted all the straps as tight as they'd go. It was useable. Jack showed her the sails and basic set up on the beach. It was extremely hot. One of the things Jack wanted to expose her to was the thrill of open water. At Lake Fairview, there was limited room to run before a shoreline got in the way. The lake Jack lived on, where they'd talked about sailing but never had, was even smaller. Jack had lived on a lake as a child, and his father had bitched about the sailing not being much but turning as the far shore came up on you. But the Banana River was big. One could sail for thirty minutes or more without changing course. It was a giant playground. Jack wanted Jen to experience that.

Unfortunately, there wasn't enough wind to trapeze, and they both ended up sitting on the black trampoline which was bone dry and hot. There were no splashes or spray to wet it, and Jen's wet feet and knees quickly dried off. It was like sitting on a grooveless rubber tire under a gazillion candlepower.

Still, it was quite lovely. Jen smiled at him a couple of times, as they'd talked about the open water many times. She'd worn a big, floppy hat, but Jack could see her face; it looked extra white. She didn't say anything stupid, which was normal for her. She understood the wind was light, and there was nothing to do but sit on the trampoline. They crabbed along for a while, and Jen laid out full length on the trampoline. It was a sloppy way to sail, but Jack didn't want to crab at her; let her save her energy for the big afternoon blow if it came. She had both a life jacket and the trapeze harness on in addition to her shorts and a long-sleeved white shirt and rubber booties Jack had bought for her. She'd complained the booties were ugly, but once she wore them quickly realized how utilitarian they were.

After another fifteen, slow minutes, Jack realized she'd fallen asleep. It was near noon. The heat increased, but the wind stayed very light. Who could say whether the big blow would come? Jack just wished for a little more air, enough to get Jen on the trapeze, while he sweated profusely.

Jack went as far as he could to the east and said "Ready about" but Jen didn't move. It was no big deal, Jack thought, the wind was light, and he could tack the boat himself and then bear away downwind. So, he did, but after the jib backfilled, he was required to go forward to pull in the new leeward sheet and the bouncing on the trampoline woke Jen up. Suddenly, things were very bad.

"Oh Jack, I'm sick," Jen said and rolled her head to the side and puked green and red and God knows what on the trampoline.

"Jen! What is it?" Jack was shocked. She was twenty-nine. They had made it through the eye of the wind, and Jack was able to bear away, but now it was hotter because the wind was behind. Every sailor knows how unrefreshing a wind from behind is. She looked over at him with eyes he'd never seen before and vomited again.

"Jen!" he scooched near and grabbed her arm. It was all clammy and wet with perspiration. "Jen, what is it?" but now he could see. She was totally dehydrated. She hadn't eaten and her blood sugar had no doubt plummeted. It was extremely hot; she was lying on a black trampoline that had to be over one hundred degrees and there was no breeze. Jack had been in quite a few near-death experiences in his life, and he immediately assessed the situation. She was helpless, and he would have to get her to the beach and get fluids into her or things could get very ugly.

"Take off your harness," he said gently. "Jack, don't leave me," she dreamily spoke. Jack had wanted to hear those words since he had fallen in love with her, but not like this.

He stayed near her and removed the harness. He clipped it on the trampoline netting. The wind died, and they were nearly becalmed, the old Hobie crawling and crabbing along at under 5 mph. Now Jack had to make a decision. He could see the long sleeve shirt was a major problem, but the only way to get it off was to take off the life preserver. If she went over, she'd die. But Jack calculated the odds of going over were very low and he still had his life preserver on so he could dive in after her as a worst-case scenario. She was limp at this point. They weren't going to tip over.

"Take off your life preserver," he ordered gently.

"Oh Jack, I'm sick," but she complied. He personally held onto the life preserver.

"Take off your shirt," he ordered

"What?"

"Take off your shirt," and he reached over and started pulling it up. The fabric was not super heavy, but still significant. She said she was sick again, but didn't fight him. She had a bra on, not a sports bra, but still there was no reason to fight him.

"Put your life preserver back on," Jack said.

"Captain, my Captain Jack. Do you love me? Old Rip, my man." She was white paste. Some of the vomit was stuck on the corners of her mouth, green like a clown, only not funny.

"Oh, Jesus Christ, Jen, how can you say that? Don't you know how much I love you? Now put on your life preserver." But she couldn't, and Jack put her life preserver on for her. His course went wrong, and he did a slow accidental gybe. Even though she seemed completely out of it, the sailor in her noticed the gybe, and she gave a faint delirious "wheee" out as the boom went overhead. So, this is it, Jack thought, before I even meet her parents for the first time, I'm going to report her death as my initial message. Fuck that. I'm Jack Forester. This girl is twenty-nine. This is not going to happen.

Jack calculated. She would do no sailing, so he was sailing alone. Shit, it seemed like he'd spent his whole life sailing alone. Better, he was sailing down wind, and he knew the big cooler was waiting. Plus, he remembered they had an outdoor shower at the rental place; sure, they did, and a freshwater hose as well. So be rational, you piece of shit, he tried to tell himself. He'd have to gybe at least once, probably twice, at most three times to get home. The Hobie 16 was terrible in light air, and it only got lighter. Jack calculated at the maximum, one hour to get back to the beach. If the wind picked up, it would be dramatically less. But one hour was too long. Here was Jen, the paragon of put togetherness puking and talking like a delirious madwoman. An hour was an eternity.

So, Jack turned his attention to the small cooler. He could splash her with Banana River water, but it was hot and brackish. She couldn't drink it, and it wouldn't refresh her very much. Jack's entire world became that very small soft cooler that he had had for years. He couldn't even remember where he had gotten it. He surmised that someone had left it with him, and it was an adverse possession. Anyway, he knew exactly what was in that small cooler: two 12-ounce cans of Canada Dry Ginger Ale, and ice, and ice melt. Actually, he wasn't sure about the latter. The old cooler might have a leak and might not be holding the ice melt. In fact, Jack saw a circular stain around it as it sat on the black trampoline and thought it might very well have been leaking all along. But the longer he looked at the stain the more he was convinced that the leak was small; there was still ice melting in that cooler. Jen's life blood. He loved Jen. But, as it was clear to Jack that Jen would not die far away, but if anything, very close to shore, he knew a decision needed to be made right away.

He resolved that if there more than twelve ounces of ice melt in the soft cooler, he would open one can and make Jen drink it. Then he would submerge it in the cooler, fill it with ice melt, and place it in her armpit. The other drink would certainly go under her other armpit. The only better thing would be her wrist, but who was going to hold it there? There was a decent chance it would be fumbled overboard. Jack was already manning a two-person boat by himself. But then, how would she drink it, horizontally laying on a black trampoline? That would not work either.

"Come here, Jen," he pulled at her armpits.

"Jack, I'm sick."

"Please. Come here, sit up with me."

She peeled her upper body off the trampoline and her face fell into the crook of Jack's neck. From the first time he had ever held her, Jen had always been perfectly clean, perfectly healthy, perfectly dressed, perfectly scented, a Venus from heaven sent to console all men solely by her touch and smell. She had face cream that probably cost a hundred dollars a jar. Now, she was a clammy, white, salty, witch talking gibberish with green splotches at the corners of her mouth. The vomit she'd spewed was under both of them, smeared on their shorts, nothing to get rid of it. Jack, sailing for two people, and holding Jen erect, could do nothing but mash them both in the vomit.

Both the main and the jib flogged, but Jack did nothing. The whole way home was downwind and there was no way they wouldn't make it. The issue was time. He opened the soft cooler, pulled a can out, and being extremely careful zipped it close. He was correct. There was some icy slosh in it. He pulled the tab, and without offering it to her hands, held it to her mouth.

"Don't guzzle," Jack said, "Don't guzzle. Slow steady."

She drank and drank. Her hair was a sweaty rag pressed against Jack. "Don't guzzle, Jen. Calm down," he said.

She drank more and then belched. Never before had he ever heard her belch. She jostled in place and farted; it sounded like a cornet projecting into oatmeal, the vomit smear on her shorts muffling her anus. Never had Jack heard her fart. For the first time in a while, there was a little life in her. Jack pulled out the other can of ginger ale.

"Easy. Easy. Now, trust me. Put this in your other armpit and give me that."

She had no energy, but it didn't take any energy to hold the can after Jack wedged it in her armpit. He submerged the empty can in the ice melt. It filled up but there was little left.

"Drink half slowly," he gave the same can back to her. She did.

"Keep holding the other one," he tried to submerge the can again but there wasn't much left in the soft cooler.

"Hold still," he said, and he held the can of ice melt in her left armpit while she held the unopened can of ice cold, ginger ale in her right armpit. They sailed for fifteen minutes. She looked better.

"Ok, drink the water," Jack said. She did and handed it back to him.

He put the empty can back in the soft cooler which had nothing left in it.

"Keep sipping," he told her, opening the other can. The other can of Canada Dry was still very cold even though it had been in her armpit for twenty minutes or so.

Her eyes were crazy, but her skin was getting back to normal.

"One more gybe," he said. It was very calm, and he was challenged to gybe at all, so light was the wind, the leeward pontoon dragging forever, the stern finally passing through the little eye of the little wind. But eventually the rig did come around.

"Ok, keep drinking, but slowly," he said handing it to her.

She obeyed, even flashing the can at him halfway to show she wouldn't guzzle. She was back. They were five hundred yards from the beach, and death had gone.

"Hey. Jen. I love you. I hope you know." He said as it became apparent that she would live.

She nodded her head yes but hung her head and said nothing. On the beach, he walked her to the outdoor shower and turned it on. She flinched at the cold in relation to the relative heat. There was a hose also and he ran it under her armpits, down her shorts front and back, and then all over her head. He got one of the beach chairs out of the truck, went down to the boat and untied the soft cooler, filled it with ice, went back to the shower, filled the soft cooler with water, turned the shower off, and helped Jen to the chair.

"Put your hands in here over the wrist," he said.

"Both?"

"Whatever, one is better than zero." He went to the truck and made Jen a big glass of ice water from the big cooler. He brought it back to her, and she was pulling one wrist out and putting the other in.

"It's unbearable, freezing." Jen said.

"Good. That will cool your blood. Here drink this slowly."

"Sit with me." Sit with me, he thought. That's the old Jen. She's back.

"Yes, but let me tend to the boat real quick." He dropped the main. He furled the jib. He raised the rudders and pulled the boat up firmly on shore. The attendant in the bikini wasn't there. He came back.

"You're so decisive," Jen said. Although she didn't present it as a compliment, and although her tone of voice suggested no admiration, he took it as a compliment, one of the few she had ever given him if in fact she had given it to him.

"What do you mean?" Jack said.

"The boat. You did exactly what was needed, no more, and came back to me."

"I care about you," he said.

"Awwww," but the tone was wrong, almost mocking, like he was a pet. She seemed not to possess, at least toward him, a timbre that was warm and loving and what he so desperately needed. He looked into her eyes, and they were back and big and deep, deep brown.

"How are you feeling?" Jack said.

"So much better."

"I'll get you some salt."

He went back to the truck. She loved chips, and he knew Doritos had a ton of salt, so he grabbed the cool ranch ones.

"Here, you go," Jack said. "These have a ton of salt. How's your drink."

"It's gone."

"I'll get you another."

She started munching, and he filled up another big ice water. The rental girl arrived from her apparent break and came over to check on them. He was afraid Jen would say something inappropriate in her state, and she was the kind of commoner that Jen had derided before. Jack complimented the attendant and told her everything was great. Jack wanted to get back to zero with the world. They didn't say anything for five minutes or so.

"These are great," Jen said, munching Doritos. After all this, it was only 2:30 in the afternoon; the sun was high overhead, scattered clouds, heavy heat. Jack felt like he'd lived several lifetimes. She was going to act like nothing happened.

"Salt." Jack said.

"I'm sorry for ruining the sail."

"The sail? You mean death?"

"Hmmm?"

"What did you learn?" Jack asked.

"Always respect the elements," she was not stupid.

"And?" He said.

"But it was calm."

"And?"

No audible response.

"The elements." He prompted. "The sun. The heat. Water or the lack thereof. Salt. Dehydration kills. Sunstroke. Heart attack. Jesus, Jen, your number could've been up. I don't care if you're twenty-nine or not; dehydration will kill anyone."

She didn't say anything for minutes.

"Thank you," she said finally.

"I love you, Jennifer. Don't you see that?" She nodded but said nothing. He went and got their lunch from the big cooler. It was obvious there would be no afternoon sail even though it wouldn't be dark until eight or so. Might as well eat lunch, Jack thought. Jen was ravenous and ate her quail salad pita bread in ten minutes, a record for her. He'd shot the quail; he'd poached the quail; he'd picked the quail; he'd made the salad—all for her. She said nothing.

They drove back to Jack's house early. It appeared not to matter to her. She never said anything nice to him. No, she recovered and never mentioned it again. He knew the weekend with her parents—which had been blown out of all proportions by Jen—was right around the corner so he figured it was the stress. Plus, he didn't know what he'd say to her anyway. He'd never saved anyone's life before.

Chapter Nineteen

PLAYING FOR A DRAW

They were blue bloods from Virginia, but he wasn't the slightest bit intimidated. He remembered going to Homecoming as a sophomore in high school with Liz Beth—a sweet, little slut from old money in Rhode Island. Her father had dressed Jack down pretty good when he showed up to get her. He remembered being very intimidated by Mr. Rhodes, and Mr. Rhodes intentionally accentuating Jack's anxiety by prolonging the period when Liz Beth would come down from the second floor in full regalia. There were two grandparents, three siblings, and a mother. Mr. Rhodes sequestered him in his study—full of very expensive shotguns, polo clubs, fencing masks, a million-dollar pool ("billiards" Mr. Rhodes corrected him) table and assorted other "very rich people" stuff. Mr. Rhodes had known the schedule exactly, knew Jack was late, knew Liz Beth was always late, and so prolonged the entire situation entirely and deliberately. Jack was very young, but he kinda liked Mr. Rhodes even though Jack was shitting his pants. Jack had done a lot of sweating, said the wrong things numerous times, forgotten to rise when the mother came to check him out and essentially proven to be the exact lowbrow that Mr. Rhodes feared his daughter might end up with. The only sniff of approval had come when Jack told Mr. Rhodes he'd get Liz Beth home before curfew.

But Jack held the trump card even if he didn't know how to play it, in fact couldn't play it. If only he could tell Mr. Rhodes that at the very same dance the year previously, Scott Holder had accidentally come in Liz Beth's face in Mr. Rhodes' driveway approximately 100 yards from where Jack was seated in the study! In fact, Jack could see out the widow to the long horseshoe driveway as he was being interrogated, but he didn't know which side Scottie had parked on. Scottie had told a few boys about it and sworn them to secrecy. Jack smiled devilishly thinking about how that little group of fifteen-year-olds had kept the story secret. They all liked Liz Beth and knew it would hurt her if it got out. Scotty had a J C Penny's collared shirt on, beige pants (not quality enough to be called slacks) and topsiders with no socks. Scotty's parents apparently didn't realize how underdressed he was. Mr. Rhodes clearly disapproved.

Apparently, Liz Beth, too, had had a little too much of Mr. Rhodes' disapproval in her childhood, and so resolved to make out with Scotty. They didn't even have any clothes off when Liz Beth's Titian hand found its way to Scotty's fifteen-year-old bulge. And what a bulge it was. Lucky Liz Beth stroked him through his pants for too long (meaning approximately two minutes), unzipped poor Scottie but didn't even get his pants off, before his cock arched through the top of his waistband as she descended completely unaware of what she was going to do. She then made the mistake of reaching inside his underwear and tenderly stroking Scottie about twice before he rocketed off in the greatest moment of his life. "Oh my God," they yelped together. She hadn't even taken her glasses off, and there was a beautiful goober on her right lens which Scottie thought meant her eye had popped out of her skull, and she was going to die right in her old man's driveway or at least have to wear an eyepatch for the rest of her life as Scotty's jism had blown her eye out. She had only a tiny amount of Kleenex in her clutch from Homecoming and used it up before she saw he was still oozing from his tip and writhing in the driver's seat. Even a fifteen-year-old prostate needs help finishing, and what was he going to do—jack off in front of her? Insist she continue? Both were inconceivable, so Scotty just sat there writhing in agony. She was mesmerized. More cum? What to do? But Liz Beth had always been a sweet girl, and her maternal instincts took over. She didn't understand jerking off, but she'd brushed her teeth regularly. "Let me help you," she whispered, making a ring with her middle finger and her thumb at the base of his cock just above the balls, and drawing the anti-tourniquet up to Scottie's screaming head. This time only Scottie yelped, and there was semen everywhere. "Poor thing," fifteen-year-old Liz Beth and her Titian hand said. Jack laughed aloud thinking back. For years, it was the greatest story he had ever heard. It was still in the top five now. Why couldn't it have been him?

But that was over thirty years ago. His soul had been brutalized in the interim. He'd practiced law for over twenty years. He'd seen his friends run through women, get married, have kids, and make a fortune while he was always the lovable loser. This would be much different with Jen's parents. Maybe they were decent people, but the only realistic way to approach the thing was to consider them the enemy.

He had two weeks to plan and used most of it. First, he decided the best he could hope for was a draw. They probably already hated him. They would never love him on the first meeting. And so, a draw was his only chance. He would not grovel, but he would be entirely accommodating. He would not use profanity even if others did. He would not make any sexual comment of any kind the entire time; he knew that any such remark would only make them resent him for fucking their dear Jennifer. He would speak only when spoken to. This was in his nature and easy anyway. Don't fuck up a good thing, he thought. Let them run on about how great they are, and so what?

He knew that would do for Thursday night, Friday all day, and probably Saturday morning. So, he resolved to prepare more. Jen, thankfully, had followed through and the schedule was Thursday evening through Sunday midday. Monday was a holiday, so they had a cushion if they needed it. He was a lawyer and this was a case: nothing more. Sometime between Saturday morning and 2:00 p.m. Sunday, someone was going to roll the universe into a ball and the subject would have to be addressed: A forty-eight-year-old man will not fuck our sweet, little baby, and you can rot in hell you son of a bitch Disney World Southerner. Jack had to be turned into "Well, he's not so bad" or "We should have trusted our Jen; she's not a baby anymore." That or something similar was the best he could do. In fact, if they turned out to be timid, *he* would broach the topic and drive it where it needed to go. He'd spent twenty years babysitting unprepared judges; this was no different. He would not go down without a fight. He expected that Jen would do her usual nothing, but it was conceivable she'd come to his aid when the crunch came. Still, she was unreliable; it was just as likely she'd stab him in the back. He resolved to fight alone without his alleged lover.

He went to the mirror in his house and rehearsed his lines and demeanor. He had been doing this for court since he was in law school. He was amazed at the number of lawyers who did not rehearse. Certain questions were obvious, easy to anticipate. Why not have a perfect answer scripted? Others were more unlikely, but still somewhat likely. What better way to show respect than to show that it had been thought of and here was the response? Jack couldn't understand lawyers who didn't prepare, especially for the obvious. The parameters of the meeting with Jen's parents were clear. He would not walk in and "wing it."

— "I never thought she was interested in me." Note—Do not say "romantically"—too sexual.

— "I have never disrespected your daughter." Note: could backfire because fucking her is probably disrespecting her, but my goodness she was nearly thirty. Even better, they would check with Jen, and she would confirm he had never disrespected her.

— "I cannot help our age difference." Note: Don't be afraid to use this early if necessary.

— "I love your daughter with my whole heart." Note: a ghastly cliché, but all available options were ghastly clichés. What counts is the demeanor not the words. Full eye contact, unwavering, even penetrating, gaze. Hold their eyes. Make them look away first.

— "I gave up looking for your daughter twenty years ago; she's too perfect." Note: risky; pretty cavalier, even ballsy. Keep in stock but use only if the timing is perfect, late, post-alcohol, as a rejoinder only to some quasi-cavalier statement by one of the parents, probably the mother.

— "I want your blessing." Note: don't try it. Way too early. Unattainable. Be particularly wary if alone with the mother as she may indulge her emotional garden and attempt to suck you into its murky ooze.

— DO NOT MENTION KIDS! Jen had told him there had been a huge blow up when she told her parents that she did not want kids. Even though Jack had had nothing to do with it, he thought it very safe to assume that they hoped Jen would change her mind. But, Oh God, *Jack's* kids? Hell no. The topic was absolutely taboo. He'd yell "GO GATORS!" from the front lawn at their neighbors before he'd get stuck in a conversation about kids.

— Basics: perfectly groomed; perfect manners; follow Jen's lead if presented; do not check phone; do not check emails; offer to assist with paying but don't fight over the bill; SHUT THE FUCK UP WHENEVER POSSIBLE.

One of the many things that ruined modern life is being picked up at the airport. No one can come to your gate anymore, and so it's either meet at baggage claim or meet at the car in the hurly burly of the traffic while a gorilla yells at you to "keep moving." Jen was useless. Jack planned. Either option was a disaster, but the hurly burly was clearly inferior. Of course, they were going to be shocked when they saw him. He was older than shit. His picture on the firm website would only partially prepare them. The situation had to be defused. Meeting them outside guaranteed a bad start. There was literally no way it could be anything but rushed, no eye contact, possibly even an accident if things went really bad. He could see Mrs. Fairfield, aghast at his appearance next to her beautiful daughter falling and shattering her elbow. He could see Mr. Fairfield, mortified that his daughter was with a Neanderthal Geezer from Red Neck Land, throwing his back out as he too vigorously hoisted the bags, yelping in pain, and everyone hearing about it all weekend. What to do?

He asked Jen if it would be okay if her parents met them at baggage claim. He could see she had not given it a second's thought. She smiled and kissed him on the cheek: "you are a worrier, aren't you?" He nodded and explained his concerns. She laughed, "God you're fucked up, Jack" and thought about it. The next day she said "Well, we could Uber and meet them at the house." Making dad and mom park the car might be worse then meeting them outside, she explained. Neither of them traveled; it was a pain in the ass; lots of walking, etc. It was the first time she had ever helped him solve a problem. He kissed her back, "God, you're a genius," and thought about it. "Jen, I need you to blame it on yourself unequivocally and then feed them some Millennial garbage against which they cannot defend. You know like an auto mechanic, ten words in they just start talking about the E37 converter and it's over." She laughed. He found the hollow of her neck and circled back to the nape nibbling. "Horny Jack. Horny. Horny. Weirdo. Nibble, nibble," he whispered. He loved her succulent neck.

"Are you going to do this in Virginia?" she asked.

"You mean get horny?"

She laughed.

"How about this?" he said and turned her around and started kneading her back.

Two nights later, Jen came through. She aggressively pushed the Uber idea with her mother, fed her a "changing gate" scenario which was utter shit, but undetectable, and sold the virtues of just waiting for their arrival. Jack listened carefully. As soon as he heard, "Well, then I must have some food ready when you get here," he knew it was locked. He would meet Jen's parents under the best circumstances possible: at their house with no time pressures, no loud noises, no strangers, no nothing. Jack smiled. He hugged Jen for three minutes, drawing her in more and more; he loved every millimeter of her. She'd solved a problem! "Thanks, Angel," he whispered, and rolled her over on the couch, squeezing her hamstrings hard while she screamed. "I didn't know a high brow like you could make such barbaric noises," he said, while she kicked at him. He kept squeezing and then got on top of her.

"Big sack of potatoes that loves you is here."

"Jack."

"Lovey dovey lovey."

"Jaaack."

He rolled onto her side and held her for a long time.

The front door opened, and Mr. and Mrs. Fairfield were both there smiling. He met their gaze, saw the disappointment, and set about rehabilitating the situation. He didn't think Jen would be as freaked out as she was, but she started with "Mom. Dad. This is Mr. Forester." They both raised an eyebrow, and he smoothly cut in and presented a medium firm handshake with: "Jack will do." Both parents smiled, and he met the father's gaze with kind eyes and no intensity.

"You must be hungry," the mother said as they all walked in. Jack scanned the expansive living room and thought of Mr. Rhodes. There was too much pause, but finally Jen said:

"Sure, Mom."

"Thank you," he said softly.

The mother went to the kitchen, and Jack noted that neither of them had instructed him how to address them. Maybe they were a little nervous themselves, Jack thought. Best to relieve the pressure, and when the mother came back with a tray, Jack said:

"May I help you, Mrs. Fairfield?" in his best Eddie Haskell voice.

It was a cue, but she didn't get it, just said "thanks" and he helped her with the food.

The father did: "Just as Jack will do, so will 'Kevin' and 'Betty' please," he said.

"Ok. Duly noted," Jack said. Again, he felt good. The father got it. He was going to be just like Mr. Rhodes.

They all ate and chatted for twenty minutes or so. Everyone had a glass of wine, so Jack had one glass of wine. But he didn't finish it. This is all business, he thought. He had always had the gift of making people laugh, but he was tight and there wasn't a single joke the whole time. Finally, Jen bailed him out when, during very strained conversation, she blurted out: "Jack was voted most humorous in his high school class."

"Not that you'd noticed," he dead-panned perfectly.

Both parents laughed, blowing off the steam. Jen guffawed, which was once a month tops for her. She was super tight. Jack met and held the mother's gaze while her laughter trailed off. He smiled and said to her with his eyes: "I'm not a monster." He didn't know how the topic got on his high school years, but holy shit that needed to be avoided.

After the *hors d'oeuvres*, Betty motioned to the bags and said "Well, this is your room here, Jack. Jen, you know where your room is." Jack's confidence grew and he shot Jen a knowing glance. He'd already argued with Jen over this in Orlando, and his prediction was accurate. There was no way they would be sleeping together, and the odds of Jen staying in her girlhood room were 99%. So, the only issue was where would her parents put Jack? There were two rooms upstairs, one room on the first floor, and three potential rooms in the basement. Jack loved basements and hoped he'd get put down there. Hell, he'd volunteer if necessary. The parents were on the first floor; they had grown tired of the second-floor master and had converted one of the first-floor bedrooms into the new master. So, that meant upstairs there was Jen's room, her brother's room, and her parents' old master. On the first floor, there was the new master, and the existing guestroom. There were three other rooms downstairs in the basement.

"What's your prediction?" he asked Jen in Orlando.

"The old master."

He snorted. "I love Millennials."

"What about it, smartass?"

"Well, I need to see the house," said Jack.

"You just snorted at me without seeing the house."

"Snorted, Jen?"

"MMmmmHHmmm," she mimicked one of his many mannerisms.

He motioned to her famous chaise, and she got on top of him and straddled him face to face.

"I love you so much," said Jack.

"How much?"

"How deep is the ocean?"

"Ouch," she said.

"It's true."

"Cliché," she stuck out her tongue. Jack thought: . . . she's a little too old for the stick out the tongue thing.

"Cliches are true."

He loved her nose and her eyebrows and rubbed the tip of his nose on them and gave her little, baby kisses. She had hard eyes usually, which he hated, but he turned it into a game he called: "Melt for me." For months, she'd said he was a weirdo, but he was so soft and so gentle, and he just kept looking at her and would not look away. Eventually, her eyes softened.

"Melty, melty, melty," he kissed her.

"Now tell me, Jerk," she said.

"Say 'jerk' affectionately."

"No," she said.

"Well, then how about 'jerk *off* '?"

"That's what you don't do anymore," but her smile was mocking.

"What a sweet thing to say, Jen. By the way, how do you know?" he gave her a questioning grin.

"You? What? You have me?"

"Say something nice," he said.

"No! Now back to the arrangements, you fucking William Faulkner or someone."

"You swear a lot more than when I first met you," said Jack.

"Jack!"

"Ok. Ok," he said. "Well, the old master seems like a long shot because that puts me in their bedroom on the second floor alone with you. Your parents aren't going to want to try to fall asleep while a strange Southerner sleeps on the second floor with their only daughter and could easily slip into her room and play hide the salami. Worse, by putting said invader on the second floor they've legitimized his presence on the second floor in general, sort of inviting trouble. The same reasoning applies to your brother's room, though not as disturbing, but on the other hand, I'm way older than your brother so maybe more disturbing. Hmm.

"Now, we have a tablespoon of incest or something horrible added to the already-putrid stew. So that's not going to happen. I'm thinking the basement is where you put little kids and/or unwelcome relatives—kinda like an overflow set-up. So, that leaves the old standard guest room on the first floor where they can keep a bit of an eye on the gargoyle."

She laughed. "God you're a mess, Mr. Forester. Sounds like you've given it some thought."

"Thank you, Betty" he said to Jen's mother in Virginia and grinned at Jen who shook her head and stuck her tongue out. She absolutely hated it when he got the better of her. He quickly exited the main room but listened intently at the cracked door. Not much happened. A couple of "I'm tireds," and "Good to have you home," and he heard Jen go upstairs. The parents shuffled about for a while, but he couldn't hear anything they said. He sensed no tension. Well, he thought, the first impression is over, and it wasn't too bad. He wanted to text Jen, but he didn't know how tech savvy the parents were. A bunch of pinging might be a turn off. Plus, Jen didn't text him. Though he never showered at night, he forced himself to shower merely to test the set-up and let any parent that cared to know he was a clean mutherfucker. When he got out, Jen had not texted.

He lay in the guest room bed and loved the set-up. Sticking him in the old guest room with the parents on the first floor seemed to de-sex the entire situation. Good. As far as the parents were thinking, he assumed, there was no way he'd have the balls to sneak upstairs and fuck their daughter right in their own house. What kind of monster would do such a thing? Jack thought of his latest porn movie *Stonewall's Second Story Stand*, where Jack would show these blue bloods who was boss by dressing up as Stonewall Jackson, leave sucked lemon wedges everywhere, sneak upstairs in full military dress, hair coiffed and pomaded, unzip (no hooks and eyes would be better) his mightiness, and feed it all into dear, sweet Jen in her girlhood bedroom. It would be bigger and more purple than anything Hemingway had ever described, irretrievably sullying the innocence of her first dreams in that room: her kindergarten crush, crushed; her first menstrual cycle, already painful and voluminous, aggravated; her saddle shoes, kicked off; her blouse, balled up; her panties (with a new odor suddenly in them) off—a point of no return. But was Stonewall Jackson from Virginia? Jack's fantasy was interrupted by this detail. He had a nagging feeling that Stonewall was from South Carolina, so the whole thing would backfire as he'd merely prove to the parents that he was as stupid as they already suspected. God, you're a dumb son of a bitch, he thought. That was the best you could do today, so stop your stupid shit and go to bed. He checked one last time, and there was no text from Jen. He hoped for a Stonewall dream and dozed off to battle his chronic obstructive sleep apnea.

He was up at seven on Friday morning, listening. His many hours on tree stands had prepared him well for this moment. How was the Fairfield house going to wake up? Jen was normally a morning person, but this wasn't normal. Surely, the parents had to be tight. His job was to ease the tension. He took a quick shower, got dressed, and sat in the chair by the door and listened. No text from Jen still, but she might not want to be the first person up. She'd been acting weird for two or three days now. No sounds except the air conditioner. The chair looked enormously old and expensive, and Jack eventually realized it was stupid to sit in it. If he damaged it, that would be a disaster. Plus, it wasn't comfortable. It was probably an antique worth a million dollars or something.

He put his tennis socks on, lay on his back right next to the door which was closed, and gently put his heels on the wall above him. He pulled at his hamstrings. There would be no mark, his back felt good, and he even got his ears within a yard of the door. Jen had said her father had to work a little on Friday, and there's likely to be a tennis game Saturday at the club. They were Ubering Sunday at 2:00 to leave. Otherwise, the schedule was open. Jack hated an empty schedule, and the older he got the more he hated it. But there was nothing he could do.

About 7:30 a.m., Jack heard some kitchen noises and heavy coughing. Former smoker, Jack wondered? There was no radio, no TV, no talking. Jack figured it must be the father getting coffee only before work. Jack heard padded footsteps cross the living room and then nothing. Jack continued to stretch on the floor and listen. Nothing. He thought of texting Jen, but didn't want to ping her awake if she hadn't turned her pinger off. Back in Orlando, he had noticed she frequently did leave her pinger on. No, let her rest as long as possible, Jack thought. He missed her, but that was stupid.

At 8:17, Jack heard some soft door noises, a distant jangling of keys, and that was it. Must be the father going to work, Jack thought. What to do? Nothing, he decided. Even if it was the mother who left, what did it matter? Jack made the bed meticulously and lay on it. He'd noticed the bookshelf last night but had not really checked it out. Now, he went over and there were many of his favorites: Tolstoy, Hemingway, Henry James, Stephen Frost, Emily Dickinson, Theodore Dreiser, Charles Dickens, a bunch of them. The books themselves looked old and beat up, but the organization of the shelf looked like no one had touched them in years: perfect groupings, tight sets, everything trimmed and upright. On another shelf, there was non-fiction, including one sailing book. It was Buckley's "Atlantic High," very tight like no one had ever read it. After his sexual fantasy the night before, Jack thought some non-fiction might do him some good—keep the mind from wandering. He remembered he'd loved "Atlantic High" when he'd read it in high school or so and started reading it again.

It was 10:13 before he heard anything. He'd never seen Jen sleep past 9, but she could be up in her girlhood room just thinking for hours; he loved that about her. More soft footsteps, which Jack decided could not be Jen's. Jen was very graceful and, if ordered, could probably adopt a light foot. But normally she had a muscular way of putting her feet down. Jack loved her feet, and he loved her walk. He'd heard it many times. But this was likely her mother, Jack thought. Stop thinking stupid shit, Jack thought, and start planning. Assuming the father had been the one to leave, Jack didn't know when he'd be back so that was a dead end, other than to keep the ears open. Jen sometimes planned, but not always.

He'd forgotten to ask her and had to assume she had nothing planned. He didn't know the mother at all, but from the stories he'd heard and the meeting the night before, Jack did not think she'd have much planned. Based on his totality of experience with women, they might well look to him to suggest something, which was a total nightmare of course. He started to think while he heard some louder and more frequent noises coming from what he thought was the kitchen. The mother making breakfast for her daughter and the big gorilla she'd brought with her, Jack thought. Hmm, possibly an allusion to Sidney Poitier in "Look Who's Coming to Dinner?" he mused. Dumb shit, he thought, way too risky. Jen would like that, and he was going to use it on her at some point, but he needed a fail safe. Eventually, he decided family pictures were a very safe bet if the two girls had nothing planned. Family pictures at night could get very emotional and lead to some tough spots, but in the morning with everyone fresh, he thought it was a good bet.

"Go ahead," he heard Betty.

"Jack, are you awake?" Jen knocked on the door.

"Yes. Good morning." He popped his head out as though he hadn't been listening for more than two hours already. He knew the mother was listening and would exhibit the highest degree of honor and formality while hopefully not saying much.

"Mom has some breakfast for us," Jen said. She had shorts on he'd never seen before, no shoes, and a simple white blouse. Her famous hair had received minimal attention.

He gave her a quick smile. "Be right there," he said, and put his tennis shoes on and combed his hair.

"Good morning, Betty," he said walking into the kitchen.

"Morning," Betty said, but she seemed to forget her husband had told Jack to call her Betty and had a quizzical look on her face.

"May I help you?" Jack said.

"Oh, well . . ."

"Jack's a great cook, Mom," Jen said.

"Yes, I remember you telling me, but maybe just set the table for the two of you."

Jack followed Jen's lead, and they sat and waited while Betty cooked. He resisted looking at Jen because he could already smell her lovely morning smell, and it would weaken him.

Betty brought three plates of English muffins, scrambled eggs, and cantaloupe. Everyone was hungry, and it disappeared quickly.

"Coffee?" Betty asked.

"Yes," they both said.

Betty laughed. "Lawyers, hmm?"

"May I clear the table for you?" Jack said

"Oh, that's nice. Thanks," she said.

Jack had always loved kitchens, and he loved this one. He had the dishes rinsed and in the dishwasher in three minutes. He left Betty alone to make the coffee, went back to Jen, and could see that it was likely nothing was planned.

"Well, what do you two have planned today?" Betty said, bringing the coffee in. There was no carafe, and there was no cream. There were some cheap sugar packets on the table, and that was it. Jack said nothing. He knew Jen was a heavy cream user and picky about sugar and honey and pretty much everything. Plus, they were lawyers; one cup was never going to cut it. On top of that, the horrible question sat. Dear Jen,

Jack thought, bail me out, please. I love you so much. It was unclear whether Betty was excluding herself or not, and he thought at least Jen could clarify that. Shit, if it was just going to be Jen and Jack that would be a cake walk. But as women so frequently do, the mother and daughter flitted about, inserted extraneous issues, clarified nothing, and had a great time doing it. Jack had wanted to see this. Jen played it cold, but he couldn't believe it. This house wasn't that sterile. Betty stroked and kissed her little girl on the top of the head as she got up from the table. Jack had wanted to grab the coffee mugs too, but the mother was too quick. He looked at Jen who was tight again.

"What do you think, Jack?" the mother said, returning in less than a minute.

"Well, it may sound a little unusual, but I thought you might show me some family albums?"

"You're kidding," Betty said.

"No."

"I'll make some more coffee." Jen said, smiling, she loved it when Jack made suggestions so she could play the critic while never offering any of her own.

So, they went into the living room, and Betty smiled and gestured at the albums on the wall.

"There's the children's books as well," Betty said, pointing.

"Well, why don't we go chronologically," Jack suggested, figuring that would burn up at least three or four hours.

It was about 11:30 a.m., and they didn't finish until 3:30 p.m. It had turned into a marvelous idea, and Betty had really opened up as was Jack's plan. Jen had a great time too. It was obvious the books hadn't been looked at in years. Jack had caught the reference to the "children's books" and as the afternoon wore on, figured those must be books devoted mostly to the kids' progressive development, with photos of kindergarten through high school and that type of stuff. There were some photos of Jen and her brother in the family books but not organized. The room was fully lit, and the phone rang from time to time. This helped things from getting too emotional. Jack very much wanted to see Jen's books, but decided it was too acute of a request and might backfire. We're going for a draw; he kept reminding himself. Don't push it. Plus, it was only the first day, and he could return to Jen's books later in the visit if things got stale. He listened carefully to see what would become of the father, but there were no clues.

They were blue bloods alright, and the books went back to the eighteenth century, all of them in Virginia. They had had slaves, but always fewer than ten, and sometimes only one or two. They did not have enough acreage to be old Virginia farmers with lots of slaves. Instead, they'd started with only a few thousand acres, which got smaller and smaller as they consolidated wealth and moved into the cities. Mother and daughter remembered the half dozen land sales that had occurred in favorable terms. Their instincts were urban, not country life, and that explained a lot. Jennifer was very urban and bitched about crowds but seemed always to pick a place where crowds would be. He'd invited her on a few outdoor adventures and her first question was always: "Where do I go to the bathroom?" That side of her came clearer to Jack through the hard-faced photos of her ancestors. He knew it was not fashionable to smile in pictures in the old days, but these ancestors had hard eyes like Jen's. Their features were sharp, boney even. Was it that none of the land deals had gone bad, or that some of them *had* gone bad but no one wanted to admit it? They were blue bloods for sure, but not the bluest. There were no cousins named Washington, Jefferson, or Madison. These were in the centuries when Americans had "honor," and Jack got the sense that somewhere along the way someone had fucked it up a little, maybe more than a little. Today, there was no "honor" and every screw up was someone else's fault. But in those days, Americans had "honor" and it was the screw up who burned and smoldered inside and the family members who silently but forever condemned the loss of family honor. Jen had glossed all this over. There wasn't a smile until the 1930s, and then a tight-lipped one.

"Well, that about does it," Betty said, closing the last book. Like the ones in the guest room, they were all meticulously organized and shelved. Jack thought this might be some bait as he knew there were still the "children's books." He did not bite.

"May I take you to lunch?" Jack said, omitting the word "buy" as he had practiced in Orlando.

"Why, it's late and oh my goodness where did the time go?" Betty said.

"Relax, Mom," Jen said, but otherwise did not help.

Betty's phone rang, and it was Kevin. It did not take long and Betty said "Well, we missed lunch too. Okay." She hung up. "Okay, your father says his half day turned into three quarters, he skipped lunch to get back, did not make it, and now wants to slum it at Langtry's."

"My favorite," Jen said.

"He remembers," Betty said.

"What time?" Jack said.

"Five." Betty said.

"What should I wear?" said Jack.

"Slacks and a button down." Jen said, very eager to answer the question.

"I'll be ready. May I help you clean up, Betty?"

"Oh that's sweet, but it's nothing. I've got it."

Jen disappeared up the stairs, and Jack went back to the guest room. He took another shower, shaved meticulously, and got dressed up to his undershirt. He had a full hour, so he enjoyed his shower and thought about Jen's father. Son of a bitch has got to be late 50s, but not quite 60. It irked Jack that he had not done the basic research to know exactly how old the parents were. It irked him that Jen had intentionally not made it clear, as though the math would change if no one put a fine point on it. Overall, however, Jack was pleased. His plan was working. There were no mistakes, and he hadn't even hit a double. But he'd been bunting and poking singles from the start, and that was going to be the best he could do. Jen did not mention a sport coat, but he'd brought his nicest one. He bought it for her after it became clear that she was not going to disappear from him. He knew Jen was embarrassed by the way he dressed but tonight would be different. She'd smiled at the coat but said nothing; he knew that meant "much better than that old shit you've been wearing, but still not great." He'd also noticed she'd never bought him a new one. If there was one thing Jen would spend money on it would be clothes so that her boyfriend didn't embarrass her. Fuck it, Jack thought. Let them tell him to take it off. He doubted the father would go to work without a sport coat. Anyway, his mother had always said, "It's much easier to be over dressed then underdressed."

"What a nice coat," Betty said.

"That shirt isn't nice enough to go with that coat," said Jen with a little miffy frown. Classic Jen, he thought. Don't fix the problem, just air it out so everyone can smell the stink; then let it linger. All downside, no upside, it was the Jen Special. But he'd practiced law for over twenty years, and even though his heart was broken and, for Christ's sake, all Jen had to do was *agree* with her mother, he let it slide off.

Betty drove. Jen sat up front. Jack was in the back. Well, he thought, the main danger tonight was the dreaded meeting with old friends. How would they explain Jack, the old man with their daughter, if push came to shove? Well, he could do nothing except be a perfect gentleman and, if necessary, possibly help Mr. Fairfield escape the situation. It would be interesting to see if any of them were prepared for such an encounter. Would they lie to avoid it? Would they try to pass him off as something other than Jen's boyfriend? It might even be one of Jen's old friends, which might mean Jen would have to save Jen. Jack hoped it wouldn't happen. Just score a draw, he thought.

Langtry's was the nicest pizza joint he'd ever been to. Everything was extremely expensive and extremely good. They even had barolo by the glass, which shocked him. There was hardly a T-shirt in the place. Jen and her mother were having a great time, and even Mr. Fairfield was much more relaxed than the prior evening. He ordered a Glenmorangie to get started, and a carafe of pinot noir with the pizza for the group.

Jack played it very tight. Finally, Jen and Betty started to carry the ball and kept the conversation going. Mr. Fairfield said very little, but he let it slip that it had been a good day at work. Once in awhile Jack could see him scanning the room for potential friends of his, likely worrying that he didn't have a great way to introduce Jack planned if it happened. Jack was prepared to go along with any nonsense that Mr. Fairfield might serve up. Jack knew Mr. Fairfield might make a little bobble, but he wouldn't completely blow it. But as Jack observed Mr. Fairfield, he guessed that Mr. Fairfield was even more nervous that an old friend of Jen's might show up and there could be real fireworks if she froze up. Jack knew Jen hadn't given it a moment's thought. She also had a proclivity to clam up, which probably would not work in the: "Who the fuck is this old man?" context in which they all found themselves. Jack tried to prepare to bail her out if things got dicey, but there were so many variables to consider. But neither happened and the awfulness was avoided at the potentially perilous public site.

So, Jack had to do no work, and the place was a controlled zoo. Jack had never seen so many millionaires eating pizza and drinking red wine. Scanning the room, Jack smiled that it was an abomination to order beer. He couldn't see a single one. Anyway, what did he care? Let it ride, he said to himself.

They ordered dessert and got home at 7. Mr. Fairfield announced he was tired and looked at Jack: "I understand my wife and daughter have set me up for you to slaughter tomorrow." He smiled, but Jack was old too.

"I understood the exact opposite," and grinned back, a touch unctuous.

Mr. Fairfield waved the conflict off with a wry grin that said: "I worked today. What did you do?"

Betty, who'd had four glasses of wine, laughed hard. Jen giggled. "Daddy, Daddy, Daddy," she said, "be nice."

Mr. Fairfield laughed, "I love you my only daughter."

"Daddy, Daddy."

"You are my only daughter."

"Everyone knows that, Dad."

"I know. I know."

There was the slightest tinge of competition, but Jack quelled the situation.

"Is that your book collection in the guest room, sir?" Jack changed the topic.

"Yes. Mostly."

"Most of my favorites. I assume Jen read most of them?" Jack, who had intentionally refrained from drinking wine, had hit a double at least.

"Why, yes," Mr. Fairfield beamed. Jen had heard the question and squeezed her father with a big smile.

"They both made me read," she said.

Betty had heard and came right over. "Yes, Jen was a constant and disciplined reader. She lapped her classes in sophomore and junior years."

"What about senior?" Jack raised an eyebrow.

They all burst into laughter, and the mother looked at him a long time with shiny eyes. He kindly returned her gaze, and held it, and his eyes told her again: "I am not a monster." She smiled warmly at Jack for the first time.

Mr. Fairfield announced his deal was 99 percent done, but there was still some "cat herding" to do on Saturday morning so he would be going to bed. "I wouldn't be drinking if I wasn't so successful," he announced.

Everyone laughed.

Mr. Fairfield's lenders were in the far East and United States "Saturday" meant nothing to the lenders. He would go in early and finish it off on Saturday. Jack had nothing but respect and again saw Jen in her father. She could get the same grim, nothing-well-stop-me look on her face, but never regarding their relationship. In any event, it was only 7:30 and something had to happen. Jack kept quiet.

Mr. Fairfield carried on for another ten minutes but then went to bed.

"How about some backgammon and popcorn?" Betty squealed.

"Doubling cube?" Jack did not miss a beat.

"Of course."

"Great. Jen, I hope you have cash."

They laughed. The mother howled. Of course, Jen had no cash.

"I'll stake her," Jack said.

"How nice."

"Bitcoin, okay?"

Betty howled again.

"Do I get to see the twin set?" Jack said.

Betty looked over at him, not understanding. To Jack's amazement, Jen also did not get the reference. Had he just fucked up?

"I understood that Jen had a backgammon set in Orlando that matched one up here?"

"Ohhhh," they said together, but Betty still seemed a bit confused.

"I know where it is, Mom," Jen said and ran upstairs.

"Awesome," Jack said but thought: too "surfer dude," watch it.

Jen came down. It was indeed the matching set about which Jen had told him. "How the heck did you remember that W . . .?" said Jen.

She was just about to call him "Weirdo" in front of her mother but caught herself. Betty noticed. For the first and only time, Jack let Jen twist in the wind. See how that feels you little brat, went briefly through his mind, but Jack's heart was too big. After some long seconds, he said, "What is the story about the matching sets?"

Betty looked at him, trying to figure out what just happened. "I don't really know. My mother gave them to me, and I just don't remember asking. Did you ask Mimi, Jen?

Jen thought awhile and shook her head. "No, I don't ever remember asking her or what the story is, just seemed like we always had them."

Jack let it roll off. "Well, they're lovely," is all he said.

They played for ninety minutes, and they had a ball. He had played against Jen of course and he knew she hated him. She was a bit of a sore loser and spoiled. Jack had known in Orlando she was spoiled, but Jen was smart, knew she was spoiled (or had been told) and now guarded against it. But, like most truly spoiled people, there was no way to unspoil them. It was obvious both parents adored her, and Jack noticed that Jen had not been asked to do one thing since they got there. Nor had Jen even offered to help anyone with anything.

Betty was an excellent player but enjoyed herself more than Jen who was more like her father. Betty didn't mind losing and whispered little swear euphemisms, but with delight, not anger:

"Shit," became "Sugar."

"Holy shit," became "Sweet sugar."

"Fuck," became "Fudge."

"Bastard," became "Buster."

And so on.

Jack was winning, and Betty was euphemizing when he made a questionable move to try to help her out. Betty pounced: "Oh Jenny! He did that on purpose to help me! Jack, you buster, I know what you're doing, helping the old lady, huh?" She was sharp, especially after five glasses of wine, and laughing.

"Well, I just felt, you know . . ."

"The first time all weekend he's been at a loss for words," Betty screeched. "Oh, Jenny, where did you find this one? Ha Ha. He must think I'm *not* married to a lawyer."

"I told you he was funny, Mom."

"Yes, and not too stupid."

"I like that in a man," they said together and laughed. Jack knew there was an inside joke on that, but he couldn't figure it out and wanted to get things back to smooth city.

"And well-meaning, loving, honest, generous, and warm-hearted," Jen blurted.

Jack wanted to scream: "WHY IS THE FIRST TIME JENNIFER HAS EVER SAID SOMETHING NICE ABOUT ME NOW?" But he said very softly: "The feeling is mutual." There was a little tension. Jen had opened the cage; the elephant was in the room. Betty was a little confused and shaken. But Jack had the shaker, so he just said, "Doubles," and in effect moved the subject back to the game.

They played on and Jack rotated off so he could now watch mother and daughter play. He thought it was relatively late, especially with all of the drinking, but mother and daughter playing each other brought a fresh boost of energy. The girls played for another hour. Jack had left all the money he'd won on the table, so Jen started gambling with it. They both accepted the most absurd doubles from one another, talked feverishly to the dice, told each other how much they missed each other, carried on 3-4 other conversations simultaneously in the way only women can do, and of course ended up with an exact split of the money. Once again, Jack felt lucky. He'd survived the brief moment of tension and then mercifully been allowed to become a bystander. He offered to bring them water, and they accepted. He tarried in the kitchen looking over Betty's set-up. Too much female bric-a-brac, he thought, but pretty darn good.

The evening ended, and he brushed his teeth. He got one red heart from Jen on the text machine and returned the same. It was Friday night, and he was pretty confident he was working toward a draw. Certainly, there were no major mistakes. Jack wondered if Jen's compliments would reach the father. Jen would say nothing—her specialty. Betty might though. He could see the marriage was strong. They were not sticking together just because they'd already been married for thirty-five years. They'd *built* something together. They *respected* one another. They were *adults*. It's what he wanted so badly with Jen, but of course there would be no thirty-five years. He noted that Betty was not spoiled like Jen. They were quite rich, but Betty still did quite a bit of work. Sure, they had illegal aliens to do the really dirty stuff, but Betty still cooked, still did laundry, still vacuumed and dusted, still organized the parties (previously cooked for, now catered), and so forth. She did not trust the illegal aliens on the chandeliers and the antique woods, either. She did all of that detailed work herself. There were family heirlooms everywhere, and Jack doubted she would let anyone touch them but herself. The house was meticulous. She took pride that her husband did *not* do anything. Jack could see her at the bridge club: "Of course, my husband does no work at the house. I do no work at the office. It's the least I can do for him."

Jack thought and planned. He had had very little to drink, but he was exhausted as he knew he would be. Tomorrow, he thought, I will be with Betty and Jen in the morning, and then tennis with the father in the afternoon at an unspecified time, which irritated Jack greatly. But he didn't panic. The time would have to be made known in the morning. It would be best if Jack did not even see Mr. Fairfield—the soft-footed, sturdy, persistent, disciplined lawyer who would close his deal on Saturday morning—before he left. What about the girls? Well, they really hadn't gone out together, so he'd encourage them first thing in the morning. What about dinner? Again, no one had said a word, which irritated Jack. He had worked for years on many cases, many weekends, many thousands of documents, many personalities, much money, yet this tired him more. He went to sleep and battled his chronic, obstructive sleep apnea.

Breakfast was perfect. Mr. Fairfield had indeed left early and determined. Jack assisted Betty in the kitchen with French toast, sausage, and fruit. He'd been allowed the honor of cleaning the table and loading the dishwasher. The girls resolved to shop and left at 10:00.

"The Uber will get you at two unless you hear from Daddy that things went badly," Jen said as they left.

"How would I hear from your dad?"

"He'll call me, and I'll call you."

"Ok. So, I'll hear from you, right?"

Jen nodded her head, yes. They left, and he had nearly four hours to kill. He stretched his back and planned. The girls were a done deal, he thought: As long as I don't aggressively screw up, the mother has seen my ass, and I can't do anything about it. Jen will not help me in any way. So, it's 100% the father. A lawyer, like me, working on Saturday, like me, to close a deal and put money in the bank. All like me. And close in age. We'd be playing, if at all, at Mr. Fairfield's private club. He'd probably paid dues for twenty years. Possibly, his family and/or Betty's were members as well. Possibly, even more distant relatives. Possibly, the fucking club had been founded by Robert E. Lee! In any event, if it was possible to see someone at Langtry's, it was much more probable at the tennis club. Hell, he would know many of the members. On the other hand, we'd be dressed for tennis so any conversation might be quite limited, and probably with other men, not women. Women seeing two men play singles had a way of knowing that a lot of conversation was inappropriate. Even doubles, Jack thought, which was way more conducive to a jerk and pull, could be competitive with all men. In any event, what was certain in Jack's mind was that as a guest no one would address him. He had only to follow Mr. Fairfield's lead. If Mr. Fairfield chatted, he would smile and hope he didn't have to participate. If he had to participate, Mr. Fairfield would likely signal him. If Mr. Fairfield moved away, he would dutifully mimic him. Not that difficult at all, Jack thought.

Now, the tennis itself. Jack was very competitive and had tennis trophies all over his house. Jen had never asked about any of them. He'd played a million matches in all sorts of competitions. He suspected Jen had only said something vague like "Jack's pretty good at tennis," even though Jen had seen all the trophies. For reasons which he did not understand and which hurt his heart, Jen made few inquiries concerning the history of his life. He also suspected Mr. Fairfield was pretty competitive, but Jack had seen no trophies. Betty had not mentioned anything about his prowess. Jack resolved that a "hit around," which he normally loathed with every fiber of his being, would be best. It would allow Mr. Fairfield to say they both had a good time without the direct confrontation of a formal match with a formal score. He got a text from Jen at 1:00: "Dad at club. Uber on schedule. Be nice." He gave her a red heart and took a deep breath.

The club was lovely and perfect without being pretentious. He was registered as a guest of Mr. Fairfield's, asked if he needed to change, declined, and was directed to court six which is where they would play. He walked over and the place was pretty empty. It was a beautiful clay court (which Jack loved, though he also loved hard court) that had been brushed by machine (probably eight-hours earlier) and sat perfectly just waiting. No one had played on it all day. Jack waited too. It was very quiet. There was a slight breeze, and a blue sky. There was a touch of humidity, but nothing compared to Florida.

Mr. Fairfield showed up within ten minutes, and they warmed up. Jack could see immediately that Mr. Fairfield was a graceful mover and a very good player, but Jack would annihilate him in open competition. But Jack bet that if Jen had said anything it was vague, and Mr. Fairfield would not know much.

"I looked up your records," Mr. Fairfield said.

"Oh." Jack said. The fucking USTA website! They forced all tournaments into being USTA, and so Jack realized the last fifteen years of his tournament life (with few exceptions) were on the website.

"Look at this print out my secretary did for me," Mr. Fairfield said.

"Oh. Well, you . . . ah . . . Thank you, sir," Jack managed.

"Two out of three?"

"Sure."

"Don't beat me up too bad, okay?"

"Ok." Jack was at a loss for words which bothered him enormously. The son of a bitch had looked him up? Why was society so bankrupt that anyone could get your records off the internet? Can't anyone sneak up anymore? Jack processed his rage, but the beauty of tennis is that there is very little rest. Soon they nodded and played. Jack resolved to beat the gentleman in a very gentlemanly way.

And so it was. The score was 6-4, 6-1 and had been a lot of fun. Jack loved tennis. Mr. Fairfield was a very good player. He could see Jen in each step. He was just not quite as good and about ten years older, so that was it.

They met at the net afterward, and there was full sportsmanship and no angst. There had been no dodgy line calls, no loud grunting, no profanity, and the day and the facility were perfect.

"House lemonade?" Mr. Fairfield said as they sat down.

"You're kidding."

"Jen didn't tell you?"

"She doesn't say much."

He laughed and ordered the lemonade. Jack assumed it must be alcoholic, but no, it was just an old recipe that had stuck from a million years ago. It was delicious and tart. There was sugar, but only a little. It was more than lemons too; there was grapefruit or something else in the mix. Jack detected something floral (lilac?) but he couldn't place it. He imagined Thomas Jefferson writing the receipt down in cursive while in the fields with the slaves, examining the fruits. It was all so ridiculous.

They drank two dainty crystal pitchers and enjoyed themselves. Jack wondered where those pitchers came from. Mr. Fairfield had closed his deal and the pressure was off. He complimented Jack on his game, and Jack could see that he was a pretty big tennis addict himself. Like Jen, he would not admit it. They were both taciturn, but Jack didn't understand the point. Even though Jack was not a transactional lawyer and did not do deals, he knew what it meant in general: There was a threshold, and Mr. Fairfield had crossed it. Sure, he had a forty-eight-year-old geezer fucking his daughter but that could wait. The deal was done. The money wired. The client is happy. It was no different from building a barn at the end.

No one came by. The weather stayed perfect the breeze even picking up a touch and whisking away some of the humidity, the light moderating, getting orangish. It was 3:30 and still no one had said a word about dinner. That irritated Jack, but he let it slide. If there were 4-5 other matches going when Jack arrived, there were 1-2 now. It was very quiet. Jack could even hear birds chirping and singing where they sat. Jack had always liked quiet and resolved to let it roll. This is the quiet and the privacy they pay for, thought Jack.

There was a period of silence between the men that was benevolent. They hardly knew each other. They'd met. They'd shown courtesy and mutual respect. One of them was fucking the other guy's daughter. It was unconscionable. He was also as old as the father (well not really) and that was obscene. How could two relatively educated, relatively honorable, relatively decent, relatively honest men find themselves in such an absurd conundrum? But now there was contented silence.

Their minds worked silently. Surely all of these things would disappear because of the will of the participants. They were tough lawyers with tough clients working in a tough world, day after day, year after year. What petty social problem could possibly upset them? Jack would pumpkin into 33. Mr. Fairfield would pumpkin into 65. Problem solved. Jack, although from Florida, was a distant relative of Chamberlin's. Jack's 32nd cousin had died at Little Roundtop—a bayonet to his red, white, and blue chest. Problem solved. Well, if not, then Jack was a celebrity, however minor, had been to New York and properly vetted by suitable jackoffs who knew suitable jackoffs, some of whom knew people that the Fairfields knew or at least knew of. Sure, it was just commercials, but he'd made a lot of money in five years. And you know, that's it. I mean, my God, he's not a simple redneck from Orlando fucking Florida, here to defile our perfect daughter? Oh God. Oh God. Problem solved.

"Well, shall we go back to the house?" asked Mr. Fairfield.

"I love your daughter with my whole heart, sir." Jack said looking directly at Mr. Fairfield from about six feet away.

"I understand," Mr. Fairfield was shaken. He had not expected Jack to take the initiative.

"I have never disrespected her," said Jack. His voice was strong but not loud just as he had rehearsed.

"I, ah. Thank you for that."

"I'm forty-eight years old," Jack continued.

"I know."

"I'm sorry."

"Me too."

"I never lied to your daughter."

"I understand."

"I never thought she was interested in me."

"I, ah. Yes. I understand," concluded Mr. Fairfield trying to end Jack's pesky proclamations.

Jack had a few other lines, but he saw Mr. Fairfield was dazed and shaken. He was not even 60, but he felt 1,000. He only had one daughter, and my God how could this happen? Jack had looked him in the eye the whole time, and Mr. Fairfield had returned the look but trailed off. They were tough lawyers, used to looking people in the eyes, but this was different. Mr. Fairfield had known that he could do nothing, but it still hurt to see the reality placed in his face. Like so many lawyers, he'd had the task of delivering bad news before, but now he was delivering it to himself. He would lose more than a million dollars? It's only money. He would lose hundreds of thousands? Shit. He would lose $100,000? Life goes on. He would lose $10,000? Fuck that; let's bargain. He would lose his daughter to a man his own age? Oh, God no. Does anyone know a hit man?

"Thank you, Jack. Please let's go back to the house," he finally said.

They left together and drove to Mr. Fairfield's house in his burgundy Jaguar with moonstone leather. It was spotless, and Jack felt dirty getting in. Neither of them had showered. Jack heard Mozart playing as Mr. Fairfield started the car, but he reflexively turned it off.

"One of my favorites," Jack said.

"Really?"

"Sure. Everyone knows the first movement, few the second, or the rest."

"How true," Mr. Fairfield said, but Jack could see he didn't know. Jack had an incredible memory in general, but when it came to the arts there were few who could match him.

It was one of the reasons why he had fallen in love with Jen, who could go back and forth with him. Jack thought it best to let the subject sit, as he didn't want to show off, or put Mr. Fairfield on the spot. But there was a little tension in the air. Jack correctly assumed that it would irritate Mr. Fairfield that some redneck from Orlando knew more about classical music than he did, though in reality Mr. Fairfield was not particularly well-versed in classical music anyway. They drove in silence for a while, but Mr. Fairfield was unsatisfied.

"Which piece is it?" he asked.

"*Eine kleine Nachtmusik*, the second movement, the romance," said Jack.

"You mean Mozart?"

"Yes."

Mr. Fairfield punched it into his car's streaming audio and up came the first movement, which Mr. Fairfield recognized immediately. He pushed to the second movement, and there it was. He listened for a while.

"Lovely. Do Jen and you play this?"

"Yes, but partially of course."

"Not enough orchestra?" Mr. Fairfield asked.

"Exactly."

"How does it sound with only the two of you?"

"Sublime."

Now they drove again, and Mr. Fairfield saw his daughter playing in his mind's eye, though he never remembered her playing this piece. For years and years, he had heard her upstairs in her room practicing. Occasionally, he would go into the room and listen. She would always smile and almost never speak.

Some of it made sense to him now, but geez, there must be violin players in Orlando that are not 48, he thought. He liked that Jack did not talk a lot. He sensed that Jack had baited him a little, a little too coy with the remarks, a little too smooth. But Jack had no idea what would be on the radio when he got in the car, so it had been both genuine alertness with a polish that had come with decades of practice. Also, Jack had not rubbed it in when he didn't know Mozart. No Goddamn spiking the football or whatever that boorish behavior from the South was called, Mr. Fairfield thought. He could see that a good lawyer had trained Jack. He liked Jack's manners, though there seemed to be a little chip on his shoulder. He'd never get that figured out this weekend, so he set it aside.

What amazed him was his daughter who was very much like him. Sure, she could get emotional like all women, but Jen had gotten his practical streak. Even as a young girl and all through her adolescence and young adulthood, she had made good choices. Her deliberations were often shared with Mr. Fairfield, and he could see she was grounded. Dating a forty-eight-year-old? Ok, but briefly and discretely. Bringing a forty-eight-year-old to his house and presenting him as a legitimate boyfriend? No way in hell.

Now he saw a little of what was going on. They had been harmless friends and she'd never given Jack a thought, until she started checking boxes and he checked all of them. He doubted his daughter was a slut, but she was twenty-nine. She'd been through high school, college, and law school—all at elite institutions surrounded by well-groomed boys and men who were after her. He knew his daughter had had at least three serious boyfriends, and he thought it realistic that she had probably had sex with 10. He knew the statistics applied to his daughter like everyone else's daughters. She had always been a voracious reader and the May/December relationship would have been well within her education. She'd moved to Orlando, the available pool of men she'd be interested in and had shrunk, and then Jack fell out of the sky. Since there had been no expectation of sex early in the relationship, he thought, they had been at ease with one another from the beginning. And it had all been so easy because they had many things in common, including the magic of music, and much opportunity to share it. Even though Jack was way too old for Jen, he was not ugly, not fat, and fairly athletic for a forty-eight-year-old. So, Mr. Fairfield speculated, there was no physical revulsion, and his daughter had had sex with Jack. Apparently, the sex was satisfactory, and now they were at his house. Jesus, Mr. Fairfield thought, how do I get rid of this poor man?

Anyway, his deal was closed and Mr. Fairfield was happy. He was too old to go to the office on Saturday and close deals. He was too old to deal with a forty-eight-year-old man who loved his only daughter. He had had a lovely tennis match with Jack, and now he would have a lovely but short evening and go to bed. He could not solve any more problems today.

The girls met them in the living room and beat around the bush as women so often do. Jack was happy when Betty gave him a little grab on the forearm, but he only smiled at her and said nothing. Jen bounced around her dad, told him he smelled bad, and kissed him on the neck. He gave her a big shoulder hug and rubbed sweat on her. Jack smelled food coming from the kitchen and was irritated that no one had said anything about dinner. He assumed now it would be at the house, but why didn't someone tell him. Anyway, they were about to break for showers, when Betty said: "C'mon boys, what happened?"

Everyone laughed, and Mr. Fairfield shook his head ruefully and said "6-4, 6-1 Jack wins."

"Oh, I told you to be nice to papa," Jen said.

"Oh, he was," Mr. Fairfield said.

"May I help you, Betty?" Jack said, walking into the kitchen.

"Oh, you don't have to."

"I'd prefer to," said Jack.

"Yes, I keep forgetting you're a chef."

"A cook, that's all," said Jack.

"Well, ok, can you prep shrimp?"

"You mean peel and devein?"

"Yes."

"Sure."

She motioned at the sink and there was a nice bag of 16/20s in there. Jack loved shrimp, and he peeled the feet and the shells in two sections and then squeezed the shank so the whole chunk of meat popped out from the tail. It irritated Jack when people threw the shank meat in the garbage can. Then, Jack quick-rinsed them again, and folded three sections of paper towels into one.

"Paring knife?" Jack asked softly.

"In the drawer," Betty said, motioning.

The draw contained an assortment of ultra high-end Japanese knives which pleased Jack greatly. He found the paring knife and slit each shrimp down the back. He then took a clean paper towel and wiped the vein out of the shrimp. A couple needed running water, but most came clean with just the paper towel. He was drying the shrimp with every wipe as well. Finally, he made another bed of two paper towels, laid the shrimp out flat across the entire expanse, and dabbed from the top with another paper towel.

"Plate?" Jack asked.

"For what?"

"The shrimp."

"Oh, just put them back in the colander," Betty said.

"Sure?" He looked over at her with a smile. The colander was wet and nasty. Even if he rinsed it to clean the pre-cleaned shrimp cack off (something you couldn't do properly without using soap), it would still be wet.

She walked over and looked. She squeezed him on the forearm again.

"Oh, my. Yes, a plate is right there," Betty said.

He laid them on the plate, clean and dry and put them in the fridge to cool. He cleaned his little area, including the colander, with soap and wiped it down.

"What else?" he said.

"Put him to work," Jen said, walking in. She looked beautiful in a sundress and bare feet, and her hair was still a little wet. He loved her very much and wanted to hold her desperately. She did not come within ten feet of him.

"Oh, Jen. You were right; he's too good to be true," Betty said.

Jack let it all roll off and said nothing. He'd never heard Jen say he "was too good to be true" or anything like it. Women said "too good to be true" all the time so Betty was just blabbing, and he was determined to make nothing of it.

"Let him cut the romaine," Jen said.

"Well that's an odd one," Betty said.

"Oh, it's nothing, ma'am," Jack said with his polished twang. "How big?"

"For Caesar salad."

"I've heard of it," Jack said quietly.

Mother and daughter laughed.

Betty had not said the romaine was also not washed, but Jack wasn't surprised. He cut the ¼ inch of bitter tips off, then the end. He pulled the outer green leaves off and rinsed them under cold water and set them erect in the colander he had just cleaned. He took the hearts and set them aside. He made a little ice bath, rough-chopped the hearts, and plunged them into the ice bath, but only for about a minute. He put the outer green leaves on the cutting board and then poured the hearts into the colander and fluffed them immediately to get the excess water off. Even though he wasn't making the salad, he wanted the hearts rough-chopped. People were always glorifying them and leaving them in little spears. Certainly, they were glorious, he thought, but they did need to be brought to heel. They didn't taste better with an end of the spear poking one in the tonsil or poking out the lips. They also had a lot of spots to hold water, and he fluffed them again after the rough chop to get them nice, cold, and dry, and rough-chopped.

Now, he took each outer green leaf, cut it longwise on the bias and folded the halves on top of one another. He did this with each leaf, trimming any ugly spots away but not meticulously. He always thought the green leaves looked worse but tasted better, so he was not worried if a little dark green or even a spec of brown was around. After he cut them all on the bias, he stacked them up in two bunches and cut them diagonally back and forth, getting large leafy diamonds and triangles of green. Then he put them in the colander with the hearts and set it next to the salad bowl which was gorgeous but porcelain and already on the counter. Jack did not care for a porcelain salad bowl; he much preferred wood. He said nothing. He didn't want any water in the salad bowl, so he didn't put the lettuce in it. Better to have it baby drip on the counter than tinkle into the virgin salad bowl.

"What else?" Jack said.

"Oh, get the big pasta pot down for me would you, Jack?" He complied.

"Good heavens, what's going on in here," Mr. Fairfield walked in with a cocktail in his hand, smiling. Jack could smell scotch again.

"Oh, Jack is doing exactly what Jen said he would," said Betty.

"A worker, huh?"

"Yes."

"Have a drink with me?" Mr. Fairfield said.

Jack pointed at Betty who waved him off. Betty loved waiving men off to do their own thing, and Jack felt good he was at least worthy of being waved off. He hadn't seen Kevin Fairfield since Jack had spilled his guts, but he could see Kevin had recovered. You did it, thought Jack. It's over. You can't do any better this weekend. Now just don't go backwards by saying stupid shit.

They went into the study, and Jack smiled as he thought of Mr. Rhodes all those years ago. Mr. Fairfield's study looked very similar. Jack couldn't remember how rich Mr. Rhodes had been, but he guessed Mr. Fairfield was either richer or he had inherited a lot over the centuries. There was a large gun collection going way way back; it even had a small cannon in it that legend had it was a gift of the Virginia army or the Virginia militia or something like that. They sipped their drinks, and Mr. Rhodes next showed Jack the book collection. Again, it was extraordinarily impressive. There was also a snooker table from Bermuda that was part of some trade deal or something two-hundred odd years ago. Mr. Fairfield had had it refelted and claimed it was made of teak and would last a million years in an air-conditioned house. Jack could see Mr. Fairfield was relaxed and having a good time. The key was to express admiration (which Jack found very easy) without becoming obsequious (which Jack also found very easy). He doubted Mr. Fairfield would say anything about Jen, and the den was not that far from the living room so there was lots of noise and they both knew dinner was imminent. Jack had spilled his guts to the father, and the father had recovered. Just play it cool, Jack thought.

Dinner was caesar salad, stuffed mushrooms, and shrimp alfredo. It was all perfect and everyone was hungry. The talk had been small, and Jack kept his mouth shut. Afterward, he asked Betty if he could clean up, and she didn't even fight him. The three of them went up to the second floor for some absurd furniture/remodel discussion which Jack longed to avoid, and Jack was all alone in the kitchen—exactly where he wanted to be. He made a big tub of soapy water and added two cups of white vinegar. He found the nicest kitchen towels he'd ever seen, and he used four of them. Nothing was all that dirty, and his first job had been a dishwasher. He'd never stopped since. It was all done in thirty minutes, and they were still upstairs. He could hear them laughing and mock crying "no, no" about redecorating nonsense that none of them were taking too seriously. Jack checked out the book collection in the living room, and after a while they all came down.

Betty had apparently forgotten the permission she'd given him or assumed he hadn't even started yet when she saw him in the living room. Either way, she let out a mock shriek when she went into the kitchen and saw everything done. "Thank you, Jack," she called.

"Yes, ma'am," he called back. She laughed, but Jack felt he let his guard down too much with the "ma'am" crack. One twang per day was enough he reminded himself.

Jen saw the whole thing and give her mother an "I told you so" look when she came out of the kitchen. More tea. It was 8:30.

"The old man is tired," Mr. Fairfield said, "A little light reading and then off to sleep."

"Too much work, honey," Betty said.

"My dad never quits," Jen said.

He waved them off and disappeared into his room. So, Jack thought, it was going to be me and the two girls again. No problem. They talked awhile and he listened. He could see that Jen was more like her father, but she was still a girl. Her mother was smart, educated, and well-mannered, but she had never known a moment's financial stress. Her father had been rich, and she had married a rich man. She had never done manual labor in her life, and had no friends who weren't very much like her. She treated her servants well but drew a firm line and never made friends with them. They called her "Mrs. Fairfield," and she did not disabuse them of it. She had not worked in business since she was in her mid-twenties and had rare occasion to have to put up with someone she hated. That the rest of the world lived differently was something she knew of only in the theoretical sense. She had not heard a man belch since she could remember. She had not heard a man fart since she could remember. Other than construction workers, she had not seen a man scratch his balls since she could remember. Plus, she did not want to remember hairy men and their giant erections. Men were here to take care of everything and then get cleaned up for goodness sakes. Her job was to honor them, continue her never-ending finishing school, and prune her ever growing emotional garden. Jack noted that between mother and daughter in less than an hour they used the word "civil" or its conjugation eight times. Not a single question was posed to Jack the entire time. Clean, smart, well-educated, well-behaved men were all that they were around and all that they respected. The rest were just gorillas and thank God they wore pants.

"Well good night, Betty and Jen," Jack said during a break in the conversation.

"Oh, no, Jack. I'm sorry. Jen you should . . ." Betty's voice trailed off as she looked at Jack.

Jack could see that she was about to say "spend time with your boyfriend" or something like that, but she couldn't bring herself to do it. Jack looked at her with deep tired eyes and a nod of resignation. Somehow, they'd been thinking the same thing, and Jack's beaten look penetrated her. Shaken, Betty had to look away.

Jen did nothing as usual.

"It's okay," he said, "Good night."

Jack went into the guest room, found *To Have and Have Not*, and read the beginning. He'd always loved it. He wouldn't be the shirker, that was for sure. He wouldn't be Eddy, that was for sure. And he wouldn't be the Chinaman, that was for sure. That left Harry, and Jack grimaced—a lovable-maimed loser, but a loser, nonetheless. Why hadn't Jen said something? Why was she so unprepared? Why did she let him twist in front of her mother? And for a scene that was entirely predictable? He was her fucking boyfriend. Her parents knew they'd been together and had been having sex for months. Could she not say one nice thing in his defense this entire fucking weekend? No, she always had to let him sit in shit while she smiled and did nothing. No battle was ever hers to fight. Jack cried for a while. He suddenly became tired with the accumulated pressures of the weekend, and revisited his basic plan to get a draw, found it solid, and slept.

Jack woke early but felt great. The dramatic decrease in his alcohol consumption combined with the stress of the situation had defeated his chronic obstructive sleep apnea. His head was clear. It was 7:15. He remembered the hurt that Jen had caused him, but he quickly recovered his game face. As he recalled, no one in this house got up very early. It was Sunday. They'd be Ubering at approximately two. Jack imagined if anyone got up early it would be Mr. Fairfield—another lawyer who couldn't sleep. But he would never come into Jack's room, and it did not appear he did any cooking. Jack perceived no threat. Although he very much wanted coffee, he resolved to read in bed until he heard some action. This would minimize the interaction and hasten the departure.

His plan worked. He read *Up in Michigan*, *Big Two Hearted River*, and was halfway through *The Short Happy Life of Francis McComber* when he heard gentle footsteps. Jack listened carefully as it could be any of them. There wasn't much sound at all. After ten minutes or so, there was none. Another twenty minutes went by before Jack heard anything, and then he heard voices. On the rare occasions she spoke freely, Jack loved the timbre of Jen's voice. She was an alto or mezzo soprano, kind of like Stevie Nicks but not husky. The pitch was lower than normal but clear and feminine. It was one of the reasons why her sing song, "I love you," sounded so fake to Jack. She also had a wonderful laugh which Jack hardly ever heard because she rarely cut loose. She was a chuckler and a smiler, not a laugher. Even when she laughed, she was forever putting her hand over her mouth to muffle it, as though it were unladylike to laugh. Listening in the guest room to mother and daughter, Jack noticed that Betty was a laugher. She had laughed easily, even strongly at times. Mr. Fairfield had the typically sinister lawyer's laugh, but still he laughed. Jack was puzzled but got in the shower.

As had been the case all weekend, he took a preposterously long shower and primped like a girl going to prom before appearing. He also made his bed drum tight, and meticulous. Of course, Betty would clean the sheets, but Jack wouldn't let her walk into a disheveled bed and thus think him a slob. Further, he swept the bed vigorously. Betty would find no cock hairs of his.

No text from Jen as usual.

It was 9:45, so he had a few hours to go. He walked into the living room, waved at Jen, who smiled from the couch but didn't say anything, and continued to the kitchen for the coffee he had been thinking of all morning. The parents were both there.

"Morning," Jack said.

"Morning," they both said.

"May I?" Jack said, motioning to the coffee.

"Sure," Mr. Fairfield said.

"May I help you with breakfast, Betty?" Jack asked.

"Oh, thank you. Yes, please cut the muffins and toast them both sides for me."

"Two a piece?" Jack said.

"Yes, please."

Jack forced himself to stay quiet. He liked Jen's parents, and he was always comfortable in the kitchen. But he was trying for a draw. Betty was busy cooking. Mr. Fairfield still got the real newspaper and was reading the *New York Times*. There was nothing to say. Jack cut the English muffins carefully and toasted them both sides under the broiler. Then he turned the broiler off, closed the door and left the muffins inside.

"Those will stay warm for fifteen minutes or so," he gestured to Betty.

"Oh good. Okay. Well fifteen minutes then."

"Anything else I can help with."

"No, you can sit with Jen," Betty said.

It was the closest to a directive that Betty had given all weekend, and Jack felt his defenses come up. "Sit with Jack" had been what she should have said to her daughter, but somehow it got inverted. But he went and sat with Jen who was reading a different section of the *New York Times*. He loved to watch her read, and she remarked on how the weekend had gone so fast (as though this were just another three-day weekend) and kept on reading.

They had eggs benedict, hash browns, and a quarter of a waffle each. The hollandaise was the abominable powdered-packet kind but Jack said nothing. The hash browns were frozen from a bag, and Betty hadn't tried to spruce them up at all. Jack was suspicious of the waffle but couldn't place it. In any event, Betty served real maple syrup, so all was not lost. Jack said nothing but thought to himself that Betty had run out of gas a little on the menu planning. She didn't have enough meals planned, and she'd served the weakest meal at the end, instead of hiding it in the middle. Of course, there would be no accountability, Jack thought.

Breakfast took longer than usual, and then Betty declined Jack's offer to help with the dishes. Jen preposterously announced that it would take her forever to pack and disappeared upstairs. Her mother followed her, and Mr. Fairfield went into his den with the briefest of words.

Jack went back to the guest room. There was nothing to do. As predicted, Jen and her mother took enormous amounts of time upstairs, and the Uber was even a little late.

"Thank you for having me," Jack said to each of the parents and looked them in the eyes.

"Nice meeting you," Mr. Fairfield said with a smile.

"So nice meeting you finally," Betty said and gave him a little, one-armed, half hug, which he carefully returned with the softest touch on her shoulder blades and a genuine smile.

They hugged their only daughter a long time. Even though she was twenty-nine, it had only been ten years ago that she had left their house. She was still very much their little girl, and they both teared up a little before they regained their composure. Jack and Jen Ubered away. It had all been very civilized. Jack was sure he had won his draw.

For reasons Jack did not understand, Jen loved Ubering. Apparently, it fulfilled some horse and carriage horseshit that went through her mind, though Jack knew if she actually had a horse in front of her and it defecated prodigiously that Jen would be the first to shriek in amazement and horror. That she would want to go to law school, and be able to get through law school, and still hold such inconsistencies in her head with ease was something beyond Jack's comprehension. For him, law school had been a one-way street, and there was no going back. In any event, he resolved with Jen, as with her parents, that a draw was probably as good as he could do. She had hardly spoken to him all weekend. She had hardly texted him all weekend. And she had provided no support all weekend. She had not touched him a single time. It was her house, her parents, and her boyfriend, but somehow it was his problem. He'd seen her turn molehills into mountains before, and he sensed nothing good could come out of the trip home.

Everything was normal, and they got back to Orlando and Jack's house by five. Jen had been friendly but pensive on the journey home. He loved her very much. He wanted to help her with her struggles. He wanted her to talk to him. But there was nothing he could do, and airports, airplanes and Ubers are not conducive to conversation.

"Well, I really enjoyed meeting your parents," he said opening the front door.

"They did too."

"How do you think it went," Jack asked.

"Fine and shocking."

He laughed as she put her bags down in the living room.

"Hug please?" Jack asked.

They hugged a long time, and Jack reminded himself to work for a draw. He hugged her in and in and in, and they kept hugging a long time more. He had a feeling she would leave and was not surprised when she did. She used the bathroom, gathered her stuff, and gave him a big kiss and another long hug and left. She was gone. Jack went for a long walk and tried to let his mind release. He loved her so much. He did not feel loved by her. Every punch was pulled. Every bet was hedged.

Every commitment was caveated. It was quite humid, and Jack worked up a good sweat and returned to his house.

He audibly laughed at taking yet another shower and sat in his sweat instead. He poured himself a big Wild Turkey. He played his violin and thought of Jen. It was seven o'clock, and he had had no dinner, but he suddenly felt old, tired, and sad. He feared Jen did not love him. There was nothing he could do. He poured another drink and played the adagio from Mozart's Divertimento K. 136. It was one of their favorites, yet Jen had not mentioned it, or any music, all weekend with her folks. They had agreed not to take the instruments to Virginia; it would just be too much to play for her parents. But the thing he felt most precious, most rare, the thing which easily crossed their age difference, which easily cured their shortcomings had not even been mentioned by her. Why?

He poured himself a short and sat on the couch and cried quietly. He was a forty-eight-year-old loser, and the efforts of the weekend and how little support he felt from his lover of twenty-nine crushed him. He knew Jen was under a lot of pressure, but fuck, *life* was a lot of pressure. If she wasn't going to handle this, where could the relationship go? She'd known from day one that everywhere they went together she'd always be twenty years younger than him and everyone would always stare. Now, it has been 18 months; Goddamnit, stand up and love your man. But that hadn't happened. He made excuses for her. He made excuses for him.

He resolved to go to bed and cry there but wanted to check his phone first. He had turned it off for hours and then turned the ringer off even after he'd turned it back on. Jack wanted to make sure his mother was ok. His mother was fine, and Jen had texted him three red hearts and a cartoon GIF of a fair maiden leaping into the arms of her suitor. Jack's heart burst and he took the phone to bed with him. He looked at the text six more times and quietly cried and blubbered. He was confused and exhausted even though it was only 8:30. He put the phone on the dresser, strapped his CPAP on, and passed out.

Chapter Twenty

THE MONSTER THEY LIKED SO MUCH

"We've got to get rid of him," Mr. Fairfield said to his wife.

"Oh my God. He's such a nice man," Betty said.

"Yes, but we've got to get rid of him."

"So, nice. So thoughtful. He touched me so softly."

"What?" said Kevin.

"When they left and I gave him a little hug, he gave me a little hug back and his hand and arm were so light."

"Geez, Betty."

"I know it's stupid, but I've had lots of men hug me my whole life and none ever like that. His hand was like a pillow. Jen said he had a way with his hands."

"What are we going to do?" he said.

It was Sunday evening at seven after dinner, and they were sitting in the living room. He'd gone to the club and then run errands, and she'd gone to the grocery store and cleaned the house. They'd both been thinking about Jack, and what they'd say to each other.

"Well, I don't know," Betty said. "Get rid of him? I mean he's so nice."

"He's almost as old as I am."

"Well no, honey; he's nine years younger than you."

"Are you kidding? He's going to be forty-nine. Jen is twenty-nine," Kevin said.

"Well, yes but you said he's almost as old as you."

"You know what I mean."

"Okay. He's so nice." Betty tried to start over.

"Yes, he is."

"He has perfect manners."

"He could be faking it."

"No. I didn't sense that at all."

"You're right. He seemed very genuine and respectful," Kevin admitted.

"He was, and he loves Jen, that's for sure."

"How do you know?"

"Well, I'm a woman. It's obvious. The way her looks at her and it's just . . . obvious."

"He told me he loved her," Kevin announced.

"You're kidding? When? In the study?" Betty's eyes were wide.

"No," Mr. Fairfield said, resigned to telling his wife the truth, "at the club."

"Good heavens. What happened?"

"We were having a lemonade, and he looked right at me and said, 'I love your daughter with my whole heart.'" Kevin choked up and the sentence came out congested.

"He did? Oh my God. Oh, he's so direct." Her eyes watered up at the thought of it. "Oh, I can see that in my mind. He looked right through me a couple of times. Oh God."

"Exactly," Mr. Fairfield said nodding his head, "And then he apologized for being so old."

"You're kidding."

"Just said it literally; 'I'm sorry I'm so old.'"

"Oh my God, that poor man. That must have torn his guts." Betty's eyes watered more.

"And then he said he had never disrespected her," Kevin continued.

"I believe that. He obviously respects her. He is so direct. He looked at me several times and I just couldn't hold his eyes for long. He looked right at me, full on, with such a, I don't know, *resolve* to him. Oh my God. Who is this man?"

"We've got to get rid of him," said Kevin.

"I can't think of anything I didn't like about him, except he was very reserved but that was normal for the situation."

"Honey, he's 48. Are we going to introduce him to our friends? Is he going to be in the family photos? He's forty-eight."

"What else?" asked Betty'

What do you mean?"

"What else did you not like about him?

"Nothing I could detect, but he seemed pretty planned out."

"Ha. *You're* just the same!" Betty said. "Now you don't like it because our daughter has fallen in love with a man who is like you."

He had to laugh. He looked at his wife and his eyes were also wet.

"You're crying, Kevin? You never cry."

"It's stupid, our little Jen," he said. "You're right, he has a steadiness about him, like he'd give you the last meal on a deserted island."

"Exactly," Betty went and hugged Kevin, "you can see he gives everything to her."

"You think she loves him," he asked.

"She never said one thing all weekend."

"Sounds like Jen. You think she loves him."

"I'm not sure," Betty began. "Up in her room, she said a lot of pleasant things about him, but she never said she loved him. She never described any single moment. Did you notice she never touched him?"

"Yes."

"Oh, that must have hurt him so much. Why would she do that?"

"She's your daughter."

"Yes, but you know, honey, she's always been *your* daughter. She never did anything for him either. Did you notice that?"

"No. What do you mean?" said Kevin.

"She never brought him coffee, or water or a drink. Nothing. She never brought him any food. She didn't offer him a footstool, a shoulder rub. She never set one foot in that guest room for three days that I ever saw."

"I guess you're right." He said.

"Nearly kicked him like a dog."

"Now, c'mon."

"You know exactly what I mean. I know it was nerve wracking for her too, but no woman in love can treat her man like dirt for three days. There was plenty of time late for her to walk him around the block and get some privacy."

They sat for a while and Betty leaned over into the crook of his arm which went around her. The grandfather clock from one hundred years ago chimed. The air conditioner kicked on. The ice machine kicked on. The cooler in the wine cellar kicked on. They sat in their appliance chamber orchestra.

"Well, we've just got to get rid of him," Mr. Fairfield finally said.

"He's so much better than I ever thought possible," said Betty. "When I found out he was forty-eight, I *wanted* to find something wrong with him—so stupid."

"She didn't pick him on accident," he said.

"Makes a little sense from that perspective."

"If only he was thirty-nine," said Kevin, fingering the gravamen of his reasoning. "That would be entirely manageable, but twenty years. My God, he'll be 70 in 20 years. Can you imagine Jen married to a seventy-year-old?"

"Goodness," Betty paused and cried a little. "Oh, poor Jack. He's such a nice man. He has something about him, a pain, deep to his roots. He's *scarred*."

"Yeah; someone kicked him hard some time in his life," Kevin was surprised at how emotional he had become. "But we just have to be frank with Jen that this is never going to work in the long run. She must be blind."

"Well, he is good looking," she said. "I never thought our baby would be twenty-nine before we had this conversation."

"You know what I mean."

Betty nodded her head, and they both sat awhile longer. It was resolved that they would get prepared and call her with the bad news. Once a decision was made, they closed ranks and unified.

Chapter Twenty-one

THE COMPLIANT EXECUTIONER

It was June 6, 2019, a week after they had returned from Virginia. Jack had waited all week for the verdict to come in, but Jen said her parents hadn't really said much. Jack took that as a bad sign. He wasn't worried about Betty, but if Kevin was going to kill him, he could imagine he would think the matter through. If the news was tolerable or even good, Jack couldn't think of why it wouldn't come quickly. On the other hand, he'd only met them for a few days. Obviously, Jack couldn't call the parents, so he had to wait for Jen to communicate. They were both busy at work, and they didn't see each other.

Meanwhile, Jen's parents had been on the phone with her every night. She figured out that her parents liked Jack, her mother, in particular, but even her father too.

"Jen," her mother said, "I have to admit that he loves you sincerely. It's obvious. But do you love him?"

"I told him I did," said Jen

"Not when you were here."

"Well, he knows."

"I don't think so," said Betty.

"C'mon, Mom, he must know."

"Can't you see how much he needs you?" asked Betty.

"That's ridiculous. Jack is very strong and tough and resilient."

"Yes," said Betty, "but to me he looks *tired* of being strong; he's *unloved*; that's my impression."

"That can't be it. Of course, he knows, I said I love him," said Jen.

"Jennifer," her father said, "it doesn't matter that much. True, it makes the decision harder, but Jen, you have to think long term. He's just too old. Twenty years; it's too much. Do you want to be stared at everywhere you go? Try to look at the situation objectively. How can it last? Do you want to be divorced at forty and looking for a new husband even if you can make this last for ten years? Same for fifty if you can make it last twenty? Everyone knows that women don't age as well as men. Whether it's fair doesn't matter; that's the way things are. Now, you're in your prime, and your ability to pick who you want is at its greatest. Jack will not last. It's almost guaranteed; the odds are terrible against you. And then what? Think about what you're doing."

Jen had not been around her father consistently for a decade. She'd been away to school and back and forth and here and there. But her father's roots ran deep in her. Jen's father was all business. This was his only daughter. His arguments were all objective, rational, repetitious, the same things he'd said to her since she was a very young girl. He never gave the bath, but he almost always tucked her in, read with her, played games with her, and reasoned with her.

Three weeks passed. The Fourth of July weekend was coming. Jack and Jen resumed their normal routine while the conversations with the parents became less frequent, but nothing had changed. Jack had been asking for weeks whether they should take a little trip for the Fourth, and presented some fly-fishing opportunities in Canada, the Dakotas and Idaho. Jen never made a decision.

Jack sensed that things were wrong, but Jen kept making love to him passionately. She even did the dishes a couple of times, and vacuumed Jack's house once. Jack was shocked but he didn't know whether it was good or bad. He knew she was lying about the parents, but again, maybe she was lying because it was going to be good or maybe she was lying because it was going to be bad. If he got aggressive and demanding, it could backfire.

It was July 1, 2019, 8:40 a.m. and they had just made love. Jack made breakfast, and Jen sat in the living room.

"Well, I guess we aren't taking a trip since you never said anything," said Jack.

"Jack, I'm sorry."

"I don't get it. I thought you liked our trips," said Jack.

"I did."

"You did?"

"I mean, I do."

"Well, what is it?" Jack asked.

"I couldn't make up my mind."

"It's only the 1st, we could pull something together today."

"I don't know," her head was down and she would not make eye contact.

"You never had any trouble picking before."

"Stop picking on me, Goddamnit!" she roared.

Jack looked over from the kitchen, and Jen's face was white and hard.

"Why do you attack me?" he asked, walking over.

"Stop picking on me," she said defiantly, but she refused to look at him.

"I'm not picking on you. If you didn't want to go anywhere, you had a million chances to say so."

"I think we should just be friends," Jen blurted out. Her face was hard.

"What is it?" said Jack.

"I can't do it. It's too much," and Jack saw the stiff, stern Jen he hated, the eyes deep brown and flat, resolved.

"I love you, Jen."

"I can't. I want us to be friends only."

"We just made love; I love you."

"I know. I'm sorry. I can't."

Jack sat and cried softly. For the first time ever, she initiated an embrace. He did not return it. He was limp. She did not cry. Her jaw was set. Jack thought he'd offer to drive her home and instead drive the car off the offramp on the freeway. It was a huge drop and they'd probably both die.

Or Jack's gun was in the center console where it always was. He should shoot her first, then kill himself.

Jack thought of all the retention ponds on the way to her apartment. Why not drive into one? She'd probably drown with her huge hair all wet. He'd have a plausible explanation why he survived. Chappaquiddick? Sounded pretty good, but he'd be alive without her. Better she survives, and he dies. If Jen didn't love him, who on earth would? No one.

He molded into the couch and cried uncontrollably. Jen could not console him and didn't really try. Her father had made it clear that the break must be unequivocal, but of course he hadn't had a date in forty years. And so, Jen soft-footed around Jack's house and grabbed all her jewelry (as though Jack might steal it) and called Uber. She had her cello and three bulging bags of bullshit, but she still left a lot. Uber arrived. Jen left. Jack cried.

EPILOGUE

The harder you work, the luckier you get, Jack's father had told him, among endless maxims of youth, to the effect that Jack was in control of his destiny. Jack's mother had nodded in assent at every maxim: A man makes his own destiny. In the United States any man can become rich, can become the president. Always be optimistic, and good things will happen. Jack was forty-nine and all these maxims had proven to be lies or, at least, incorrect—dreams, fantasies, delusions, at best impractical. In his entire forty-nine years, Jack had never once done anything seriously wrong with any woman, yet they had rejected him constantly and continually. Yes, he was awkward. Yes, he said the wrong thing. Yes, he could be blunt. Yes, he had demanded an answer from time to time. But the punishment had always been capital.

Now, he had met the woman of his dreams and, despite the work Jack had put into it, it was gone. Jen didn't care how much he'd worked. Jen didn't care how much he'd paid. Jen didn't care how much he loved her. Jen didn't even care that Jack had possibly saved her life, that doldrum day on the Banana River, on the black trampoline, with a small hangover, having eaten no breakfast, dehydrated, covered in clothes, disrespectful of the elements of which Jack had warned her.

None of that mattered. Jen had thrown him in the dumpster, and hard work, ambition, and optimism meant nothing, and were indeed totally useless and irrelevant.

It was July 1, at 4:22 p.m. He had tried to get his mind off the morning by mowing the big lawn. He drank a lot of water, but it was brutally hot, and he was dehydrated. Now, Jack sat in his house alone. He poured himself another double Wild Turkey. He was sure he would never hold her again. He'd seen that hard look before. She was never coming back. If they ran into each other by chance, she'd give him her fake smile and get it over with as soon as possible. Jack started crying. He poured himself another double. The bottle still had quite a bit in it. Jack got on his phone and scrolled through his photos of Jen. He had thirty-eight of them, and he was only with her in six. He had taken the rest.

Jack kept crying. He knew he would wake up feeling like shit and feel like shit all day tomorrow, but he poured himself another double. He already felt like shit so what difference would it make? He knew as the weeks went by the dozens of little objects and signs of Jen that were in his house would prick and slice him over and over. After that, there would be periodic other memories for months, each a shot of diarrhea for him to take, fading, fading, and finally fading into nothing but memories in Jack's mind. He poured himself a triple and smashed his knee against the coffee table on the way back to the couch, but somehow didn't fall, half the drink sloshing down his pant leg. On the couch, the couch where Jen and he had spent so much time, his pant leg reeked of booze. He ate some chips that Jen had left on the coffee table, but even the bag smelled like Jen, and he sobbed. He hadn't changed his shirt from mowing the lawn and sweat had caked from the air-conditioning. Now, the shirt had a puddle where Jack's tears had run off, chin down, blubbering snot mixed in with bits of chips. Jack passed out with all his clothes on.

Jack's apneas woke him at 2:37 a.m. He went out the front door to urinate and started vomiting violently until he dry-heaved. It was warm, buggy, and extremely humid out. This took a long five minutes, and he wanted to urinate badly the entire time. What was left of his brain said start urinating, but he fumbled his belt buckle and started pissing in his pants. Once he started, he couldn't stop. He kept fumbling and pissing, only getting his pants down at the very end, his weak prostate intermittently squirting out the last 10 percent or so. Mosquitoes gorged on his head, neck, and ears. He staggered to his bed and passed out again. At dawn, he discovered that he had left the front door open all night, but no one had come in to conveniently kill him. He walked into the living room and an opossum scurried out the front door. Also in the living room, eating the rest of the chips, were two raccoons on the sofa near where Jen used to sit.